About the Author

During the COVID-19 pandemic, I was stuck in the house like so many of us. I decided to pass the time by writing something fun and totally out of my comfort zone. After putting the book down for several months, I was encouraged by family and friends to complete the book. Upon completion, I decided to use the pen name Libby Rose to honor my late mother. I am a mother of two grown adult children, and I am "Nannie" to my five beautiful grandchildren.

A Simple Hello

Libby Rose

A Simple Hello

Vanguard Press

A CIP catalogue record for this title is
available from the British Library.

ISBN 978 1 83794 151 3

*Vanguard Press is an imprint of
Pegasus Elliot Mackenzie Publishers Ltd.*
www.pegasuspublishers.com

This is a work of fiction. Names, characters, businesses, places, events and
incidents are either the product of the author's imagination or used in a
fictitious manner. Any resemblance to actual persons, living or dead, or actual
events is purely coincidental.

First Published in 2023

**Vanguard Press
Sheraton House Castle Park
Cambridge England**

Printed & Bound in Great Britain

This book is dedicated to everyone who wants to do something out of their comfort zone.

I would like to acknowledge and thank my very loving family and friends who encouraged me and gave me feedback every step of the way.

Chapter 1

"Oh my God, I see the truck. He's here. Those arms. Those magnificent strong arms. Oh, how do I look? How's my breath? Am I having a good hair day?" Those were the only thoughts that went through Diane's mind when she saw David the deliveryman's truck outside her classroom.

They had never met or even exchanged hellos, but that was about to change.

David was a former Army Ranger who still looked like he could kick any Taliban's ass. He had not one ounce of fat on his body and the way his jeans molded to his thighs and manhood was all Diane could think of.

Diane left her classroom in hopes of timing her walk into the building as David got out of his truck.

Perfect timing. Jackpot! David jumped out of his truck, tugged on his belt to readjust himself and slid his hands over his flat chiseled stomach to smooth out his tightly fitted t-shirt. Diane groaned silently.

David was in her direct path but, instead of saying hello and introducing herself, she shied away. She kept her head down but then a loud bang came from the truck, which made Diane look up at the exact moment David was walking past her. Today's walk to the main office was about to change everything.

Their eyes met and Diane was transfixed on David's smile. "Did I startle you?" David asked in a deep soft voice. "If I did, I apologize."

"No, no, not at all," Diane said almost too scared to answer.

"I'm David," he said as he wiped his hand on his tightly fitted pant leg and then extended it to her as a greeting.

"I'm Diane," she said nervously as she met her hand with his. They looked at each other and held the stare into each other's eyes a little longer than a usual greeting. They smiled and then they both nervously let go of their hands.

The silence was short but seemed like an eternity. It was a little awkward for both. "Well then," said David. "I guess I better be going. I have to deliver these books to the library."

"Oh yeah, of course. Me too. I need to get back to class myself," Diane said with a girlish grin totally forgetting where she was for a moment. She squinted her eyes, bit her bottom lip, took a deep breath and began walking away.

"Hey, Diane," yelled David making Diane turn around, "Maybe next time, let's see if we can talk a bit more and get to know each other a little better." Diane smiled as she nodded yes. David winked, smiled then walked away. Diane's mouth dropped open in disbelief and she swore she just had an orgasm.

Diane beamed throughout the rest of the day. She wanted so badly to tell her friends at school but knew it would be a bad idea. They would tell her he was a player and not to bother because he probably has a girl in every school that he flirts with.

David was definitely a hunk and all the teachers talked about him when he came to the school. He was always very professional and very polite. He always said good morning or good afternoon to anyone who he walked past.

Was Diane just crushing badly on him? Was she making more out of a common hello and introduction? Hell, she didn't even know if he was married with kids! But a girl can dream, right?

The following week, Diane saw David's truck outside her classroom window but she was unable to leave to sneak a quick glance at his well-chiseled body and to get another chance to look into his deep, dark blue eyes. She was totally bummed.

Later that day, long after David's truck was gone, Diane took her class to the library where she got an unexpected surprise.

Jenny, the librarian, who was one of Diane's friends, said, "Girl, I couldn't wait to see you. I have something juicy to tell you."

Diane laughed thinking it was school gossip and said, "Uh-oh, who did what to whom?"

"No, my friend, it's not about anyone from school. It involves you!"

"Oh, crap! Seriously? What the hell? What did I do now?"

"Don't worry, it's all good. Let me get the kids situated on the computers so we can talk," reassured Jenny.

Diane sat shaking her head wondering what this could be about. "Okay, Jenny, you've kept me wondering too long. What's up?"

"Well, you know that hunky deliveryman, David?" Jenny began.

"Uh, yeah!" Diane replied.

"Well, girl, he was asking about you today."

"What?" Diane said with her mouth hanging open.

"Yeah, he came in to drop off the new shelving and when he was done, he asked me about the cute little blonde teacher."

"You're crazy. He did not."

"Oh, yes, he did."

"Oh. MY. God. Jenny. Seriously?"

"I'm as serious as a heart attack," replied Jenny as she put one hand on her heart and one hand up to the sky.

"Why would he ask you about me?" Diane asked Jenny curiously.

"I've known David since last year. He knows my husband." Diane sat in shock. She could not believe her luck.

"Well, what did he ask? What did he want to know? What did you tell him? Tell me everything!" Diane eagerly asked.

Jenny laughed. "He wanted to know if you were married and when I told him no, he wanted to know if you had a boyfriend or if you were dating."

"So, I guess that means he's not married or dating," Diane asked Jenny.

"Well, I know he's not married. I'm just not sure of the whole dating thing. Let's just say, I'm sure he goes out!" said Jenny with a quizzical look on her face.

"Oh, I'm sure he does," smirked Diane. "Well, I think it's very interesting that he asked about me. When is he coming back?" Diane said with a chuckle.

It was a very long rest of the week and beginning of the new week. Diane anxiously looked out her classroom window frequently to see if the delivery truck was there, but no truck.

"Hmm, I don't understand, Jenny, he usually comes on Wednesdays but he's nowhere to be found," Diane said while having lunch.

"Don't worry," reassured Jenny. "Maybe his schedule changed but I guarantee he'll be back this week."

Chapter 2

Early afternoon the next day, there was a knock on Diane's classroom door. "That's odd," thought Diane. "No one knocks." Since her students were in art class, Diane got up from her desk to open the door. To her surprise, it was David. Diane was lost for words. "Oh, hi. What's up?" Diane asked nervously.

"I just thought I'd come by and say hi while I was here," said David. Diane quickly looked out her classroom window.

"Your truck? Where's your truck? You usually park it right outside my window."

David laughed. "Oh, today, I had a delivery for the office so I parked in the front of the school. Got to keep you guessing!"

"Yeah, I guess you do," Diane said as she unknowingly bit the side of her lip.

"Well, I know you're busy but I couldn't stop by the school without seeing you and saying hi."

Diane just stood there not knowing what to do or what to say. Then, finally, she said, "Oh, thank you, that's so sweet." As soon as those words came out of her mouth, she cringed to herself and thought, "Thank you. That's so sweet! OMG, how lame?" David smiled, said goodbye and turned around and left.

Diane couldn't believe what just happened. Could she have been more childish? "Oh, my goodness," thought Diane to herself. "He's never going to make a special trip to my classroom again. I'm such an idiot!" Diane sat at her desk with her head down and eyes tightly closed.

Soon after, Jenny excitedly came running through Diane's classroom door yelling, "Oh my goodness, oh my goodness, Diane! You're not going to believe who just left the library!"

"Who? What? Are you okay?" asked Diane as she quickly lifted her head off her desk. "David, David just left the library. He's been there talking to me about you for the past fifteen minutes."

"Oh my God, are you serious? He came by my classroom to say hi and I was a complete idiot when he left. I'm so embarrassed. What did he say?"

"Oh, he definitely doesn't think you're an idiot. He is totally crushing on you. He said he can't stop thinking about you and he really wants to get to know you better!"

Diane let out a scream of excitement and started jumping around like a silly teenager. "He wants to get to know me better? He can't stop thinking about me? Oh my goodness," Diane said as she nervously shook her hands. "Okay, tell me everything he said. And tell me everything you said back to him. I can't believe this! I really can't!" Diane said to Jenny as she shook her head from side to side.

"Well," started Jenny. "He told me that he came by to say hi and all he could think of was your adorable smile and big brown eyes."

"Go on, go on," encouraged Diane.

"He also said that you were very nice and not like the other ladies he sees at the other schools."

"Aww, really? That's so sweet. But how am I not like the others?" said Diane.

"Yeah, it was sweet but… "

"But what?" Diane said in a worried tone.

"Well, I got the impression that he's used to women throwing themselves at him," Jenny said as she crinkled her nose. "He also mentioned that he didn't think you were into him and he wanted me to find out if you were!" laughed Jenny. "I totally gave him the impression that we never mention him."

"You know, Jenny, I really think I could use this to my advantage," Diane said with a sly smirk on her face.

"I know, right," said Jenny. "I think, as much as it's going to kill you, just play it really cool with him right now. Make him work for it!" Diane nodded yes with a big smile, then both Diane and Jenny laughed.

Chapter 3

The following week couldn't come quickly enough. All Diane could do was fantasize about being in David's masculine arms and having him press his body into hers. She would sit with her eyes closed imagining their first kiss and the smell of his masculine body.

As Diane was teaching math, she was sidetracked when she heard the sound of a large truck. Her heart started beating faster and she got the feeling that a thousand butterflies were flying around in her stomach. "Geez," thought Diane. "How old am I? I'm not in high school anymore. Pull it together, Diane, and see what he's going to do."

Fifteen minutes had passed since she saw the truck drive up. No knock at the door. No surprise visit. Did she miss him? Did he leave? "Damn, it's been over a week since I last saw him." Diane got nervous and began watching the clock, just waiting for her hour-long break to come. Her students would be going to music. Her lesson plans were done for the following week. All she had to do was go to the front office, check her mailbox, and turn in a report to the counselor. She had it all figured out but it would all be for nothing if he had already left the school.

One o'clock finally came. Diane walked her class to music, looking side to side for a glimpse of the hunky deliveryman but he was nowhere in sight. She walked over to see if his truck was still there and, to her surprise, it was!

A small smile appeared on her face. She clenched her fist and said, "Yes." Diane quickly went to the office to check her school mailbox but got caught talking to the secretary about last night's HEAT game. From the office, she quickly walked to the counselor's office to drop off her report. Thank goodness the counselor was on the phone, so all Diane had to do was smile, wave, and place the report on her desk.

Diane wasn't sure where to go from there. Should she walk around school looking for him or should she go back to class to play it cool like she and Jenny had discussed?

Diane decided to go back to class. She paced back and forth and couldn't focus on anything but David. "Oh, I hate feeling this way," Diane said out loud. "This is absurd. I told myself I would never again lose myself or make myself crazy over a guy. Especially a guy I don't even know. Come on, Diane, your whole conversation consisted of, hello, how are you?"

Diane decided to go to the library and tell Jenny this whole David thing was dumb. She decided she was too old to play games.

Diane was basically talking to herself as she walked into the library and then, stopped suddenly in her tracks when she saw David talking to Jenny.

"Well, well, well, speak of the devil," Jenny said smiling.

David quickly stood up and said with a huge smile on his face, "Hey, Diane."

"Oh wow! Hi, guys," Diane replied. "I was just coming in to say hi to Jenny."

"Oh, you were, were you?" said Jenny. "Look guys, I have to get ready for my next class so I need to get up, but why don't you both stay and talk?" Jenny said with a very mischievous grin on her face as she walked away from the two of them.

"I'd like that," said David to Diane.

"Yes, that sounds nice. I have about twenty minutes before I need to pick up my class. What about you, David? Do you have time to talk or do you need to get back to work?"

"No, no, I'm good. I'll make time to talk to you," David said with the sweetest look on his face.

Everything Diane thought earlier about this whole David thing being absurd was soon forgotten.

Diane didn't know how to start the conversation so she began with the good old, "Where are you from? Where did you grow up?"

David politely responded, "I'm from New York and grew up just outside of the city." David reciprocated and asked the same of Diane. She promptly responded that she was born and raised in Miami.

The small talk was frustrating David. He wanted to get down and dirty. He wanted to find out exactly what type of girl Diane really was. Could she really be as nice as she seemed? Could she be as innocent as she looked? Those are the things David wanted to find out and he was determined to find them out soon.

Diane was secretly thinking the same things about David and also wondering if he could really be that nice. But she also had other thoughts swirling around in her head. "I wonder if he is a good kisser. I wonder how his body would feel next to mine. I wonder if he's a good lover."

"Oh, my goodness," Diane said as she looked up at the clock. "I need to get going. I'm so sorry and, before I pick up my class, I need to go back to my room, so again, David, I apologize but I'm going to have to leave."

"I'll walk you to your class," David anxiously said. "It's on my way out."

"Great!" Diane said and the two of them left the library without saying goodbye to Jenny.

Diane opened her classroom door. David asked, "May I go inside with you?"

"Sure," Diane eagerly said. She walked in and, before she had walked five feet into her room, David gently grabbed her arm. Diane looked back. She stood still and looked deeply into David's big blue eyes. David got a little closer. He reached his hand towards her face and softly caressed her cheek with his strong fingers.

He drew her body close to his and softly asked, "May I kiss you?"

Diane went limp but was able to nod and whisper, "yes." David's hand slowly moved towards the back of Diane's neck. All of his fingers except his thumb gently held the back of her head. His thumb softly moved over her lips. Diane's eyes closed and she moaned softly. David knew he was in control. He softly kissed her bottom lip and Diane soon softly kissed back. David knew exactly what he was doing. One kiss. One soft, sweet kiss.

David pulled back and said, "Diane, as much as I want to stay and as much as I would love for us to be somewhere other than here, I need to go and you need to get your class."

Diane caught her breath and, for an instant, had forgotten where she was. "Oh my God, David, you're right. We both need to go."

"But I need to see you again, Diane. I need to see you again soon. When can I see you outside of school?" Diane couldn't think straight but she knew that this coming weekend, she was going to be out of town with her girlfriends from high school.

David asked for Diane's number and as he left her classroom, he stole another kiss, winked and told her he'd call. Diane stood in her room with her eyes closed and her hand over her mouth and she asked herself, "What the hell just happened?" Diane giggled and left the room to pick up her students.

Later that night after she got home from school, Diane nervously anticipated David's call. Hours went by, no call. Diane tried to tell herself that guys don't call when they say they will. But that didn't help. After several more hours of waiting, Diane kept thinking out loud and talking to herself saying, "Maybe he is a player and he played me like a fiddle. Man, I fell right into his trap. What a fool?" Diane screamed and couldn't believe history was repeating itself. She always fell for the bad boys. The tough guy who knew when to be nice and when to sweet talk. Diane went to bed angry and frustrated with herself.

Chapter 4

The next morning, Diane had a workshop at another school. She wondered if she should tell Jenny what happened and especially about the kiss. She decided not to because she didn't want to look like a fool. Diane couldn't concentrate and was in a fog most of the morning.

During a fifteen-minute break, Diane decided to sit outside on one of the benches. She checked her phone, hoping that there would be a message or even a call from David but there was nothing. Diane grew more hurt. She shook her head in disbelief and said, "I can't believe I did it again. God, I'm such a fool!"

"Did what again? And what on earth is making you think you're a fool?" a voice from behind her said.

Diane quickly turned around. It was David. "David, what are you doing here?"

"Well, I guess I could ask you the same question," he said joking with that dazzling smile.

"I'm here for a workshop," Diane said in a short tone.

"I'm here because this is another school that I deliver to," replied David. Diane's mind quickly wondered if there was another naïve woman here that was being played for a fool by this handsome man.

Diane abruptly stood up and decided to excuse herself by saying, "Good to see you, David, I really need to get back to my class." Diane walked away without turning around.

David looked extremely puzzled and said, "Diane, is everything okay? Are you all right?"

Diane decided to stop and turn around. "Yeah," she said with a small smile. "Everything is great. I really need to get back. 'Bye, David."

Diane sat in her workshop trying very hard to not think about that incredibly soft, sexy kiss she and David shared not even twenty-four hours ago. She kept replaying in her mind David walking her back to class, coming in and passionately kissing her. Did she have the right to be hurt and upset with him because he didn't call, especially when he never said when he'd call? Wasn't she supposed to be playing it cool? She definitely wasn't because all she could think of was being just another girl from a different school earning him another notch on his belt. She shared a kiss and now she was becoming needy and insecure. What she just did outside to David was everything she said she didn't want to do but yet showed how very fragile of a woman she really was.

Meanwhile, David was wondering why Diane was so short with him and why she didn't appear to be happy to see him. David thought to himself, "Did I move too fast? Did she not like the kiss? What went wrong?"

David tried to retrace every step. "Okay, let me think. She came into the library. We talked. I walked her back to class. I kissed her. I asked her for her number and said I would… holy shit, I said I would call her. Damn it, I never called! That's got to be it! Diane probably thinks I didn't want to talk to her and that all I wanted was a cheap kiss. Oh man, I need to fix this and fix this fast!"

After David finished his delivery, he took out his phone and found Diane's number and quickly sent her a text,

Diane, I'm sorry I didn't call you last night. I had every intention but I work a second job from four till midnight. I was slammed and when I finally got a break, it was way too late to call you. I'm sorry.

David waited for a response most of the day but didn't hear back from Diane. Diane had her phone off because she was in the workshop.

Hours went by without hearing from Diane. David decided to call Jenny and spill his guts. He told her about their talk, the kiss, the promise of a phone call, not calling because of work, and today's cold shoulder encounter.

"Jenny, I didn't mean to mess up. I really like Diane but do you think she's overreacting? In my defense, I never told her what day I'd call, even though I had every intention of calling last night. Why didn't she tell me what was wrong when she saw me this morning?"

"David, my friend, listen. When you tell a girl you're going to call, we think it's the same day, especially if we want to hear from you. Diane's been through some pretty rough relationships. She's very guarded. She let her guard down. She allowed you to get close for just a minute. I know it seems to you that it was only a missed phone call and that would be fine if it was just in a passing conversation, but you kissed her and knowing you, it wasn't a peck on the cheek."

"No, it sure wasn't," agreed David as he shook his head and smiled. "It took all of me to stop at one kiss."

"You need to talk to her plain and simple. Explain what happened. I'm sure after you talk, things will be better. Give her a call tonight. She probably has her phone off or on silent because of the workshop. Once she gets out, she'll see your message and she'll probably feel better but she'll probably feel like an idiot for overreacting. Oh, by the way, do you work tonight?"

"No, not again until Thursday," said David.

"Good, then maybe ask her out to dinner and make it up to her but take it slow. Please, David, take it slow before you sleep with her." David agreed. He thanked Jenny for listening and for the advice. He hung up and waited for Diane to text or call back.

Diane couldn't get out of her boring workshop fast enough. "Why do they make me sit through classes I could teach with my eyes closed?" She got into her car, took out her phone and turned it on. She had three missed text messages. Two from her substitute complaining about her class and one from David. She gasped as she read it three times. She placed her phone on her heart, looked up, and closed her eyes and thought out loud, "Are you kidding me? There you go again, overreacting. Oh my God, instead of brushing it off and giving him the benefit of the doubt,

28

you thought the worse. Damn it, Diane. You always do that! When are you going to realize all men are not alike?" Then she realized the most obvious. "Ugh, why would he have come over to me if he didn't want to see me? He could've avoided me altogether but he didn't and he looked so happy to see me." Diane felt so bad. She was so mad at herself. She decided to call Jenny.

"Oh, Jenny, thank goodness you answered. I need to talk. I've made the biggest mistake."

"Does this have anything to do with David?" Jenny said from the other side of the phone.

"Yes, how did you know?" Diane eagerly asked.

"Well, I've got to be honest. He called me and told me everything."

"Oh, Jenny, I made a huge mistake. I really blew it. I really overreacted. I feel horrible. What did David say? Does he think I'm a crazy bitch? I just can't believe I acted the way I did. I had no idea about a second job. I didn't even give him a chance to explain. What the hell is wrong with me?"

"Okay, first of all, calm down. He doesn't think you're a crazy bitch. He called me to figure out how he could make this right. He sincerely wants to fix this and feels really bad," explained Jenny.

"Well, what should I do? Should I call him or wait for him to call me again? Is he working tonight?" Diane frantically asked.

"If I were you, I'd send him a text asking if he has time to talk and then go from there, but do it after you get home and relax."

"Thanks, Jenny, I really appreciate the advice and thank you for listening to your crazy friend. I'll let you know how it goes tomorrow."

"You better," Jenny said laughing and ended the call by saying, "Talk to you tomorrow and, remember, to just talk from your heart and let him explain and, whatever you do, don't read too much into anything. Just be you. Play it cool and everything will be all right."

Chapter 5

Diane changed into a pair of sweats and poured herself a glass of wine. She was pacing up and down her hallway trying to get the nerve to call David. "Okay, I'm ready. I'm going to make the call," she said out loud.

Diane hesitated as she picked up the phone but then said, "Oh, what the hell, just do it!" Diane entered David's number and pressed send. Her heart was racing and she wasn't sure how she was going to start the conversation. But after only two rings, David answered his phone.

"Hi, Diane," David said in a soft but manly voice. "I'm so glad you called."

"Hey, David," Diane began. "I'm glad I called too because we both really need to talk about everything that has happened since yesterday.

"Yes, we do need to talk but I was hoping we could talk in person. Have you had dinner? Or maybe we can meet for a cup of coffee or a drink? I really think it would be best to see each other." Diane looked down at her sweatpants and frowned. As far as she was concerned, she was in for the night.

"A cup of coffee would be nice. Where and when were you thinking about meeting?" Diane said and hoped for at least an hour or two from now.

"There's a quiet little bakery slash coffee shop near Ashford Drive. Are you familiar with it?" David asked.

"Yeah, I think so. Isn't it near the new town hall?" Diane replied.

"Exactly," said David then asked. "How about seven? Does seven work for you?" Diane agreed with the time. It would give her time to shower, dress, and eat a little something before they met.

Diane hung up the phone and stood in place, jumping up and down like a five-year-old. "It's not a date. It's just to smooth things over," she said to herself. "What do I wear? Oh, my goodness, what do I wear?" thought Diane. "I'm going with my black jeans and white peasant blouse." Diane decided.

Diane arrived at ten-to-seven. She was ten minutes early and decided to go in and sit down to wait. No need to wait, David was already there waiting for her.

"Oh, wow, David, I thought I was early. Have you been waiting long?"

"No, not at all. It's just the soldier in me. I'm always early. I was raised that if you're on time, you're late!" Diane smiled and sat down across from him. David had chosen a booth in the back of the bakery, where they had some privacy to talk.

"May I get you a cup of coffee? How about a brownie or maybe a doughnut? They have great eclairs here."

"Oh, my, well, definitely a cup of decaf. I'll wait on the treats, if you don't mind," Diane said. David smiled and left to order at the counter. Diane looked around at the people inside. There were couples, families and college kids just hanging out.

David came back with coffee and a sample of treats. "I couldn't resist. They all looked so good!" Diane laughed at David and then it got quiet.

David stared into Diane's eyes. Diane smiled and they both began to talk at the same time. They both nervously laughed and Diane said, "You first."

"Diane, let me first say that I really like you. I think you're one of the prettiest women I know and I'm so sorry for not calling you. I should've at least sent you a hello text or something last night. Like I said in my text earlier today, I work a second job. I'm a bartender on the beach. We got extremely busy and, to boot, we were short-handed. All I kept thinking about was how much I wanted to talk to you, that fantastic kiss we shared and how much I wanted to get to know you better and to see you outside of school, but by the time I got a break, it was late and I didn't think it was right to call you at that time. When I saw you this morning, I was so surprised and couldn't believe it. I was just happy and surprised to see you."

"Oh, David, I'm so embarrassed. I'm so sorry. I had no right to overreact. I really like you too and I have to admit that you have to be one of the best- looking men I know," Diane nervously said. "I just jumped to conclusions. I thought that maybe you were the type of guy that was looking to put a new notch on your belt buckle."

David laughed and said, "No, Diane, that's not me. My mom raised me to respect women. I just got lost in the moment and had to kiss you. At first, I thought I was moving way too fast and you didn't like it but, to be honest, after that kiss, I thought, no, she definitely kissed me back." David and Diane both laughed and finished their coffee and treats. "You know, Diane," David began. "I wasn't going to tell you this but I have to be completely honest with you. I first noticed you at school a few months back."

"Oh, my goodness! Really, David?" Diane said with a huge smile on her face and feeling really good about herself.

"Yeah," said David and continued, "I know this might sound a little unsettling but I even remember what you wore and how you had your hair."

"Seriously?" laughed Diane.

"You wore your hair clipped up on one side and you were wearing a blue and yellow sundress."

"Wow! Firstly, I'm honestly shocked that you even remembered something like that and, secondly, I'm kind of freaking out but in a good way. That's just crazy!" Diane said as she gushed with excitement.

"Well," began David, "You took my breath away." Diane's heart just seemed to melt as she gazed into David's eyes.

It was getting late. They talked for over two hours and even though neither of them wanted to leave, they knew it was time to go. David walked Diane to her car. They stopped and David opened her car door but, before she got in, David took both his hands and placed them softly on Diane's warm face and said,

"God, you're beautiful." Diane gently closed her eyes. David's lips touched her lips. They started with small teasing kisses. David's right hand moved slowly to the back of her head where he slightly grabbed her long hair. Diane silently let out a soft moan. David pulled back from Diane's lips because he knew if he continued, his manhood would explode out of his pants. He already had a hard-on and knew it was time to go. "Diane, I better go or else I can't be liable for what I will do.

Diane softly said, "I know, me too." Before Diane got into her car, they kissed one last time.

"I'll definitely call you tomorrow," David said confidently. "I'm so glad we did this."

"Me too, David. Good night."

"Good night, Diane," David said as he slowly walked away.

On the way home, Diane could still feel the touch of David's lips. She also got chills as she remembered his swollen manhood pressed up against her body. She knew he left at a good time. She also knew that next time wouldn't be that easy for either one to leave.

It was a long painful drive home for David. His manhood was swollen tightly in his jeans and he knew that if he hadn't left when he did, he would've taken Diane passionately right there in her car. She was way too classy for that and then he quickly fantasized about making slow, intense love to her. David quickly got out of his car and ran to take an extra cold shower.

Chapter 6

The next day at school, Diane couldn't wait to share the good news with Jenny. Over lunch, the two women giggled like young schoolgirls. "I'm so glad you guys spoke and cleared the air but, Diane, my friend, promise me you won't overreact when he doesn't call. You have to play it cool. You guys really don't know each other yet. I can say that David must really like you. When he called me yesterday, he sounded like he had just lost his puppy. He sounded pathetic."

"Wait. Jenny, he called you? I didn't know that. He never mentioned it to me."

"Seriously, Diane? You don't remember me telling you that David called when you called me after your workshop?"

"Dear God, Jenny, it totally slipped my mind. Refresh my memory."

"You're so crazy but, yeah, he was sick to his stomach, thinking he ruined your relationship before it had even gotten started."

"Oh my goodness, he's such a sweetie," Diane said as she clutched her chest. "I feel so bad. I didn't realize how I made him feel."

"The boy has got it bad for you. Don't think otherwise," Jenny said as she smiled, got up from the table, grabbed her lunch bag and left. Diane stayed seated, closed her eyes and reminisced about the way she felt last night.

Later that evening, Diane received a text from David, Hey, sweetie, can you talk? Diane quickly responded with, Yes, and a smiley emoji. Within several seconds, her phone rang. Diane made sure she was comfortably laying in her bed.

"Well, hey there, handsome," Diane said smiling. "I'm so glad you called."

"I've been thinking about you all day, Diane," David softly said. "Well, to be honest, I haven't stopped thinking about you since I left you last night."

"Oh, I know, me too!"

"So, beautiful, can I see you this weekend so we can continue where we left off?"

"David, I would want nothing more but I'm not going to be in town this weekend."

"What? Where are you going?" David said frustrated.

"I just can't believe the timing, David. I'm so upset. Every year for the past fifteen years, my friends and I take a trip and this year's trip just happens to be this weekend. As a matter of fact, I'm taking Friday off because my flight leaves at ten a.m."

"Oh, man, that's horrible. Well, I mean it's great for you but I was so looking forward to being with you this weekend. May I ask where you ladies are going?"

"I know, David, I would love for this trip to have been over or have been last weekend, but the flight, the rental car, and the hotel has already been booked and paid for. This year we're going to Nashville for a Keith Urban concert and we're staying at the Gaylord Opryland Resort."

"When will you be back?"

"I'll be back Monday afternoon. There's no school Monday so it works out where I only get to take one day off."

There was a silence but then Diane anxiously said, "How about the following weekend? Let's make plans for that weekend."

David hesitated then said, "Diane, you know the other night I told you I was an Army Ranger, right?"

Diane slowly answered, "Yes, I remember."

"Well, I'm no longer in the Army but I'm in the National Guard and, every month, I am away for one weekend and guess what weekend that falls on?"

"Oh no! You're kidding me?"

"I really wish I was, Diane, and, to boot, I'm scheduled to work tending bar all next week because it's Bike Week." More silence on both ends of the phone.

"Well, are you scheduled to come to the school next week?" Diane said hopefully. "You know, even if I'm not scheduled, I'll make a special trip to see you."

"I'd really like that, David. I really would."

David and Diane spoke for another half an hour, getting to know a little more about each other. They laughed. They joked and told each other things they liked and disliked about the world but were very careful not to get political. It was getting late. Diane accidentally yawned and that was David's clue to say good night.

"Diane, I'm going to let you go so you can get some sleep. I usually don't talk on the phone this long to anyone but, with you, it's easy and comes very naturally. Sleep well, beautiful."

"Good night, David. Sweet dreams."

Diane lay in bed trying to take in all that was said tonight. She couldn't believe that she wasn't going to be able to be with David for at least two weeks. "Two full weeks without being in his arms? I'm not sure if my body can handle that!" Diane laughed and then said, "I hope David can wait that long and doesn't find a replacement for me." She worried a bit, then finally drifted off to sleep.

Diane woke up in a good mood, knowing that today she would see David and, tomorrow, she would be off to Nashville with her friends for a fantastic weekend of good music, good food, good friends, and good times.

Before she left her house, Diane received a text message from David, Good morning, sunshine. What time is your break today?

Diane replied, Hey, handsome. My break is from one till two.

Great, going to try very hard to be there, David answered. Diane answered back with a smiley kiss emoji.

Diane was having an amazing day at school. Her students were behaving. They were answering all her questions and she was smiling from ear to ear. The only thing that could make this day more perfect was seeing David and that was about to happen.

Diane heard his truck and saw it pull up. She looked at the clock. It was twelve-fifty. "Wow!" she thought, "He's not playing when he says he's always on time." She finished her lesson a couple of minutes early just to make sure she had time to freshen up and pop a piece of gum in her mouth. The kids lined up. They walked quietly in line and she dropped them off at art class.

She walked past David who was still inside his truck. He smiled down at her and said, "Hey, you. You look amazing. I have to finish this delivery and then I'll come to see you. Give me about twenty minutes."

Diane smiled and said, "That's great. That will give me time to do a few things." Even though Diane had nothing to do, she didn't want to sound too eager.

Diane made it back to her classroom where she finished getting things ready for the substitute tomorrow. She had everything labeled and was over-prepared but she wanted the day to go smoothly for her students.

Diane looked at the clock and it was already one-forty. "Oh, man, where is he? What's taking him so long?" Diane was growing very impatient and popped another piece of gum into her mouth. She wanted to see David. She was hoping for another kiss even though it would be unprofessional to have the delivery man in her classroom and make out with him.

Five minutes later, there was a knock at her classroom door. Diane knew it had to be David. She opened the door with a smile and there stood a student from another class. "Hi, Ms. Walker. My teacher wanted me to give this to you."

Diane smiled and said, "Oh, thank you, sweetie. Tell her I appreciate it." Diane stepped out of her doorway to check to see if she could see David down the hall.

As she looked to the right, she saw his smiling face walking towards her. Diane lit up and said, "Perfect timing."

David looked deep into her eyes and replied, "You can say that again."

They entered Diane's classroom. David looked to the left and then to the right. "Is it all right to kiss you? Is anyone else in the room?"

"Yes and No. In that exact order," Diane said as she moved closer to David's body.

"Dear God, Diane all I've been doing is thinking about you and having you in my arms and your lips on mine."

David softly pushed Diane against the wall and began kissing her. He passionately explored your wet mouth and gently kissed her bare neck. Tingles ran through Diane's body. Her nipples were hard and erect. Diane's neck was her weakness. She pulled away panting softly and said, "Oh, my God, David. I can't believe I'm saying this but we have to stop. I'm not going to be in any condition to pick up my class and finish out the day."

David looked down at his pants and agreed. His swollen loins were bulging in his tightly-fitted jeans. Diane wanted so badly to reach in and touch him but knew that would only make matters worse.

"Damn, girl," David said as he took a deep breath. "You are something else. I want you so badly. Are you sure you have to go out of town this weekend?" he said as he smiled.

Diane bit her bottom lip and frowned like a three-year-old. "I do David. I have to go. I'm so sorry." David held Diane close in his arms but made sure it was just a simple hug.

"Well, I think I'm able to walk now without scaring a young child." Both David and Diane laughed and were able to see some humor in all of this. They walked to the classroom door. David kissed Diane on the lips and then on her nose. Diane giggled. "I'll call you tonight during one of my breaks."

"I'd like that very much and I don't care what time you call, just try to call." David placed his hand on Diane's face. He said goodbye and then walked out of her room.

Diane stood with her back against the wall, her arms crossed on her chest, her eyes closed, and her mouth slightly opened just enough to let out a satisfying moan.

David made it to his truck. He sat stunned then pulled down on the crotch of his pants and smiled a huge smile. He uncharacteristically took out his phone and sent the following text to Diane, I miss you already! Diane sent back a kissing emoji.

For the remainder of the day, Diane wore a very soft contented smile on her face. Her cheeks were still flush and she feared others would know her secret. She didn't dare tell Jenny. She didn't want her to accidentally let it slip while talking to other teachers.

Chapter 7

Diane's day was over and her vacation was about to begin. She was very excited to see her girlfriends again but sad she was going to miss out on time with David.

When Diane got home, she packed her suitcase with fun, flirty outfits. She made sure not to forget her cowboy boots since they were going to be visiting the Grand Old Opry for the Keith Urban concert. First, she called Anne, her oldest friend from school. They talked for a few minutes just to verify flight times. They would wait to catch up until they saw each other. Diane called Sara next. Sara was Anne's friend first. They had met in middle school but they became good friends when Anne reintroduced them their freshman year of high school. Lastly, Diane called Luna. Crazy Luna. All four met in science class their sophomore year and have been as tight as thieves ever since. All four girls went their separate ways after high school, all to a different college but always kept in touch and made a pact that every year, no matter what, they would find one weekend out of the year to reconnect and catch up. No boyfriends, no spouses, and no children. Just the four amigos.

Luna is happily married to her college sweetheart. They married soon after graduation and moved to Atlanta for her husband Jim's job. Luna has eight-year-old twin boys. She put her career as a hospital administrator on hold after the birth of her boys. She wanted to be a full-time mom but, just recently, the hospital gave her an opportunity to work from home. She was hesitant at first but now Luna is loving life.

Sara is recently divorced with no children. She needs this girls' trip more than any of the girls. She's been a bit depressed even though she has a great job as a top journalist for a major newspaper in New York City.

Anne, is happy-go-lucky. She lives in Houston with her fiancé of five years. They are yet to set a wedding date. They both love being in the "engaged" phase of their relationship. Anne is a curator at an art museum.

All four girls live four different lives but they are connected because of their strong friendship. When they get together, they're one. They laugh. They cry and they give each other constructive criticism. They candy-coat nothing. They tell it like it is, even if it hurts.

It was getting late and David had not called. Diane didn't worry because, after today, she felt a little more secure with him. She knew he was going to be busy all night. At about ten-forty-five p.m. Diane crawled into bed. She had her suitcases packed. She checked in for her flight. She touched base with all the girls and made sure the hotel and rental car had been confirmed. She was ready and now the only thing that could make this night any better would be to hear from David. She checked the clock before she closed her eyes and was startled when her phone rang.

"Hi, David."

"Hey, sweetie. Did I wake you?"

"No, as a matter of fact, I was just lying here thinking the best way to end my day would be to hear from you and, boom, you called."

"I don't have a lot of time to talk but I did want to call to say good night and tell you again how much I enjoyed seeing you today. It didn't end like I wanted it to but you'll just keep me wanting more."

"Aw, David, I know. It wasn't easy for either of us."

There was silence for a few seconds then David asked, "What time does your flight leave again?"

"Ten a.m."

"Before you board, call me. I'd love to hear from you."

"I definitely will, David."

"Well, babe, I need to go. You sleep well and I'll talk to you in the morning."

Diane smiled peacefully and said, "Good night, David."

"Good night, Diane."

Chapter 8

Diane got up bright and early and showered. She dressed comfortably in a pair of loose-fitting jeans, soft t-shirt and slip-on shoes. She made herself a cup of coffee and gathered her things before calling her UBER. She was ready to see her friends and begin her girls' trip.

On the way to the airport, Diane wanted so badly to call David but decided against it because she didn't want her driver to eavesdrop on their conversation. Diane and her driver made small talk throughout her trip to the airport.

Diane checked her bags at the curb and, since she had pre-TSA clearance, she was able to walk straight to the checkpoint without any problem. She was already checked into her flight and she had her boarding pass ready on her phone. Diane quickly found her gate and found a seat. She had about forty-five minutes before the flight would begin boarding and decided to send David a text to see if he could talk,

Good morning, handsome. Do you have a minute to talk?

She waited several minutes for a response then her phone rang. "Hello," smiled Diane as she answered the phone.

"Hey, beautiful. Are you at the airport or did you decide not to go?" laughed David.

Diane giggled and answered, "Yeah, I'm at the airport and just waiting to board. I'm so happy I got to talk to you before leaving."

"I'm glad I was able to call. I've been so busy training this new kid. I don't know how you teachers do it!" David and Diane both laughed.

"So you're busy, right?" asked Diane.

"Kind of," said David but added, "I just had to hear your voice before you left. Will you call or text when you get there?"

"Of course, I will, David." There was a small pause then Diane said, "Well, I'll let you go. Have a good day and don't be so hard on the kid."

"Ha, ha! I won't. Okay, sweetie. Have a safe flight and I'll talk to you later."

"Talk to you later, David. 'Bye." Diane dropped the phone to her heart, closed her eyes and smiled softly.

Diane sat waiting to board her flight still sporting a soft smile on her face. She stared into space thinking of David, their passionate kisses, his gentle touches and his stiff, large manhood. She shook as tingles rushed through her body.

Diane arrived safely in Nashville and, soon after touching down, she sent a text to David,

Landed safely. I'll call later XOXO. David responded with a heart emoji.

Diane was the first to arrive. She retrieved her luggage and set out to find the gate where Anne's plane would be arriving. She patiently waited while people-watching, which was one of her favorite pastimes. Diane waited about twenty minutes. Then she saw Anne walk out.

Anne nervously looked from side to side and, when she saw Diane, she let out an excited, "Hey!" They embraced and each wore a huge smile. Next, Luna was arriving from Atlanta. After getting Anne's luggage, they made their way to Luna's arrival gate. The two ladies sat and caught up a little because it was a rule between the four that no special news or new news was shared unless all four girls were together. Anne looked at Diane and said, "What's going on? You look so happy. It's written all over your face."

Diane smiled and said, "You know the rules; no news until everyone is together."

Both girls chuckled and Anne said, "I can't wait because I know it's going to be good!"

An hour went by with small talk about work and family. Finally, Luna's plane landed. Both girls were waiting patiently for her to walk out from her flight. Luna, the craziest of the bunch, yelled happily when she saw her friends. She yelled so loud that people stopped to stare. The three girls hugged with excitement.

"You girls ready to go have some fun?" said Luna. "I can't wait! I love my boys and my husband but mommy needs a break and a couple of drinks."

"Some things never change," laughed Anne.

"Okay, so where do we go to pick up Sara?" asked Luna.

"Her flight gets here in an hour so we have time to grab a drink and a quick snack," said Diane.

"Sounds good to me, Diane," replied Luna. "Let's go and see what trouble we can get into!"

Anne shook her head and said, joking around, "Who brought the bail money?"

Finally, an hour passed and the girls made their way to Sara's gate. They sat close to the walkthrough so they could jump out and surprise her. Girls will be girls. People were walking out two by two and in groups but no Sara.

"Where the hell is she?" Luna asked in a sharp voice. "If that girl missed her flight, I'm going to kill her."

"No, no, here she comes," said Diane.

"She's not even looking straight ahead," added Anne.

"Who is she with?" asked Luna. Sara walked straight past the girls and was in deep conversation with a gorgeous older man.

"Um, excuse me. Do you remember us?" Luna sarcastically asked Sara.

Sara turned around and yelled, "OMG, ladies! I'm so sorry." She laughed and hugged all three of her friends. "This is Edward Smithfield. Edward and I sat next to each other on the flight. Edward, these are the friends I was telling you about. This is Luna."

"Nice to meet you," said Edward.

"This is Anne and this is Diane."

Edward shook the girls' hands and said, "It's a pleasure meeting you. Sara told me all about your trip. Have a great time in Nashville. It's a great city and my hometown. If you need anything while you're here, just give me a holler. Sara has my business card. Sara, my dear, it's been an absolute joy sitting and talking with you." Edward hugged Sara and he walked off.

"Are you kidding me? Damn, girl, what a gorgeous man," said Anne.

"I know, right?" said Sara smiling from ear to ear.

"You better spill about Mr. handsome," laughed Luna.

"There's nothing to spill," Sara said as she batted her eyes and laughed.

After a very long day, the girls finally reached the hotel. "Oh, my goodness, this hotel is absolutely amazing! I've never seen a hotel this beautiful," Diane said with her eyes wide and mouth open. The girls checked in, got their room keys and went straight to the room. The girls dropped their luggage and plopped on the beds. "What a long day" sighed Diane.

"Oh, don't you party pooper out on us, missy. The night hasn't even begun!" Luna said as she seemed to get her second wind.

"Okay, so what's the game plan? Sara, I know you have a whole itinerary set for us," joked Anne.

"Oh, you bet I do," answered Sara. "So, tonight, I figured we'd have dinner and drinks here at the hotel bar. Catch up with each other's news and gossip. Tomorrow, I made reservations for a lunch on a riverboat cruise and, of course, tomorrow night, Keith Urban but, before the concert, I was thinking about having a fun day exploring the city. Sunday, I thought we would tour the Jack Daniels Distillery, do some more sightseeing and have dinner and drinks at a local place. You know, I can always call Edward!" The girls all laughed and even though they gave Sara a hard time for being so organized, they were happy she planned things out. "We're all flying out Monday afternoon so we can do some morning exploring if you want. I left that open," Sara laughed and the girls got ready for the evening.

As Diane was getting ready, she looked at her watch and thought about what David would be doing. She decided to send him a text, Girls all arrived safe. At the hotel. Thinking of you. David quickly responded, Can't stop thinking about you. Call me when you get a chance.

Diane's heart raced as she closed her eyes. Her thoughts quickly went to being in David's strong arms with his lips gently on hers.

"Hello, earth to Diane," Luna whispered in her ear.

"Oh, my, I'm sorry. What?" said Diane startled.

"Where were you? Or should I ask, who were you with?"

Diane smiled mischievously and said, "In due time, my dear. In due time."

Chapter 9

The girls walked into the hotel's main restaurant and bar. It was more beautiful than they had anticipated. They ordered drinks, appetizers then, finally, dinner. They laughed. They danced a bit. They joked and then they began sharing and giving advice when it was needed.

Sara was the first to spill her guts. She talked about her recent divorce and how much she still cared for her ex-husband. She also mentioned briefly about her new assignment at work. She was working on an investigative piece about the federal government, so she really wasn't at liberty to discuss too much. The girls didn't press for more information and understood how important her writing and job were. She was also debating whether or not to call Edward, the man from the flight. The girls encouraged her to spread her wings and go for it.

Up next was Anne. Anne shocked all the girls when she told them that she and her fiancé, Tom, had set a wedding date.

"Well, it's about damn time!" Luna exclaimed.

"Oh, my goodness, that's fantastic. I'm so happy for you," added Diane.

"What finally changed your minds?" Sara asked curiously.

"Age," said Anne.

"Age? What do you mean, age?" Luna questioned.

"Tom and I sat down one day and started thinking and talking about the future. We figured if we wanted children we should consider our age. We both don't want to be too old to play and have fun with the kids."

"But you're not too old," stated Luna.

"I know, but, guys, Tom is in his forties already. I think he was hearing his clock go tick-tock." The girls laughed.

"Well, I'm excited. When's the big day?" asked Diane.

"November 30 of this year. It's a Saturday. In Houston. Small, small, small wedding. Just very close friends and family. Maybe thirty people at the most and I was hoping that you, Diane, would be my Maid of Honor and, ladies, I was hoping you would be my bridesmaids."

"Oh, my gosh, of course. Yes, I'll be your Maid of Honor!" exclaimed Diane. Both Luna and Anne hugged Sara and agreed to be in the wedding.

"Well, how do I top that announcement?" Luna said laughing. "I'm the boring housewife and mom."

"Oh please," said Sara. "I'm sure you've got some juicy news for us."

"Okay, here goes. Jim and I are loving life. He just made VP at the brokerage. The boys are doing well in school and the hospital asked me back."

"What?" That's fantastic!" Anne said as she jumped up.

"What are you going to be doing there? I thought the long hours of administration were too hectic while raising the boys?" questioned Diane.

"Well, that's the good thing about this job offer. I'll be working from home. It's thirty hours a week to start and if I feel I can handle more, then they'll give me more."

"Wow!" remarked Sara. "That's unbelievable! I say, take the offer."

"Yeah, I've been really thinking about it and especially during my flight, when I had some alone time. Jim says go for it. So, you know, I'm going for it!" laughed Luna and then ordered another round of drinks.

Finally, it was Diane's turn to spill her guts but just as soon as she was going to begin, David sent her a text. Diane grabbed her phone. "Wait a minute, guys, I need to read this real quick." The text read,

Hey babe. Missing you and thinking about you.

Diane smiled and bit her bottom lip. "Oh, no, chicka. You better spill. We know something's up when you bite that bottom lip of yours," remarked Anne.

Diane quietly giggled, raised her index finger and said, "Wait, I need to respond."

"Oh no, this is going to be good!" Luna said as she turned to the other girls and high-fived them. Diane thought for a minute before responding then wrote,

Hey, handsome, I miss you too. I haven't stopped thinking about you since I left. Having a late dinner and drinks with the girls. I'll call tonight.

David responded, I can't wait to hear your voice. Have fun but not too much fun. Lol

Diane sent back a kiss emoji.

All three girls closely watched and waited for Diane to put her phone away. They were staring at her like cougars ready to pounce on their prey.

Diane nonchalantly said, "What?" and then laughed.

"Spill your guts, girl!" shouted Luna.

"Who is this person that's making you beam?" added Sara.

"Details now!" demanded Anne.

"Okay, okay, but, first, what time does the restaurant close?" asked Diane.

"Who the hell cares? Just spill!" snapped Luna.

"All right, his name is David. He's a former Army Ranger."

"What does he do now?"

"Where did you meet?"

"How long have you known him?"

"Is it serious?" The girls were bombarding Diane left and right with questions.

"Hey, wait a minute. Geez, give me a chance to finish. I thought we always said NO questions until the person finished. I haven't even gotten started."

"Sorry, sorry, go on," said Anne.

"I'll keep quiet. I promise," said Luna.

"I'm sorry, we're just so excited you've met someone. Go on. Finish!" added Sara.

Diane took a deep breath and began "He works for a delivery company that services my school. I noticed him a couple of months ago when school started but never had the nerve to say hi. He would look at me and smile and, of course, I would smile back but there was no conversation until two weeks ago."

"What does he look like?" Luna curiously asked.

Diane started with a huge smile on her face, "He's about six foot, two hundred pounds and, oh, my goodness, does he know how to fill out a pair of jeans!" The ladies all giggled.

"Keep going, keep going," demanded Anne then asked. "Have you been out?"

"Is he a good kisser?"

"Kisser? Forget that. How is he in bed?" Sara eagerly asked.

Diane blushed, slightly giggled and then continued, "Do you want me to finish telling you about David and how we met?"

"Yes, of course," the ladies said in unison.

"Okay then," snapped Diane. "Zip it until I'm finished!" Diane took another deep breath and started once again, "I finally got the nerve to walk out of my room when I saw him pull up. I guess you can say I timed it perfectly. It was a casual hi at first, then I found out that he started asking questions about me. I have a friend, the librarian, who he talks with because he knows her husband. One day,

I walked into the library when he was in there. We talked for a few minutes and when I had to leave, he walked me to my classroom and before he left, he kissed me and I almost fainted. It was one of the most gentle but sensual kisses I've ever had."

"Damn girl, I'm drooling. Continue," Luna said softly.

"Before he left, he took my number and said he would call. Of course, I thought he meant he was going to call that night."

"Oh no, I guess he didn't?" asked Anne.

"No, and, of course, in the usual Diane way, I jumped to conclusions and thought the worst. Well, luck would have it that I had a workshop the next day at another school. I was bummed and didn't want to be there. I was on break and guess who saw me and came up to me to talk?"

"Who?" asked Sara.

"Sara, don't be dumb. It had to be David, right? Right, Diane? It was David?" wondered Luna eagerly.

"Yes, it was David and I was a complete and utter bitch to him. I was so wrong for acting like that. The poor guy didn't even know why I was so short with him." Before Diane could continue, the waiter came by the table to ask if the ladies needed anything else.

"Another round?" suggested Luna.

The ladies agreed and Diane continued, "Well, after I was short with him, he called Jenny, my friend the librarian, and, according to her, he sounded like he had just lost his puppy! He told her how I treated him at my workshop. Then he realized, after going over in his mind, the time we spent in my classroom when he said he would call but didn't. He understood why I was upset but what I didn't know, is he also tends bar on the beach and worked that night. By the time he was able to call it was too late and he decided not to call."

"Oh, my gosh, so much drama already. So how did this work out?" asked Anne.

"Well, after he spoke to Jenny, he sent a text apologizing and explaining what happened. Long story short, I called him. He asked if we could meet for coffee to talk. We did. We had a nice time. He walked me to my car afterwards and kissed me so passionately that I wanted him to take me right there on my car!"

All the girls laughed and all Luna could say was, "Damn girl!"

"After David found out that I was not going to be in town this weekend, he was upset because he had something "special" planned. Ladies, for a minute and only a minute, I was upset too because I knew what I was going to be missing." Diane blushed and laughed out loud with her friends. Diane continued, "He made a special trip to my school yesterday just to see me and to steal another kiss. I don't know if it's because I haven't been kissed in a while or if he kisses me in forbidden places that make the kisses unbelievably sensual or maybe it's all of the above." Diane stopped for a second, looked up to the ceiling and said, "I think, it's all of the above." Diane let out a soft grunt and smiled. "So, that's my story. It's still extremely early. I have no expectations and I'll see where it goes but I do know I'm going to have fun!"

After having a delicious dinner and drinks and, especially after catching up, the girls decided to make their way back to their room. They had a big day planned for tomorrow and needed a good night's sleep.

Luna called her husband and spoke for a while. It was almost embarrassing listening to their love fest. Anne was almost as bad when she called Tom to say goodnight. Sara debated on calling Edward, just because she was feeling left out. She decided against calling, for now. Diane wanted so badly to call David but she wanted to do it privately. She wasn't sure if he was still working, being a Friday night on the beach, so she sent him a text, Hey, handsome, I'm in for the night and just wanted to say goodnight.

Minutes later, her phone rang. It was David. The girls let out a unanimous, "Aw!" Diane got up, smiled and took the call in the bathroom.

"Hi, David, are you still working?"

"No, sweetie, I'm actually on my way home. So, did you have a nice dinner with the girls?"

"Oh, yeah, it was great catching up with them. They're really a great group of girlfriends, that I don't know what I'd do if I didn't have them in my life."

"Yeah, that's special. I feel the same way about a group of guys I grew up with. Maybe, one day, you'll meet them and I'll meet your friends." Diane smiled at the thought of a future with him but she was determined to only think in the now… for now. "So, what's on the agenda for tomorrow? Anything exciting?"

"Sara made reservations on a river boat for lunch, some sightseeing, and the Keith Urban concert at night."

"Now that sounds like a full day!"

"Well, when Sara makes plans, she never disappoints."

There were a few seconds of silence then David said, "I really wish you were here with me. I can taste your lips and, oh, how I'd love for you to be in my arms."

With her eyes gently closed, Diane softly moaned and said, "Yes, David, that would be great. I'd love that too."

"Well, sweetie," whispered David. "I'm going to let you go get some sleep. You sleep well and give me a call or text when you can."

"I will. Goodnight, David."

"Goodnight, Diane."

Diane walked out of the bathroom with both hands crossed over her chest and yelled, "He's so freaking adorable. God, I can't wait to be with him. The man gives me tingles just talking to him. Can you imagine what he'll do to me in bed?" The girls laughed. They were all super tired from traveling and drinking. They said goodnight and went to bed. Diane stayed up trying to visualize being with David. She went to sleep with a smile on her face.

Chapter 10

The girls woke up ready to have fun. The first thing on Sara's agenda for the girls today was a riverboat lunch cruise on the Cumberland River. The cruise is a two-and-ahalf hour music fest of great music, ranging from bluegrass, country, blues, and R&B. The food is reported to be some of the best Southern Cuisine one could ever eat. The girls were excited and looking forward to spending time on the water.

Before Diane left, she sent a quick text to David, Hi sweetie. Heading to the lunch cruise. I'll call later. Have a good day. XO

David responded soon after, Have a great time. Send a pic if you can. XO

Diane and the girls were waiting in the lobby for their UBER to arrive when they ran across Edward, the older gentleman, who was sitting with Sara on her flight to Nashville.

"Oh, my goodness, Edward," Sara said as she walked over to him. "I can't believe you're here."

"Wow, Sara. Small world. Where you, ladies, heading?"

"We're heading to the riverboat lunch cruise on the Cumberland River," said Sara.

"Oh, that's a good one. You, ladies, should enjoy that. What's up after that?"

"We're going to the Keith Urban concert later tonight," Luna said eagerly.

"Well, isn't that something? Ladies, when you get to the door, mention my name and hand them this pass." He handed the pass to Sara and said, "This should get you backstage to see Keith. If you have a problem, just call me." The girls looked stunned.

"What? You know Keith?" asked Diane.

"I run his security detail. Well, not me personally, but my company does."

"Oh, wow, okay. Thank you, Edward," said Sara in disbelief.

"No problem, ladies. Enjoy your lunch cruise. See you tonight."

The girls climbed into their UBER and could not believe their luck. "This shit is unbelievable," Luna said as she shook her head. "Sara, I'm so glad you weren't a bitch to that man on the plane." The girls laughed as they arrived at the riverboat.

The cruise was everything they said it would be. The music was fantastic and the food was amazing. They took several pictures and Diane took a few selfies for David but didn't send any. The girls had a couple of hours to kill before they had to get ready for the concert. They walked through downtown Nashville and enjoyed the sights and the shopping.

Back at the hotel, the girls decided to up their game on what they were wearing to the concert just in case they got to meet Keith. Sara decided on a pair of black jeans and pink blouse. Luna wore blue jeans and a white lace halter top. Anne decided on white jeans and a black fancy t-shirt. Diane decided to go with a cute little sundress with mid-calf high boots. All four girls topped off their look with a cowboy hat. They were ready for fun.

When the girls reached the concert hall, they were hesitant to use Edward's special business pass. "What if he is a fraud?" Sara said nervously.

Luna quickly took out her phone and said, "I can't believe we didn't think of this earlier. I'm going to Google this man." Luna quickly googled the name Edward Smithfield. "Oh, hell, yeah, this dude is the real deal. Use the pass." Sara handed the pass to the man taking the tickets. He smiled and asked how many were in the party. Sara told him four and was then handed four backstage passes. The man gave the girls instructions on where to go after the concert. The girls stood in disbelief and couldn't believe their luck.

For two hours, the girls sang and danced to the music of Keith Urban. They were having a phenomenal time. "This is one of the best concerts I've been to!" yelled Luna.

"I can't remember the last time I had this much fun," shouted Diane.

"Let's get to the backstage to meet Keith," said Anne.

"What are we waiting for? Let's go!" demanded Sara.

The girls timidly walked to the backstage and through the security checkpoint. They each handed their pass to the security agent standing in front of the door, where they were allowed to enter.

"Oh, my, this is so exciting! I still can't believe our luck," Anne said as she led the way.

"Whatever anyone does, please make sure you don't embarrass me or Edward," said Sara as she looked directly at Luna. All the girls laughed.

"Sara, hey. I see you and your friends made it."

"Oh, Edward, this is so great. Thank you so much."

"No problem, Sara. Why don't you and your friends grab something to eat and drink and when Keith comes out, I'll make sure he comes over to say hello." The girls walked over to the large tables of food. There were all kinds of sandwiches, shrimp, chicken, hot and cold entrees; just a smorgasbord of food and desserts. The girls each grabbed a plate and dug in. They made small talk with the other invited guests and then, about a half hour later, Keith came out to meet his fans. The girls were star-struck. They shook his hand and he was happy to take pictures with all the girls.

"I can't believe how nice he is," smiled Diane.

"So much fun!" cheered Anne.

"Best night ever!" beamed Luna."

"Let's go find Edward to thank him," suggested Sara. The girls searched but couldn't find Edward. They decided to head back to the hotel.

When they got to the hotel, Sara left a thank you note for Edward at the front desk. She was hoping she would get a chance to thank him personally before they left.

The girls got ready for bed and talked about their fantastic night. They viewed the pictures and decided which ones were Instagram approved. Luna and Anne decided to call home to speak to their better halves. Diane picked a couple of good pictures to send to David.

She sent this text along with the pictures, Hi, David. We had a wonderful time. Got to meet Keith Urban. SUPER night. Can you talk?

David responded, Wow, you look beautiful. Looks like you and the girls had a great time. Still at the bar. It's crazy here on a Saturday. Call you tomorrow?

Diane was disappointed she couldn't speak with David but she was glad he liked the pictures. Diane and the girls talked about their amazing day and soon fell fast asleep.

Chapter 11

The next morning, the girls woke up, still in disbelief that they met Keith Urban in person. "Okay, ladies, this is our last full day together. Let's make it a good one," said Luna in a happy voice.

"I don't know what we can do to top yesterday but I'm ready," said Anne determined to make this day count.

"Remind us again what we're doing today, Sara," asked Diane.

"I have us scheduled to tour the Jack Daniel's Distillery and hoping we can visit the Grand Ole Opry."

"You do know that the distillery tour is a seven-hour bus tour right?" questioned Luna.

"What? Wait. Seven-hours? Ew, I don't want to be stuck doing that," moaned Anne.

"Yeah, I'm going to have to agree with the girls, Sara," said Diane.

"No problem, I didn't get the tickets yet so we're good. Are you guys still interested in the Grand Ole Opry tour?"

"Why don't we just walk around the city and sightsee? I don't want to be stuck doing one particular thing. I just want to get as much time with you guys before we leave tomorrow."

"Aw, Luna, I couldn't agree more." Said Anne.

The girls spent their day doing a number of things. They had lunch in a quaint little restaurant near a winery, which they visited afterwards. They walked into a few touristy shops and ended the day visiting Madame Tussauds, where they had fun taking pictures with the waxed singers. All in all, it was a great day.

When the girls got back from their day of sightseeing, a note was waiting for Sara at the front desk. It was from Edward. He had arranged dinner at the hotel, in the main restaurant, for the girls. The note read, Sorry I had to leave early last night. I'm back in NY. Please accept this offer of dinner for you and your wonderful girlfriends. It was a pleasure meeting you all. I hope to be able to see you in the near future. Edward

"Wow! Someone has it bad for you, Sara," laughed Luna.

"That's crazy!" smiled Diane.

"It sure is," wondered Sara then asked, "Who's hungry?" The girls laughed and went upstairs to shower and change for dinner.

While Diane was waiting for the girls to get ready, she decided to take a chance and call David. She was surprised when David answer the phone saying, "Hey, beautiful, what's up? Are you enjoying yourself?"

"Hi, David. Yeah, I can honestly say I'm enjoying myself. This is probably one of the best girl trips we've had. Did I call at a bad time?"

"No, I have a few minutes to talk. You're coming back home tomorrow, right?"

"Yes, my flight gets in around three-thirty. So, I should be home, hopefully, by four. Will I be able to see you tomorrow?"

"Sweetie, I would want nothing more but, remember, it's Bike Week here on the beach so, right after work, I'll be up here but I'll see you Tuesday at school."

"Oh, I'd like that very much especially knowing my students have library from one till two," Diane said giggling.

"I guess that means I have to control myself when I see you?" laughed David. Diane smiled. "Well, sweetie, I need to get going. Call me before you leave for home tomorrow."

"I will, David. Have a good night. 'Bye, handsome."

"'Bye, Diane. Good night."

The girls had a fabulous last evening together. They laughed, joked and reminisced about their high school days. The dinner was absolutely delicious. The desserts were to die for and the drinks were plenty. This girls' trip was definitely one for the books.

Later that evening, Sara called Edward and thanked him for his kindness. She also accepted an invitation to have dinner with him after she got back to the city. Sara had a date!

Morning came too soon for the girls. The girls were packed and each one was ready to get back to reality. The four girls had different flight times but traveled to the airport together.

Luna was the first flight back to reality. She was heading back home to Atlanta to her life as a mommy of twin boys, devoted wife and, now, working woman. She was ready to tackle her new world. She hugged her friends tight, said her goodbyes and walked away.

Anne was next to board her flight. She was anxious to get back to plan her wedding but would deeply miss her time with the girls.

That left Diane and Sara; both girls who have been unlucky at love but, with any luck, that would soon change. Diane encouraged Sara to give Edward a chance and to look forward to new adventures. Diane told her that after what she's been through, a messy divorce, she deserves happiness. Diane and Sara sat for about thirty minutes talking about the pros and cons of these two new men in their lives. It was time for Sara to board. Diane and Sara got up from their seats, hugged and promised to keep each other posted on their upcoming dates.

Diane sat down at her gate and checked the flight schedule. Everything was on time. She sent David a text,

I'm at the airport waiting to board. Can't wait to get home. I'll text when I'm back in the 305. Xoxo

David's response was: Safe flight, sweetie. Talk to you soon. Xoxo

Diane's flight was ready to board. She bought a magazine to read so she'd have something to do during the two-and-a-half-hour flight. The flight wasn't full so she was able to have the whole three seats to herself. She thought having the magazine to read would take her mind off of David but it didn't. She missed him. She missed his deep blue mesmerizing eyes. She missed his warm smile. She missed his strong arms. "Oh man," she sighed silently. "I think I've fallen too soon for this man. I don't even know him but I can't think of anything more that I would want than for him to make passionate, unbridled love to me." Diane's body got tingly and wet as she fantasized about being with him.

Diane closed her eyes for what she thought was just a minute but was woken up when she felt the plane touch down. "Oh, my, I guess I needed that little nap," she said to herself as she gathered her carry-on.

Diane listened closely to the flight attendant as she gave the location of the baggage claim for her flight. She waited patiently for her fellow passengers to leave while she remained seated. She decided to text David that she had arrived,

Hi, handsome. I just landed. I'll be home in about an hour. I'll call you later so we can talk. Can't wait to hear your voice.

David didn't respond right away so she figured he was busy. She got up from her seat and made her way out of the plane and to baggage claim. She took the escalator down, which was easy access to outside, where she could catch an UBER home. Once at baggage claim, she waited until the conveyor belt started. She waited patiently for her luggage to appear. Diane had placed a bright yellow ribbon on her luggage so she could spot it among the countless other pieces of luggage that were making their way out.

"Excuse me, ma'am. Do you need any help with your luggage?" said a strange but familiar voice coming from the back of her.

"Oh, no, thank you," Diane said before turning to look at the person. "David!" Diane screamed happily as she completely turned around to see David. "Oh, my God, what are you doing here? How did you know where I'd be? Oh, my goodness, I'm so happy to see you!" She hugged David tightly.

"Hi, babe. Surprise! I've missed you and had to see you," David said as he smiled his million-dollar smile.

"But don't you have work? It's the middle of the day?"

"Babe, don't worry about it. Just tell me which piece of luggage is yours," David said laughing.

Diane pointed out her luggage to David. He picked it up with ease as his t-shirt sleeve rolled up, exposing his large biceps. Diane smiled, bit the side of her lip and slightly moaned to herself. David took Diane's hand and, together, they walked out of the airport and to David's truck.

"I still can't believe you're here picking me up. How did you know where I'd be?"

"Well, my dear, there's a new little tool called the internet," laughed David. "All I did was Google flights from Nashville to Miami leaving and arriving at the times you told me, then I looked at the different baggage claim locations and found you standing there."

"Wow, I'm very impressed."

David stopped in the middle of the parking terminal and said, "I can't wait any longer. I need to kiss those lips!" and he did. Diane felt a rush of energy go through her body. They arrived at David's truck. David opened the door for Diane and placed her luggage in the back. "So, my dear, how about directions to your house?" Diane smiled and happily obliged. David took Diane's hand and held it tight. She smiled from ear to ear.

Chapter 12

During the ride home, Diane was nervous; not that David was taking her home and that they may finally finish what they started, but she was more worried about the condition of the house. She silently thought, "Is my house visitor ready? Did I leave clothes on the floor? Did I make my bed before I left?" Then her mind jumped to, "How long will he stay? Do I have any food to offer him?" Diane was a mess and she tried quickly to claim herself down.

David asked if she was hungry and if she wanted to stop to grab something to eat. Diane had only had breakfast and her stomach was beginning to growl. "That sounds great, David. I am a little hungry."

"Do you have any diners or delis near you?"

"Well, there's a little family-owned restaurant right before my house."

"Great! Why don't we stop there for a quick bite?" suggested David. Diane nodded and gave him directions to the restaurant.

David and Diane sat across from each other and smiled. Diane's smile was sweet and almost timid, while David's smile was mischievous with nasty thoughts of what he wanted to do with Diane.

Diane was careful about what she ordered. No onions or garlic. She knew there was going to be some heavy kissing and action pretty soon. Diane settled for a bowl of chicken soup and a small house salad. David, on the other hand, didn't seem to worry about what he was eating. He decided on a huge Italian sub.

David and Diane talked about her trip and all the cool things she and the girls did. David told Diane about some of the crazy things that happened at the bar. He was making small talk during and after dinner but he really wanted to leave to begin his night with Diane. He picked up the check and threw a five on the table.

"Well my dear, are you ready to leave?" David anxiously asked Diane.

"Sure, let's go," she answered with a smile. "I wonder what awaits me at home and, gee, I can't wait to see what's waiting for me at school!" They both laughed.

David followed Diane's directions to her home. Diane lives in a townhouse in a much sought-after, well-maintained neighborhood. Her home is two-story with two bedrooms and two baths. She has a large kitchen and a nice size living area. All a young single woman would need.

David parked his truck and helped Diane out. He gathered her luggage and followed Diane to her front door. Luckily, Diane's AC was programmed from her phone and, while at the restaurant, she turned it on. The house was cool and inviting.

They walked into Diane's home. Diane put her purse on the small table next to the front door and said, "Well, this is my house."

"It's very nice," David said as he looked around.

"Thank you, David."

"But you know what's nicer?" David paused and then said in a very sexy voice as he moved closer to Diane, "The owner." Diane's heart started beating faster the closer he got. When he reached Diane, he softly pushed her against the wall and said, "I can't resist you any longer. If you don't feel the same way, please tell me now so I can leave before it's too late."

"Oh, no, David, I definitely feel the same way!" That's all David needed to hear.

David took Diane's wrists and placed them over her head. Diane let out a small moan. He began kissing and exploring every part of her mouth. Diane dropped her arms and placed them around David's head. She held the back of his head in her hands and she slightly grabbed his hair, pulling it gently. David continued kissing Diane, then moved down to her neck, where he moved up and down with his hot wet tongue. David started to unbutton Diane's blouse. She could feel her nipples becoming erect and hard. He moved down towards her full, plump breasts and took one of them into his mouth. He ran his tongue over her hard nipples and Diane let out with a loud, "Oh, my God!"

David stopped to quickly ask, "Where's your room? Where's the bedroom, Diane?"

Gasping for air, Diane said, "Upstairs, go straight then turn right!" David scooped Diane into his arms and quickly climbed the stairs to her room. The curtains were slightly open letting just enough light into the room where he could see the bed. He placed Diane on the bed as he stared into her eyes and he began removing his t-shirt. Diane was transfixed on his hard abs and chest. She began to slip out of her already unbuttoned blouse. David sat down next to her and removed her lace bra. Her breasts stood there hard and firm. David began exploring her neck and holding her right breast in his hand as he tugged gently on her nipple. Diane had never felt such passion. Diane was completely lying down on her bed when David made his way to Diane's stomach. As he slowly traced her belly button with his tongue, his hands reached up, grabbing her breasts and playfully squeezing them. Diane lifted her hips slightly so he could remove her pants and underwear. She lay there anxiously anticipating his next move. David stood up and, without taking his eyes off Diane, removed the rest of his clothes. He looked like something from a Greek god painting. "He was perfect," thought Diane as she gazed down to his abundant manhood.

They both lay in the bed together. David slowly, over and over, kissed every part of Diane's body. He was fully in control. Listening to her soft whimpers, made him want to please her even more. He continued teasing her until she begged him to be one with her. When they finally joined as one, Diane let out a joyous cry and David a joyous moan. Diane and David moved together in perfect harmony. Diane felt electricity run through her body. David took her to places no other man had even attempted to come close to. Diane's nails softly dug into David's back as drops of sweat formed on his forehead. He was breathing heavily, not because he was out of shape, no way, but because he was giving one hundred percent of himself to satisfy her. Each was exhausted but unwilling to give in and stop. It felt too good and too right. The moment they each climaxed, they lay in each other's arms, speechless. David kissed Diane's cheek then the side of her mouth. He ran his fingers down her shoulder and arm then clutched her fingers and hand and held them tightly. Still speechless, all they could do was smile at each other. They lay in bed, with Diane snuggled beneath David's neck. She traced his chest with her fingers. She never wanted this evening to end.

There was little to no daylight left peeking through the curtains. David finally broke the silence. He looked deep into her big brown eyes smiled softly and said, "My sweet beautiful Diane." He ran his finger over her lips, tracing her mouth and continued saying, "As much as I wanted this to happen, I never imagined it would. I never thought we would be right here sharing this moment together."

"Oh, David, I know. From the first kiss we shared in my classroom, I could only fantasize being with you. My fantasy wasn't even this good." They both chuckled and David kissed Diane's forehead.

"I can't believe I'm asking this question but what time do you need to get up in the morning?" David asked.

"Oh, I don't even want to think about going to work tomorrow. Ugh, six a.m."

"I need to get up at five. As much as I do not want to leave, I think I better, for both of our sakes."

"No, I totally understand but how about a shower before you leave?"

"Sounds good to me." David and Diane both entered the shower together. Seeing Diane's body in full light, stirred emotions and he was quickly hard and ready for round two right there in the shower.

Diane, dressed in a robe, walked David to the front door. He grabbed her face with both of his strong hands and kissed her passionately good night. "Sleep well, my beautiful Diane."

"You too, David. Good night and get home safe. Oh, by the way, thank you for picking me up from the airport." They laughed. David kissed Diane on the tip of her nose and left.

Diane raced back to her bed to smell David's scent. She cuddled in the sheets, holding on to the pillow that strongly smelled of David.

Chapter 13

The sound of the alarm came way too fast. Diane took one last inhale from the pillow of David's scent before getting out of bed. She slowly walked into the shower, where she closed her eyes and reminisced touching and washing David's hard erect body. She got chills while standing under the hot water. She turned the knob to cold and said, "Get it together, girl." And then laughed. She quickly dressed, made a cup of coffee and dashed out of the house. Reality was about to set in.

Diane got to work about twenty minutes before the students arrived. Her classroom looked like a bomb went off. Chairs were scattered, papers were on the floor and, from the looks of it, the work that she left was undone. She sat down at her desk and read a vile note from the substitute. She was disgusted by how this person left her room and talked about her kids. She called the front office to report her substitute and ask that this person never be allowed to sub in her room again. Diane decided to chuck all the work that she had assigned and start from scratch. "Gee, what a way to start my morning after a wonderful girls' trip and fabulous night with David." She ran around her room, picking up papers off the floor and getting it presentable for her class. She was just about done when she heard her phone ping. It was a text from David, Good morning, beautiful. Can't stop thinking about last night. Can't wait to hold you again. See you later.

Diane's face lit up and smiled. She responded, Hey, handsome. Last night was incredible. I've been thinking about you since I woke up. You're just what the doctor ordered this morning. See you soon. XO

Diane's students started trickling into class. As each student entered, they were happy to see Diane and walked up to get a hug from her. Even though she was extremely upset with them, she always had time to hug her students. She would deal with them soon enough.

After morning announcements, the pledge of allegiance and attendance was taken, Diane got up from her desk holding two notes. Her students' eyes got big and their faces went numb.

"Can anyone guess what I have in my hands?" she began her speech. She promptly read both notes exactly the way they were written to her by the substitute. She didn't mince words. She let her students know how upset she was at, not only their behavior, but how they left their classroom. She tied the discussion nicely into the daily journal writing assignment. Each student was to write to explain their behavior, good or bad, on the day she was gone. During the writing lesson, everyone, including the teacher, wrote in their journals, which meant Diane had to get out her journal. Instead of writing, Diane took the time to daydream about her night of passion with David. When journal time was up and the lesson was over, there wasn't one word written in her journal.

Jenny joined Diane in her room for lunch. Jenny wanted to know all about her trip with the girls. Diane quickly went over each day's events and showed her pictures from the weekend. Jenny went crazy when she heard about Diane's visit to the backstage of Keith Urban's concert.

"Wow, I'm so jealous. What a great weekend," said Jenny.

"Well, that's not all that was crazy," Diane timidly responded.

"Oh, no, what happened?" Jenny curiously asked.

"David surprised me by picking me up at the airport."

"What? Are you serious? Do tell," Jenny said grinning from ear to ear.

"First, did you have anything to do with this?" Diane asked.

"I swear, this is the first I'm hearing about this."

Diane started telling Jenny the details, "I was completely in shock when I saw him standing there behind me. He started off by asking if I needed help with my luggage. I didn't even know it was him until I turned around. It was so surreal."

"Okay, then what happened next?" Jenny eagerly asked.

"We went over to that little family restaurant by my house for a bite to eat."

"Okay, then what?"

"Then he brought me home. Jenny, we weren't in my house five minutes before he asked if I was basically ready to take it to the next level. He was so sweet when he said that if I wasn't ready, he would leave before anything happened that I wasn't ready for."

"Aww, he's such a sweetheart," purred Jenny. "Okay, go on. So, did you take it to the next level and, if so, girl, you need to tell me if it was everything you thought it would be."

Diane signed happily. "Oh, Jenny, it was so much more. That man's body is what romance novels are made of. He knows exactly how to please a woman. He was gentle and forceful, in a good way, when he needed to be. Afterwards, we took a shower and round two happened under the warm waters of the shower head. It was the best night I have ever had with a man. I think he's ruined it for any man that comes after him!" Diane and Jenny squealed with laughter as if they were young schoolgirls.

"When are you going to see him again?"

"He's supposed to come here today to see me. He works all week at the bar. It's Bike Week and, this coming weekend, he has his National Guard duty."

"Oh my goodness, so you aren't going to be able to "BE" with him for at least another week? But, by the way you've explained things, he gave you enough to tide you over for a while." The girls laughed and Jenny left. Lunch was over, which meant only another hour to go before David was to arrive at school.

Diane took her class to the library. Jenny gave her the thumbs up and told her she'd understand if she was a few minutes late picking up her class. She winked at Diane and Diane rushed off to the bathroom to make sure she looked good. Diane sat at her desk reading reports, checking papers, and looking over her lesson plans for the rest of the week. She kept looking outside and out of the window for any sighting of David and his truck. She was growing more and more upset that she might not see him. She kept her phone close, in case he sent a message or even called. She looked several times at the text he sent her in the morning, saying he'd see her so she didn't let her mind run wild with suspicion. Diane got a call in her classroom saying she was needed in the office.

"Damn!" Diane said as she hung up the phone. Diane walked quickly to the office. When she got there, the principal wanted to see her, to ask her to represent the school at a Town Hall meeting Thursday after school. She was honored. She got all the necessary information and left to go back to her classroom. She didn't see David's truck and was bummed as she slowly walked into her room.

Diane lit up when she saw David sitting at her desk. "Oh, my goodness! You're here! I didn't think I was going to see you."

"I said I'd come."

"That you did," said Diane as she walked over to her desk.

David stood up and kissed and hugged her. "It's so good to see you and have you in my arms again. I can't

85

stop thinking about last night. I really wish I could've stayed the whole night."

"Yes, me too," sighed Diane.

"I'm sorry I couldn't get here sooner. I know your break is almost over and I have knucklehead in the truck waiting for me."

"Where is your truck?"

"It's in the front of the school. I don't have a delivery here today. This is a special trip," David said as he grabbed Diane back into his arms.

"I'll take what I can get. So, you're working tonight, right?"

"Yeah, four to midnight."

"That must be so hard on you after working all day," said Diane.

"It can be sometimes but I'm one of the partners and, until the business takes off, one of us has to be there at all times. I drew the short straw. It won't be for long." Diane smiled and nodded. "Well, sweetie, like I said, I have the knucklehead in the truck. God knows what damage he's causing."

"Oh, don't be so hard on the kid," Diane said as she nudged his shoulder. David rolled his eyes and laughed. He gave Diane another soft, open mouth kiss but didn't want the kiss to get too involved because he knew he would have another hard time leaving her and he really didn't want to walk out of her room with a boner. As he left, he turned around and said, "I'll call you later." He smiled and walked confidently down the hall.

Diane looked at the clock. She had five minutes before it was time to pick up her students. She decided to get them early.

Jenny had them seated and ready to go but, as soon as she saw Diane, she jumped up and asked, "Did he come? Did you see him?"

"He just left but he was only here for a few minutes. No deliveries here today."

"Oh, so it was a special visit?"

"Yes. Yes, it was, Jenny," Diane said as she beamed from ear to ear.

Chapter 14

When Diane walked into her house, she went right to work unpacking her luggage that she didn't get around to doing last night. She did a load of laundry but decided to sleep another night on the sheets with David's scent.

Diane relaxed the rest of the evening with a glass of wine and leftovers from her freezer. She decided to call Sara to see if she connected with Edward but, unfortunately, she didn't answer so Diane left a message.

Diane could hardly keep her eyes open. She looked at the clock. It was ten and figured she'd shower and go to bed. Diane lay down clean in the dirty sheets. She rolled slowly on the sheets, remembering where David made love to her just last night. She picked up the pillow with his scent and took in a deep breath. Her eyes were closed and her body limp. Her phone rang. It took her several rings before she answered. It was David.

"Hello," Diane answered in a sleepy voice.

"Oh, no, sweetie, I'm sorry. I woke you."

"No, no, it's okay, David. I was just lying in my bed reminiscing about last night."

"Man, I would love to be right there next to you right now."

Diane smiled and then asked, "So, is the bar real busy tonight?"

"It's been crazy busy but it's a good thing."

"Oh, I'm sure," remarked Diane.

"Hey, sweetie, do you have plans Thursday night? I decided, since I'm leaving Friday afternoon, I'd take Thursday night off and, hopefully, spend it with you."

Diane thought then said, "Oh, God, I have a Town Hall I need to go to after school. It starts at four and lasts until seven. We just can't catch a break." Diane sounded very disappointed.

"Sweetie, no, that's fine, we can still see each other. Seven o'clock isn't too late. I can pick you up at eight and I'll have you home and in bed before eleven."

Diane giggled and said, "Will I be in bed alone?"

"Ha, ha! Well, that's totally up to you."

With a smile in her voice, Diane softly said, "Well, then I guess we'll just have to see."

David reminded Diane that he wasn't sure if he was going to be able to see her tomorrow during his scheduled deliveries. Since he was taking Friday off, his delivery orders were going to be doubled but he promised Thursday night, he'd make it up to her. Diane softly whispered good night to David. David hung up and smiled.

Wednesday's workday was uneventful. It came and went without any problems or excitement. Diane missed the butterflies in her stomach when seeing and having David come to her classroom. She wondered how on earth they were going to top Monday night. She knew that their date on Thursday night was going to end in bed with the two of them having wild, passionate sex. She also wondered if there was going to be more to them than just great sex. She knew it was too early to figure it out and, in the meantime, she was just going to enjoy herself and David.

David sent a couple of basic texts to Diane throughout the day. He was extremely busy busting his ass delivering around the county and training the young kid. Diane totally understood and knew they would talk later in the evening.

It was getting late. Diane was already showered and in bed. She still had not heard from David. She fell asleep with her phone close by but she never got that good night phone call.

The first thing Diane did when she got up in the morning was check her phone. "I can't believe it. He never called." Diane wasn't mad, she was worried. She knew he was working hard pulling double duty to get deliveries out and complete because he wasn't working on Friday, and then he had to go to the beach to tend bar late into the night. She wasn't going to jump to any conclusions. She was going to wait to see if he would call later or, at the very least, send a text.

Diane left for school dressed extremely professionally. She had on a light blue mid-calf length dress with black heels. She had to look the part since she was representing the school at the Town Hall meeting later that afternoon. She made sure she had a pair of flats with her to wear during the day.

As she pulled into the school parking lot, her phone rang. It was David. "Hey, you," Diane said as she answered the phone.

"Hey, babe. I'm so sorry I didn't call last night. It was one of the longest days I've worked in a very long time. I got to the bar late and, once I was there, things were nonstop."

"No worries, David. I was just worried about you. I knew you had a lot of work. You must be exhausted. Are you sure you still want to go out tonight?" Diane bit her lip and said silently, "Please say you still want to go out!"

"I wouldn't miss seeing you tonight. Being a little tired isn't going to stop me. You can't get rid of me that easily."

Diane laughed and asked, "So, are we still on for eight?"

"Yes, ma'am, unless you've changed your mind."

"You're so funny, David. I'll be ready."

"Okay, babe, then I'll see you then. Have a good day at work and have a great Town Hall."

"Thanks, David. See you soon and don't work too hard!"

"'Bye, sweetie."

"'Bye, David."

There were hundreds of people at the Town Hall. Diane was given a report that she had to read and discuss. She made small talk with one of the county commissioners and spoke with several other teachers and principals from nearby schools. Diane was so thankful that her part was before intermission. She decided to leave soon after intermission had started.

Diane raced home, jumped into the shower and put on a cute little jumpsuit. She fixed her hair so it fell loosely on her shoulders and she made sure she sprayed her best perfume in all the right places. Diane rushed to get ready because she knew David would show up early. She remembered what he said the first time they met for coffee, "If I'm on time, I'm late!"

At seven-forty-five, the doorbell rang. Diane opened the door and she was in awe. She had only seen David in jeans and a t-shirt. Tonight he was wearing black dress slacks that molded to his muscular thighs and a tucked-in light blue button-down shirt which accentuated his flat stomach and made his eyes appear to be as blue as the ocean. His sleeves were neatly rolled up right before his forearm. He took her breath away.

"Well, handsome, come in."

"Well, beautiful, don't mind if I do." David kissed Diane on the cheek and walked into the house. "You look great, Diane, and your house, it's so nice."

"But you saw it the other night."

"I didn't really get a good look at it on Monday night. I was only interested in seeing you." They both laughed. Diane grabbed her purse and out the door they went.

David drove to a quaint little Italian restaurant not too far from Diane's house. It was dimly lit, soft music was playing in the background, and it definitely had a romantic vibe. They sat at a table located close to the back. David pulled out the chair for Diane. She was very impressed.

Diane looked around and said, "This is so nice. I've seen it from the highway but I've never been here before."

"I'll be honest, I asked Jenny for advice on a nice place to take you that wasn't too far from your house."

"Well, she sure picked a good one!"

"She sure did."

The waiter came to the table and handed David and Diane menus. Diane ordered the baked ziti and David ordered the lasagna. They each had a glass of red wine with dinner. During dinner, they discussed David's upcoming weekend with the Guard, his partnership in the bar and his job with the county. He never brought up old girlfriends or relationships. Diane talked about teaching and her thoughts about going back to school to become an administrator. They talked about dream vacations, favorite movies, and fun things in the news. Diane never mentioned any of her old boyfriends or past flames. It was a great dinner, where they both got to know a little bit more about each other.

They both declined dessert knowing that dessert was waiting at Diane's house. David helped Diane out of her seat and held her hand as they walked to his truck. Diane glanced at the time on her watch and she thought to herself, "Nine-fifteen, yes, that's plenty of time." Before David started his truck, he turned to Diane and placed his right hand on her cheek.

He looked deep into her eyes and said, "You look so pretty in the moonlight, Diane." And he began softly kissing her lips.

Diane kissed him back and then said, "You know my house is just minutes away."

"That's all I needed to hear." He smiled, put the truck in drive and drove to Diane's house.

David walked Diane to her front door. As she opened the door and began walking in, David stood outside.

Diane turned around to him, looked shocked and said, "Aren't you coming in?"

"No, I don't think so, not tonight, Diane."

"Oh, oh okay," Diane said in a very disappointed tone. "Well, I had a wonderful evening. Thank you for dinner."

With a huge smile on his face, David jokingly said, "Diane, seriously? You don't think I want to come in! I was joking. Wow, that was way too easy!"

"Oh, ha, ha, David. Not funny. My heart sunk to the floor." Diane playfully hit his arm. David lifted her up, closed the door with his foot and carried Diane to the couch.

Chapter 15

David and Diane both sat quietly on the couch feeling the pull to be together. Just as David leaned in to kiss Diane, CLICK, David pulled away. Diane laughed. "That's the timer for the lights."

David laughed then said, "Are there any timers going off in your bedroom?"

"No, we're good if that's where you want to go?" David smiled. Diane stood up and extended her hand towards David. He placed his hand in hers and they walked upstairs to Diane's bedroom. In the back of Diane's mind, she was so happy that she finally washed the sheets from the other night.

David and Diane both sat on the edge of Diane's bed. David put both his hands on Diane's face and began slowly tracing her lips with his moist, warm tongue. Diane could feel her body beginning to react. She felt goosebumps throughout her body and her nipples were becoming hard. David began to undress Diane by slowly unzipping her jumpsuit allowing it to gently fall to her waist. Diane stood for just a moment and wiggled the jumpsuit to the floor. She quickly sat back down on the edge of the bed in only her panties and bra. The smell of her perfume filled the room. David stood up and slowly unbuttoned each button on his shirt. He looked down at Diane and licked his lips. His shirt dropped to the floor, exposing his well-chiseled arms and abs. Diane, now extremely sexually aroused, stood up, looked David directly in the eyes and unzipped his pants. She slid her hand into his pants just outside his underwear before they fell to the floor. His manhood was hard and throbbing. It felt like a caged animal waiting to be released. As David moaned in delight, Diane knew she was in charge, even if it was for just that moment. She slightly massaged his shaft still trapped beneath his underwear. She looked deep into his dark blue eyes. She pressed her lips together then slightly poked her tongue out and whimpered softly. She took both hands and slid his underwear down. The beast was fully released.

With both of his strong hands upon Diane's shoulders, he brought her close to his warm masculine body. Diane was still dressed in her bra and panties. He reached behind her back and quickly unsnapped her bra. He bent down and kissed her erect nipples. She slipped her own panties off in the heat of passion. David smiled. He lay down and brought Diane on top of him, where she straddled his lower body. David took both his hands and gently caressed her perky bosom. Diane let out a moan as her back arched forward. David was so aroused that he grabbed Diane passionately and, in an instant, they had changed positions. David was now in command and on top of Diane. He kissed her mouth and her neck. He made his way to her shoulders and then to her breasts. Diane was moaning with delight. He ran his wet tongue along her stomach and then down to her sweet essence. He tasted her sweet juices and kept coming back for more.

Diane was squeezing the sheets beneath her. Every part of her body was electrified and on fire. Right before her body was about to explode in ecstasy, David stopped and said, "You're not coming without me." He mounted Diane. She let out a moan of sheer delight as David entered inside of her. Her fingers pushed deep into his muscular back. David grunted every time he pushed himself deeper inside of Diane. As they both climaxed together, David yelled out a powerful, "Oh, my God!"

Diane yelled out, "Yes, David, Yes!"

Out of breath, David collapsed to Diane's left side. Diane had both hands on her heart as she thought it might jump out of her chest. Both were breathing heavily and said not a word for a few minutes. David finally got up on his right forearm and looked slightly down at Diane. He ever so gently brushed the hair from her closed eyes and kissed her nose.

Diane smiled, opened her eyes and only managed to quietly say, "WOW!"

"I don't want to leave you, Diane. I want to stay right here with you but I know you need to get up early for work tomorrow and I have to be at the base by five a.m."

Diane grabbed David's face and pulled him close to kiss him. "I don't want you to leave either." It got quiet. They held each other in bed without a word between them.

David finally got up and began dressing. "No shower this time?" questioned Diane.

"Babe, you know if we get in that shower together, we're not coming out for a while. As much as I don't want to, I need to go." Diane slipped on her robe, fixed her hair and walked David to her front door. They hugged each other tightly and kissed each other goodbye. Diane watched David walk to his truck and, as he got in and looked at Diane, she blew him a kiss.

David rolled down the window and yelled, "I'll call you when I can. I'll see you Monday."

As David drove off, still smelling Diane all over his body, he hit the steering wheel. "Damn it! I can't believe that cute, little school teacher has me this crazy. What am I going to do if I'm deployed back to the Middle East again? I didn't want to get attached. I didn't want to start having these feelings. Shit! I'm fucked!"

Diane ran back to her bed and grabbed the sheets where David had just been. She took a deep breath to drink in his musky scent. She wanted so badly to keep his scent on her body and, as much as she didn't want to, she headed to the shower. She let the warm water run over her still-tingly body and sadly washed his scent away. She got into bed and held the pillow with David's scent close to her all night.

Chapter 16

Morning came way too fast but it was Friday. Diane and Jenny had lunch together as normal. They talked about Diane's dinner date with David. Diane reminded Jenny that David would be gone all weekend because of his duty with the Guard. Jenny offered to go out with Diane or have Diane come over to her house for dinner. Diane said she'd think about it. Diane had planned on catching up on housework and calls to the girls.

Jenny got home from work and asked her husband, Vic, if he knew anything about David and his National Guard duties. Vic said that he knew David was a former Army Ranger who served in Afghanistan. He said he knew that he was specially trained but didn't know what he was trained in. He also mentioned that he didn't like to talk a lot about his time as a Ranger. Vic also told Jenny that David was a pretty important guy and did quite a bit for the country.

"Oh, wow, I had no idea," said Jenny. "But he wouldn't have to go back to Afghanistan, would he?"

"To tell you the truth, that's his biggest fear but he knows if he's called up, then he's on his way!"

"Oh crap, really? I wonder if he said anything to Diane about that."

"Jenny, honey, I'm sure it hasn't come up and, besides that, it's David who needs to tell her not you! They've only gone out a few times, so, knowing David, that's something he's not going to bring up anytime soon because it may never happen. So, please leave well enough alone."

"Don't worry, I'm not bringing anything up. I was just curious. Diane really likes him. She's been hurt so many times in the past. I just wouldn't want something like David going to the Middle East to ruin things."

"Again, honey, not your/our problem."

Diane kept herself busy Friday night by cleaning her house and doing laundry but not the sheets from last night. She wanted one more night of smelling David's scent to keep her company. Around ten o'clock Diane got a weird text from David. It read, I'm about to be in a location with no phone service. I'll call when I can XOXO

"What? No phone service? Call you when I can?" Diane said out loud. "What the heck?" Diane poured herself a glass of wine and sat on the couch. She reached for the phone to call one of the girls but realized it was a little too late. She'd call tomorrow and get their take on things. She went to her room, where she snuggled in the sheets and turned on the TV. She fell asleep thinking about David and how he made her feel last night.

Diane slept in later than normal. She stripped the bed of the dirty sheets and replaced them with nice clean crisp ones. Her phone rang. She ran to get it, hoping it was David. No, it was Anne.

"Hey Anne, how's it going?"

"Hey, stranger," replied Anne, "What's going on? How's the hunky army man doing?"

"Ha, ha. He's actually on duty this weekend with the National Guard."

"What do you mean? I thought you said he was out of the Army?"

"He is but he's in the reserves. He goes away once a month for some type of training. I got a text from him last night and he's at a location where there's no phone service."

"Sounds like he's training for some heavy shit! I always thought the Guard stood close to home when they did their training but what do I know?" suggested Anne. Diane paused for a few seconds, bit her bottom lip and wondered what he was really up to.

"Diane, you still there?"

"Oh, yeah, sorry. So how's the wedding planning going?" Diane asked in order to change the subject.

"It's going great and it's scary how things are falling into place. That's why I called. I wanted to fill you in on the plans and run a few things by you."

"Great, I'm all ears." Anne and Diane talked for over an hour about the wedding plans.

Anne ended the conversation by asking, "So, David, will be coming to the wedding, right?"

"I sure hope so. I haven't really asked him but he does know about it. I'll ask him later this week after he gets back."

"Great, let me know."

"I will. Give Tom my best. Talk to you soon. Love you, my friend."

"Love you too, Diane, and take care."

Diane decided to clear her mind and go jogging at the nearby park. She put her hair back in a long ponytail, wore an old t-shirt, jogging pants, and put on her new running shoes. She decided to leave her phone at home.

Diane was gone for a little over an hour. As she entered the door, she could hear her phone ringing. When she picked it up she saw an unfamiliar number. The first thing she thought, David was calling. She quickly checked to see if there was a message. There were two and they were both from David. The first voicemail said, "Hey, sweetie, not sure where you're at but I wanted to call and say hi. Sorry, I missed you. I'll try back later." Diane's heart melted. "No, no, no, I can't believe I missed his call." She quickly played the second message, "Okay, sweetie, this is the second call. I really wanted to talk to you and hear your voice but I guess your message is all I'm going to hear. I'll have to try back tomorrow. Going out on night maneuvers." At the end of the message, David blew a kiss. Diane was so angry at herself and yelled, "I never go anywhere without my phone and the day I do, I miss not one but two calls from David." Diane sat down and cried.

She played the messages over and over just to hear his voice.

To feel better, she called Luna to see how she was doing. Luna always made her laugh and told her exactly how she felt. She never held back and that's what Diane needed. Luna was excited to hear from Diane but couldn't talk for too long. The boys had a late soccer game and she was responsible for the snacks and she still needed to get things ready. It was a light conversation that ended with the promise to call each other later next week. Diane lay down on the couch to take a much-needed nap but, before she closed her eyes, she listened to David's voicemails one more time.

Diane's phone rang and woke her from a dead sleep. She jumped up and hoped it was David calling. It wasn't. It was Sara calling from New York. "Oh, my goodness, girl did I wake you?" Sara asked.

"No, I was just taking a little nap. I went jogging."

"You went jogging? What's wrong? You only go jogging to clear your head. What up?"

"Everything is fine. I promise. So, to what do I owe this pleasure of speaking to you?"

"Well, first of all, tell me how things are going with David. Are they still hot and heavy?"

"They are," Diane said smiling. "He's gone this weekend for National Guard training. I'm bummed because while I was out, I missed not one but two of his calls and I won't speak to him until, hopefully, tomorrow. He's in an area where phone service is spotty and is, right now, doing night maneuvers or at least that's what his messages said."

"Hmm, did he mention if he was out of the country?"

"No, why?"

"Oh, no reason, I was just wondering."

"Sara, I've known you more than half my life. I know you like a book. What's going on?"

"Well, there's just been talk about a military strike in the Middle East amongst the journalists here. I'm sure David has nothing to do with it. He's out of the Army, right?"

"Yeah, that's what he said."

"Okay then, nothing to worry about. Forget I said anything. Now, let me tell you about Edward." Sara went on and on about Edward and how fantastic he is and how he's been really good for her during her nasty divorce. The girls spoke for a good forty minutes. "Diane, I know you're still thinking about what I said earlier. Please don't worry and, besides, it's just hearsay. Promise me you won't give it another thought."

"I promise. Listen, you and Edward keep having fun. Tell him hi from me and, if you hear anything, let me know."

"You know I will. Love you, girl."

"Love you too. 'Bye." Diane sat staring into space when she got off the phone with Sara. "Oh God, what if him being gone is something more than just a routine weekend? What if he has to go the Middle East, like she said? Don't make yourself crazy. Just shake it off and wait until he gets home," Diane said to herself as she got up to make herself something for dinner.

Later in the evening, Diane decided to call Jenny. She asked her if she wanted to meet for Sunday brunch. Jenny agreed. They planned to meet before noon. Diane not only wanted to get out of the house and meet with her good friend, she wanted to know if Jenny knew anything about David's role with the National Guard.

Chapter 17

Diane and Jenny met at an outside restaurant near the neighborhood park. The weather was nice and there was a small band playing in the background. The conversation was about work and family. They people-watched and talked about the people as they walked by. It was all in fun and they never said anything mean about a person. After lunch, the two friends took a walk in the park and visited the local farmers' market. They both bought a frozen lemonade and sat on a park bench under a large shade tree.

Diane hesitated but then asked, "Jenny, how well do you and Vic know David?"

"Well, like I said a few weeks ago, I've only known David for a little over a year. Vic's known him for a number of years. I think they may have met at the gym but I honestly don't know. We really don't discuss him. Why? What's up?" Jenny was praying Diane wouldn't ask anything about the Guard or about the Army.

"Well, it's David," started Diane. Jenny got a little tense. "He's away this weekend, you know, with the Guard. I totally get it but I just thought it was some training that he did here locally. But I was wrong. He left a message yesterday saying that he was going to a place where there might possibly be no phone service and then he said he was going out on night maneuvers. That to me doesn't sound like "weekend duties". That sounds important and to boot, my friend who is a pretty well-known journalist in New York City said it sounded pretty suspicious and wanted to know if David had ever mentioned the Middle East to me. I'm just really worried right now and my mind is racing."

"Oh, Diane, don't worry. David would've told you if he was going somewhere dangerous. He's only going to be away for the weekend, right? He'll be back tomorrow. It's probably just specialized training. Our world is crazy right now. They're just probably brushing up on skills."

"Yeah, you're probably right. I'm sorry to dump this on you. I really like David and I'm really beginning to have feelings for this man. Lord help me!" Both girls chuckled and then got up. They decided to walk around the farmers' market one last time before heading back to their cars.

Diane was glad she met up with Jenny. She felt a little better about David and his weekend "warrior" duties, but, still, in the back of her mind, she had doubts, especially after not hearing from David all day and into the night.

Monday morning came hard and strong. Diane didn't sleep well and, when she checked her phone, there was no message or call from David. She was in a grumpy mood and needed to snap out of it before school started. Her students were well behaved which made things a bit easier. She ate lunch alone because Jenny had a meeting downtown and wasn't in the building.

As she walked to the main building to pick up her students, she noticed the delivery truck entering the school. Her heart started beating fast and she picked up her pace. She began to smile from ear to ear. As the truck got closer, she realized it wasn't David driving and her smile disappeared.

She questioned the driver where David was and he replied, "No, David didn't come to work today. I'm on my own." Diane's heart sunk to the ground. "Oh, my God, where is he?" She tried to call him but the call went right to his voicemail. Diane was sick to her stomach and it took every ounce of courage and concentration to get through the day.

Diane got home earlier than usual because she just didn't want to stay at work. She needed to go home in case she started to cry. Right now, she just didn't know what to think. Every scenario, from David dumping her to David getting hurt, was going through her mind. She called Jenny but she wasn't home yet and didn't answer her phone. All of her friends were at work so she had no one to talk to. She changed her clothes and was thinking about going for another jog to clear her mind when her doorbell rang. She opened the door and David, who was holding flowers, was standing there smiling. Diane's face lit up and then she burst into tears.

"Oh, no, babe, that's not the reaction I was going for." David hugged her tight. Diane buried her head into his chest. David pulled her slightly away and asked, "Sweetie, what's wrong?"

"I was worried sick about you. I didn't know what was going on or when you were coming back."

"I'm back, babe, and I'm fine. Not a scratch on me."

"When I missed your calls I just figured we'd talk later that night, but, not being able to contact you, was scary especially when you said you were going on night maneuvers."

"Right now, Diane, I just want to forget this past weekend and make up for lost time with you. We can talk about it later. How about staying in tonight and ordering a pizza? Oh wait, were you going out?"

"No, I'm good. I was going to go for a jog to clear my mind but no need to now."

David smiled and said, "Come here you. I've missed holding you and kissing you."

"You and me both," whispered Diane as she passionately kissed David.

"I don't know about you but I'm starving. How about I order that pizza now," suggested David.

"Sure, babe, that sounds good to me." David ordered the pizza over the phone while Diane turned on the nightly news. There was a segment on the growing number of US troops being sent back over to the Middle East to provide a presence of strength. Diane glanced over at David who was watching the news very intently.

"I bet you're glad you're out of the Army? Right?" asked Diane.

"Well, one isn't really out of the Army when you're in the Guard. You can always be called up," said David in a somber tone. "But let's not talk about that now. All I want to talk about is that pizza." Diane sat down next to David and smiled a small smile as a million little things were going through her mind.

While eating the pizza, Diane caught David up on Anne's wedding plans and Sara's dates with Edward. He asked her what she did this past weekend. She told him about her brunch with Jenny but she never mentioned the questions she asked Jenny about her concerns she had about him going to a location with spotty to no phone service for weekend training, and she didn't mention what Sara said about her hearing rumors about more troops heading to the Middle East. She wanted so badly to ask him about the news report and how it connected to what Sara said but she didn't. She wanted to keep the mood light. There would be time for questions and, hopefully, honest answers.

Chapter 18

Weeks went by with David and Diane spending more and more time together. David agreed to be Diane's plus-one at Anne's upcoming wedding. This would be the first time they would travel together but, more importantly, the first time he met "the girls".

"I think meeting the girls is going to be scarier than going into battle," David said as he chuckled.

"They're going to love you," said Diane as she kissed David sweetly on the cheek.

Two weeks before the wedding while David and Diane were out to dinner, David received a phone call. When he saw the number come up on his phone, a look of gloom and fear washed over his face. Diane looked worried. She'd never seen that look on David's face before.

"Babe, excuse me. I need to take this call outside." David got up from the table and walked away. Diane sat at the table alone and deflated. She began to worry. She'd been hearing more and more news stories calling for more troops to the Middle East and Sara had confirmed that more US troops were being called up. David walked slowly back to the table after his phone call and tried to make everything seem that all was fine, but Diane noticed something was off with him and asked,

"Hey, babe, is everything all right? You look pretty worried. What's wrong?"

"Can we talk about it after dinner, when we get to your place?" responded David.

"Sure, of course," Diane said as a part of her heart sank knowing something was wrong.

It was a quiet drive to Diane's house. David held Diane's hand tightly the entire drive. Diane sensed something bad had happened or David had troubling news to tell her. Every time she wanted to say something, she stopped. Her thoughts were filled with several questions but she waited patiently until David was ready to talk. Diane knew it wasn't going to be good.

David drove into Diane's driveway and put his truck in park. He glanced at Diane and smiled. They both opened their own door and hopped out. David put his keys on Diane's table that was near the door and Diane placed her purse on the counter. David took Diane's hand and walked her to the couch. They sat down and Diane looked very nervous.

David, still holding her hand, smiled and began by saying, "I'm so sorry for being quiet and ruining our evening."

Diane interrupted, "No, David, you didn't ruin our evening but I do know something is upsetting you. Can I help? Do you want to talk?"

"We definitely need to talk, Diane."

"Okay, well, I'm here. I'm listening." David thought long and hard about how to tell her his news.

"There's really no easy way to say this."

"David, you're scaring me. Whatever it is, just say it."

"Okay, my Guard unit has been called up. I, we, head to Afghanistan in two weeks."

"What?" Diane paused then continued, "That's not funny, David."

"No, it's really not but, unfortunately, it's true." Diane's face went blank and she looked pale. "Diane, are you going to be okay?"

"No, no, I'm not. I have so many questions. Why you? Why do you have to go? I thought you were out of the Army."

"I am but I'm specially trained in counter-terrorism and hold a special clearance with the intelligence department. When I left the Army for civilian life, I was told I could be called up within five years of leaving. This is my fourth year, so they definitely kept their word," David said with a sarcastic chuckle.

"What do you do for the Army? What are your responsibilities?" asked Diane.

"What I do with the Army isn't really important. Diane what is, is that I'm not sure how long I'll be over there. I have a meeting with my commanding officer next week to discuss my orders."

"I just don't know what to say, David."

"I know it's hard to take in. I figured something was up when we went to Panama to train for the weekend last month."

"Oh, so that's where you were."

"Yeah, in the jungles of Panama." Diane lay her head on David's chest. David slowly rubbed her arm as they quietly sat in the dark. After about an hour, David decided to go home. He had a lot to figure out but leaving Diane behind was going to be the hardest.

As he left, he held Diane close, and said, "I know I laid a lot on you tonight and, for that, I'm truly sorry. We have a lot to think about but, in the meantime, we have Anne's wedding to look forward to. We're going to have fun and not think about this until afterwards. Agreed?"

"Yes, agreed," answered Diane as she kissed him goodnight.

"I can't fucking believe my luck! I knew it. I fucking knew it!" David said as he drove home. "I can't ask her to wait. I can't ask her to put her life on hold. I can't ask another woman to give up so much for me. I can't! I won't!"

Diane ran to her bed. She put her head in her pillow and began to sob. She cried so hard she had trouble breathing. "Why? Why is this happening to me? Why can't I catch a break? Oh, my God, why is this happening?" Diane cried herself to sleep.

Chapter 19

The next morning, Diane's eyes were puffy from all the crying but she put on a brave face at school. "Hey Diane, what's wrong? Did your hunky boyfriend keep you up all night and not allow you to get enough sleep?" asked one of the office staff.

"No, I watched "The Notebook" on TV last night. It gets me every time. I went to bed crying." Diane playfully frowned then threw up her hands and walked away.

Diane couldn't wait to see and talk to Jenny at lunch. She had to tell her everything. "Girl, what's wrong? Why the puffy, sad eyes?"

"It's David."

"Oh no, what did he do?"

"He did nothing. His unit has been called up. He's heading back to Afghanistan in two weeks!"

"No, Diane, you can't be serious. We were just talking about this a few weeks ago."

"I know," began Diane. "His unit went to Panama for training and, apparently, even though David isn't in the Army anymore, he still has a five-year commitment to them. He told me he's trained in counter-terrorism and holds a special intelligence clearance. Jenny, I'm just sick to my stomach over this."

"Yeah, I kind of knew about David's special training. Vic told me a little bit about what he knows from what David has told him in the past."

"You knew about this and didn't tell me?"

"No, Diane, I only knew he was specially trained in something. I didn't know what. Vic did say that David is a pretty important guy and has done a lot for our country. He also said David doesn't like to talk about his time over there. Honey, I'm so sorry. What are you guys going to do? How are you going to handle being apart from him when you just started getting to know him?"

"I have no clue," sighed Diane. "All I do know is that we're still going to Anne's wedding this weekend. David said he didn't want to discuss anything until after we got back. He also has a meeting next week with his commanding officer to discuss his orders. Everything is up in the air."

David and Diane enjoyed a wonderful quiet dinner at David's place. He was a wonderful cook. David had a one-bedroom apartment that was nicely decorated, with very cozy pillows, tasteful wall art, and comfortable furnishings. Diane always felt a feeling of warmth and love when she went over to visit. After dinner, they discussed the flight plans to Houston and hotel accommodations for Anne's wedding. Once the details were clear, David led Diane into his bedroom where they quickly fell into each other's arms. David held Diane close and made love to her as if it was the last time they'd be together. His movements were more forceful and he was so much more in tune with her body than ever before. Diane was also more willing to give more of herself after learning about David leaving for Afghanistan. She wasn't holding back. Their love-making was more passionate and more erotic. She gave David all that he wanted and so much more.

The next morning, David arrived at Diane's house to pick her up for the airport. He arrived a couple of hours early so they'd have plenty of time to check in and grab a bite to eat before their flight. Diane met David at the front door with a huge, bright smile on her face.

"Good morning, lover," she said as she kissed his smiling, handsome face.

"My goodness, someone is in a very good mood this morning and I might be a little upset because I had nothing to do with it!" David said as he laughed and then reached for Diane to pull her closer to steal a kiss.

"Oh, you definitely have something to do with my good mood and cheerful smile. I'm going to be spending my entire weekend with you and I can't wait!" Diane said as she kissed David back.

"I'm really looking forward to this weekend too and I don't believe I'm going to say this, but I'm also looking forward to meeting those girlfriends of yours!"

"Ha, ha, very funny! You're going to love all of them. I guarantee it!" said Diane as she grabbed her purse and luggage.

David and Diane arrived at the airport, checked in and had plenty of time to sit, talk and eat breakfast. David inquired about the weekend's itinerary. "I think you're more excited about this weekend than I am," Diane laughed as she softly reached for David's hand.

David smiled, looked deep into Diane's eyes and said, "I'm so damn glad I had the courage to kiss you those many months ago in your classroom. I never dreamed I'd be this happy. Diane, I really think there's no coming back from you. You're the one." Diane smiled and her heart melted. As David began to lean towards Diane to give her a kiss, he was quickly distracted by a group of soldiers walking by.

"Oh, wow!" sighed David sadly. "Seeing these troops walk by definitely puts things into perspective." Diane got up, walked across the table, sat next to David and hugged him tightly.

She whispered in his ear, "Everything is going to be all right. We're going to get through this." As they released their embrace, David reached for Diane with both of his strong hands and gently placed them on her face and softly said,

"I love you, Diane Walker."

Diane's face lit up as she whispered, "I love you too, David Anderson."

Their two and half hour flight to Houston was unusually quiet. Both David and Diane sat holding hands, only releasing them when the beverage cart came around. Their conversation was light. Neither one of them brought up the three little "BIG" words that were professed to each other just a short time ago, but knew it had to be addressed. Those three words could either break or make their weekend getaway in Houston for Anne's wedding.

Chapter 20

David and Diane got off the plane and headed for baggage claim. As they waited for their luggage to arrive, David turned to Diane and, with a smile on his face, said, "Does this bring back any memories? "Excuse me, ma'am, do you need help with your luggage?"" Diane laughed as she repeated the question in a deep voice. Both David and Diane burst into laughter. David passionately looked at Diane, grabbed her by her waist, kissed her then whispered in her ear,

"I meant what I said back in Miami. I love you."

Before Diane could respond, a loud voice cried out, "Walker, Anderson party?" David and Diane turned around. There was a large man dressed in a coat and tie, holding a sign with their names largely printed in deep black. It was the car service driver that Anne had arranged to pick them up.

"Wow, your friend, Anne, is going all out for us. I've never had someone pick me up from an airport holding a sign with my name on it. I feel so fancy," David joked as he and Diane walked over to the driver with their luggage.

Barry, the limo driver, was quite the funny man. He had both David and Diane laughing with his jokes and comments about the city and its people. They both needed a good laugh and the distraction.

They arrived at the hotel still laughing and joking. Barry jumped out of the limo to open the door to let both David and Diane out. After Barry gathered their luggage from the trunk, David reached into his wallet and generously tipped Barry.

"Hey, man, thanks so much. If you need a car service during your trip or a ride back to the airport, give me a call," said Barry to David as they shook each other's hand.

David and Diane slowly walked into the hotel looking around in awe of the hotel's beauty. "Oh, my goodness, David, isn't this hotel beautiful?" Diane said as she slowly walked while looking around and up at the ceiling.

"It sure is, Diane. It's absolutely, beautiful," David remarked. As they approached the front desk, Diane heard an excited scream.

"Diane Walker, my gorgeous friend, you've arrived!" Diane looked around to follow the voice and saw her crazy friend Luna waving her arms frantically.

"Luna, you crazy chick," Diane said as she smiled and gave Luna a hug and a kiss.

"Well, well, Miss Diane, who is this good-looking man you have by your side? Is this the amazing David?" Luna jokingly asked.

Diane sheepishly smiled and said, "Yes, Luna, this is David. David, this is my crazy yet amazing friend, Luna."

"Hi, Luna. It's a pleasure to meet you. Diane has spoken so nicely about you and all her friends," David said as he extended his hand to Luna.

"Oh, hell, no, David. No handshake. I'm a hugger!" Luna said as she leaned in and gave David a big hug.

David smiled and Diane laughed as she said, "See, I told you!"

"So, Luna, what about Sara and Anne, have they arrived? And where's that wonderful husband of yours? I'd love for the guys to meet."

"Jim is upstairs trying to file a last-minute report. He'll be down in a few. As for Sara; she is here, but I'm not sure where. Oh, and by the way, Edward is with her!"

"Ew, really. Good to hear!" said Diane smiling.

"Anne called me this morning and she isn't checking in until after four p.m. She's running around doing last-minute things with Tom for the rehearsal dinner tonight," added Luna.

"Okay then," said Diane as she slightly grabbed David arm. "We're going to check in and head up to our room and get settled. How about we all meet at the bar in an hour? And, in the meantime, I'll give Sara a call to let her know we're here and about the plans," suggested Diane.

"Sounds good to me," said Luna with a smile and added, "It was so nice meeting you, David, and I'm looking forward to talking with you later."

David nodded his head and grinned as he said, "Nice meeting you too, Luna."

"Well, so what was your first impression of Luna? What did you think?" Diane asked David as they entered their hotel room.

"She seems great!" David said as he turned to Diane and added, "But I'm a little upset with you."

"Upset with me? Why on earth would you be upset with me?" Diane said as she frowned at David.

David slowly walked over to Diane and as he reached to hug her he said, "You told Luna we'd meet in the bar in an hour and that's not nearly enough time for me to properly make love to you!"

Diane softly smiled at David as she said, "We can be late."

"Oh, there's no doubt that we're going to be late," David said as he scooped Diane into his arms and placed her on the beautifully decorated king-size bed.

There wasn't much time after their love-making session for them to take a shower, so both David and Diane quickly combed their hair and put back on the clothes they wore earlier.

"I'm glad we didn't shower."

"Really, David. Why?"

"Now I can smell you on me for a few hours longer," replied David as he gently slapped Diane's ass as they left the room.

David and Diane entered the bar where Luna and her husband, Jim, were waiting at a table. "Diane. David," yelled Luna. "We're over here." David and Diane walked over to the table. Jim got up and shook David's hand and hugged and kissed Diane.

"Nice to meet you, David. I'm Jim. Luna's better half."

"Hey, man, it's nice to meet you," David replied.

"So, what did Sara say about meeting us here before the rehearsal dinner?" Luna asked Diane.

"Oh, my goodness," Diane said as her eyes went wide. "I forgot to call her."

"I figured you would," joked Luna. "And from the looks of you two, I can kind of figure out why." Diane blushed. Luna laughed and David lifted his shoulders with a boyish grin.

"No worries, I called her. She and Edward should be here soon."

The two couples sat talking casually waiting for the others to join the party. Both Diane and Luna abided by the, "No new news without all four being their" rule. Fifteen minutes later, the bar erupted in jubilant screams as Sara made her way to the table.

"Oh, my goodness, look at you two! I've missed you both so much!" a joyful Sara said as she hugged Diane and then Luna. All three women wore smiles on their faces as they giggled in delight to be together. "Edward, you remember Diane and Luna?" said Sara as she put her arm around Edward's shoulder.

"I sure do. How are you, ladies?"

Sara continued, "This is Luna's husband, Jim, who I must get a hug from!" Sara quickly gave Jim a bear hug.

"And, this must be the new man in Diane's life. Diane, please do the honors." Diane stood next to David as she introduced David to both Sara and Edward.

"Sara and Edward, this is my boyfriend, David," David smiled and reached to shake Edward's hand who was standing the closest to him.

Sara devilishly said, "Don't try that handshaking stuff with me. I need a proper hug." Sara went over to David and gave him a proper hug.

"Wow, your friends do like to hug," David said as the six of them laughed and sat down for a round of drinks. After about thirty minutes of sharing airport and flight experiences of the day, Diane received a text message from Anne.

"Hold on, guys, I have a message from Anne. Hey, sweetie, dealing with a couple of issues concerning Tom's family. We'll see you at the rehearsal at seven-thirty. Give my love to the girls. Can't wait to meet David.

"Well, okay. That's my cue to go up to our room for a shower and to get ready," said Luna as she and Jim were the first to stand up to leave.

"Yeah, I hate to leave but, Edward, I guess we should get on up to our room too," suggested Sara. David and Diane stood as well and walked to the elevators with the others.

Once in their room, Diane put her purse down and plopped on the couch. "I didn't get a good look at the room earlier. It's nice, don't you think?"

David sat down next to Diane, gave her a kiss, closed his eyes and said, "Very nice."

Diane gently nudged him, laughed and said, "David, my love, you are so bad."

"Bad, you want to see bad? Come here, my pretty," David said as he picked Diane up and walked her into the bedroom, where they quickly undressed and then spent the next twenty minutes passionately making love under the soft, warm shower.

Diane quickly got dressed into a soft pink floral dress that hit right below the knee. Her strappy sandals accented her slender calves. She wore her hair in a stylish messy bun with pieces of hair loosely hanging to frame her flawless face. David wore black dress slacks with a thin black and white striped button-down dress shirt that, when tucked in, showed off his well-chiseled abs and defined arms.

"Should I wear a tie?" asked David.

"No, it's very informal tonight. Oh, and may I say, sir, you look very handsome."

"Why thank you, beautiful lady. And may I say, you look absolutely amazing." The two of them stared into the mirror, smiled at one another and left for downstairs. While in the elevator, David looked at his watch and said, "This is more like it."

"More like what?" Diane asked.

"Well, this is the first time all day that we'll be on time."

Diane laughed and said, "I'm really surprised we are. I wasn't sure we would ever leave that warm shower. You definitely can't put a time limit on making love."

"With you? No way," said David. "I'd be late the rest of my life if I knew you'd be the cause of it." David and Diane both smiled as the elevator doors opened.

David and Diane walked through the lobby and out the side door into the garden area where the gardens were transformed into a beautifully arranged setting. As they looked around to take in the beauty they heard, "Diane, Diane, over here!" Diane looked to the right and saw Anne waving her arms.

Diane's face lit up as she looked at David and said, "That's Anne. Come on let's go!" Diane had a pep to her step as she went over to Anne. The two girls squeezed each other in a bear hug and squealed with delight as they let go. "I'm so happy to see you. God, you look fantastic!" said Diane to Anne.

"Look at you! My goodness, you look amazing!" added Anne as she turned to David and asked curiously, "Is this the man I need to thank for making you look so happy?"

Diane laughed and introduced David to Anne, "David, this is the bride-to-be and my oldest and dearest friend, Anne."

"It's a pleasure to finally meet you, Anne," David said as he extended his hand to Anne.

Anne put her hands on her hips as she said,. "Diane, didn't you tell this handsome man that we're not hand shakers, we're huggers!" All three laughed as Anne and David gave each other a welcome hug. Anne, being in the middle of David and Diane, grabbed both of their forearms and walked them over to Tom, her fiancé, who was talking to one of the hotel workers.

"Diane, you gorgeous thing, you come here and give me a hug!" said Tom as soon as he saw Diane. Tom lifted Diane off the floor and spun her around. "It's so damn good to see you."

"It sure is Tom. It's been way too long. I'd like you to meet my boyfriend, David."

Tom and David gave each other a firm handshake and Tom added, "You have a good one here, David. She's a real gem."

"That I definitely know," David said as he smiled at Diane.

"What are you drinking, David?" Tom asked as he gently slapped David's shoulder. "Let's let the girls catch up and go find the bar." David smiled and agreed with Tom. "Sweetie, I'll be back in a few. I'm taking David. The man looks thirsty," Tom said as he kissed Anne and began to walk away.

"Babe, would you like something to drink?" David asked as he put his arm around Diane's waist and kissed her cheek.

"No, thank you, dear. I'm good." The two couples smiled at each other as the men walked away.

Chapter 21

"Oh, my goodness, Diane! David is a hunk. He's so darn handsome!" Diane smiled at Anne as they both were distracted by Luna and Sara calling to the both of them.

"Hi, guys," Diane said as all four girls kissed and hugged each other.

"We're all here and I'm so excited," Anne said nervously as she saw the officiant walk over to her.

"Good evening, Anne."

"Hi, Marcus. I'd like you to meet my three wonderful and dear friends of mine. This is Sara, Luna, and Diane. Ladies, this is Tom's wonderful friend, Marcus. He's going to perform the ceremony."

"Hello, nice to meet you all," Marcus said as he shook all the ladies' hands and exchanged pleasantries. "How about in the next ten minutes or so you gather everyone up so we can get this rehearsal underway."

"Sounds good!" said Anne as Marcus walked towards the still undecorated ceremonial wedding arbor. "Guys, I'm so nervous. Where's Tom? Do you see him? He needs to be here. He needs to get all his people ready."

"Calm down, Anne," said Diane as she gently hugged her. "It's all going to be great. It's going to be everything you ever wanted. Luna, can you go into the lobby? No, I mean, the bar. Tom and David went to get a drink about fifteen minutes ago. I'm sure they're still there."

"No problem. I'm on it!" said Luna as she quickly walked away.

"Sara, can you please go find Edward and Jim, and try to gather anyone who is waiting in the lobby and have them meet us out here so we can get started?"

"I sure will."

Diane and Anne sat down on a nearby bench. Diane put her arm around Anne and said, "Hey, you, it's not like you to be so nervous. You're the cool-headed one in this group. I mean, what do you have to be so worried about, you're only getting married and spending the rest of your life with the man who totally adores you? You're one lucky lady and Tom, well, he won the lottery when he found you." Anne lifted her head and Diane softly fixed a strand of hair that was hanging in Anne's eyes.

Anne smiled at Diane as she said, "You always know the right words to say to me. I'm just nervous."

"But that's normal, Annie. You're going to be and do just fine." Diane softly kissed Anne on the forehead. Both ladies got up, smiled at each other and walked hand in hand over towards the wedding arbor where everyone had started to gather. Everyone took their place as the rehearsal began. David couldn't take his eyes off Diane as she stood so beautifully with the wedding party.

After the wedding rehearsal, the wedding party and a few family members gathered in the private dining room for the rehearsal dinner. The room was set up with two long banquet tables, a bar with a bartender, and a buffet of both hot and cold entries with servers. Off to the side of the food was a beautifully decorated cake for dessert. Soft music was playing in the background. The setting was both friendly and joyful. David and Diane sat next to Anne and Tom. Luna and Jim were across from the soon-to-be bride and groom, and Sara and Edward were across from David and Diane. The journalist in Sara wanted badly to talk with David about his involvement with the Army but knew the rehearsal dinner was not the time or place. She would try to get him alone for a few minutes tomorrow or before the weekend was over.

Laughter filled the room. Jokes and stories were told about the awesome foursome. David found out a lot a fun things about Diane's childhood and past. It was getting late when Luna asked, "Isn't someone getting married tomorrow?"

"Not until six p.m.," laughed Anne.

"Do you guys want to get together for brunch, say eleven a.m., before we go into hair and makeup?" asked Sara.

"What a great idea. Sounds good to me," said Diane.

"I know of a really good sports bar in town if any of you guys are interested in hanging out tomorrow for lunch," suggested Tom.

"Well, I definitely don't need hair and makeup, so I'm in," said Jim as he took a last drink of his beer. Both Edward and David also agreed to meet.

"So, how about one p.m. in the lobby?" asked Tom.

"You all better be back in plenty of time to get ready and make sure you're sober!" Luna jokingly demanded.

"Yes, mommy. We will," laughed Tom and added to Anne, "Come on, babe, let's get you to bed. This is the last night I get to sleep with a single woman." Everyone laughed as all four couples left for their rooms.

Chapter 22

The next morning, Diane woke up to David on his side propped up on his forearm, looking down at her as he watched her sleep. "Well, good morning, my sunshine," he said as he brushed the hair out of Diane's eyes.

"Good morning," Diane said as she smiled up at David. "How long have you been watching me? Was I snoring? Was I drooling?" she jokingly added.

"No, I was just watching you. Soaking your beautiful face all in," said David as he bent down and kissed Diane on her forehead.

"What time is it? Have I slept the morning away?" a worried Diane said.

"No, as a matter of fact, it's pretty early. It's only seven-thirty. So, we have a little time on our hands before you have to get ready to meet the girls for brunch."

"Do you have any idea what we can do in the meanwhile to pass the time?" Diane smiled as she put both her hands around the back of David's head and drew him in close to kiss his soft full lips.

"Well, something just popped into mind," laughed David as he began to passionately kiss Diane. He started exploring her wet warm mouth which then led to soft kisses on her neck that made Diane release a soft moan. He then made his way down to her full breasts and erect nipples. At this point, Diane's moans were louder and more distinguished. Her back was arched as he slowly kissed his way down to her wet womanhood. He teased her with his strong warm tongue as she kept her hands strongly entangled in his hair. She was about to let out a scream when David gently entered her.

"Now, now, my sweet girl, calm down and make love to me," David said in a deep sexy voice. Diane's body gladly welcomed David. Both Diane and David's bodies moved in perfect cadence as their bodies became one. "My God, I love you, Diane," David panted as he released his juices into Diane.

Fully exhausted, Diane let out a loud moan as she climaxed and added, "I love you, David, so very, very much." They both collapsed in exhaustion next to each other. Their breathing was heavy and labored. They lay next to each other holding hands, eyes closed, with smiles on their faces, saying not a word as their bodies returned to feeling normal and the electrical pulses firing off inside had subsided.

After ten minutes of silence, David quietly said, "Hey, sunshine, would you like to join me in the shower?"

"Hmm, I think I would like that very much, sir," Diane happily said as she sat up, got out of bed and walked towards the bathroom.

"Hey, hon, can you get the shower started while I call room service for some breakfast?"

"Sure can, but just coffee for me please. Remember, I'm meeting the girls downstairs for brunch in about an hour." Diane paused, looked at David with a smile on her face and said, "To think, this all started with a simple hello," as she started the water.

Diane was makeup free, had her hair in a loose ponytail, and wore a pair of jeans and a t-shirt when she walked out of the bedroom.

David looked up from his breakfast and said, "How do you do it?"

"Do what?" Diane answered.

"Look so damn cute," David said with a smile. Diane bent down and kissed David on top of his head.

"Well, the natural glow I'm sporting comes from a special blend from the "erotic sex de la David in the morning" line. I highly recommend it every morning." Both David and Diane laughed. Diane sat down across from David and poured herself a cup of coffee. "So, I have brunch with the girls from eleven to twelve-thirty then hair and makeup at one p.m. You have lunch with the guys at one and I'm sure you'll all do something else afterwards, so I guess I won't see you until the wedding," said Diane.

"Where are you going to get ready? Won't I see you then?" questioned David.

"No, babe, Sara has a room where we're all getting dressed and taking pre-ceremony pictures."

"Fancy, fancy!" said David. "So, do you trust me getting dressed all by myself?"

Diane laughed as both David and Diane got up from the table and walked over to each other. Diane put her arms around David's waist and said, "I have no doubt in the world that you are going to look extremely handsome, even though I have no idea what you're wearing. I'm sure you will be the envy of every man."

"Well, I definitely wasn't expecting to hear that," laughed David. "I'll do my best." Diane grabbed her bag, kissed David goodbye and left to meet the girls downstairs for brunch.

David had just sat back down to finish his coffee when his phone started ringing. "This is David Anderson, how can I help you?"

"First Lieutenant Anderson, how are you, son?"

"Lieutenant Colonel Jefferson, sir, I'm well," David responded, almost standing to attention. "How can I help you sir?"

"I'm sorry to call while you're out of town but it's imperative that we meet to discuss your orders for next month."

Without hesitation, David answered, "I'll be back in Miami Sunday night, sir. You name the day and time and I'll be there."

"Good to hear, Anderson. I'll see you at the armory this Wednesday at zero nine-hundred hours."

"Thank you, sir. See you then," said David as he hung up the phone and slumped down in his seat. He sat with his head down, buried in both his hands. After a few minutes, David hit the table in anger and yelled, "Why? Why the fuck now?" He ran his fingers through his hair and thought out loud, "I can't tell Diane. This will ruin her weekend. This is going to have to wait. It's going to have to wait until we get back." And with that, David went into the bedroom to get ready to meet the guys.

Chapter 23

David was sitting in the lobby looking at his phone, when he heard, "Hey, man, how's it going?" Jim said as he took a seat across from David.

"Hey Jim," David responded as he put his phone away.

"Have you seen any of the other guys?"

"Nah, just sitting here waiting and killing some time."

Jim looked at his watch and said, "Man, I thought I was early. How long have you been here?"

David laughed and said, "Not long. It's the Army in me. I'm always early."

"I think it's a great quality for anyone to have. I respect that. Now, where are the other two knuckleheads?" Jim said as both he and David laughed. About five minutes later both Edward and Tom showed up.

"Hey, sorry guys, I've been dealing with a security issue at work. I apologize for being late," Edward said as he reached to shake hands with each of the men.

"Yeah, me too. Sorry, I've kept you guys waiting. I had a last-minute call from the hotel about the table set-ups."

"No worries. David and I were just shooting the shit about life but, since you guys were late, the first round is on you both," Jim said as all the guys made their way out of the hotel.

All four men piled into Tom's new Tesla. "Nice ride, Tom," said Jim.

"Thanks, man. I love it. I'm doing what I can for the environment and I love the gas mileage." The car erupted in laughter. After driving for about twenty minutes, Tom pulled into a waterfront restaurant. "It may not look like much on the outside but the food and the lunchtime band are the best around," said Tom.

"Looks good to me," said David.

"Hell, I'm not picky," added Edward.

"As long as the beer is cold, I'm good," laughed Jim. The men were seated outside with a view of the lake. The band was set up not too far from their table but wasn't playing for another hour.

"Hi, good afternoon. I'm Becky and I'll be your waitress today. Could I interest you gentlemen in our two for one special on all bottle beers going on right now? If so, what can I get you guys to drink?" The young pretty waitress said. Jim started off by ordering Heineken, followed by David ordering Bud Light, and then with both Edward and Tom ordering Miller Light.

"I've got to remember to take it slow today," said Tom.

,"Why is that man? It's not like you have anything important to do today," laughed Edward.

"Anne, and probably my mother, will kill me if I show up with even a slight buzz."

"Nah, we're just here for a nice lunch and killing time while the girls are fancying it up at the spa," added Jim.

"I don't know about you guys but I'm ready for some of those killer ribs I smell cooking," said David.

"Damn, is that what I smell? I second that," added Edward.

"Hell, yeah, I'm in for the ribs too," both Tom and Jim added. Becky came soon after with their beer.

"So, have you gentlemen decided on what you're going to have for lunch today?"

"Well, Becky, it's unanimous. We're all going to have the ribs," said Tom.

"Great choice," Becky said as she placed plenty of napkins down on the table. "I'll put your order in right now," Becky said as she walked away.

"So, David," began Edward. "We hear that you're an Army Ranger."

"Well, I was in the Army and, yes, I was a Ranger but I'm no longer serving actively," answered David.

"You're in the Guard now, right?" asked Tom.

"I am," said David not feeling too comfortable with the line of questioning.

"Any chance of you being called up for this mess going on in the Middle East?" asked Jim.

"There's always that chance. You never know when Uncle Sam is going to call," replied David just as the plates of ribs arrived. David quickly turned the subject towards the mound of ribs that were in front of all the guys. "Damn, Tom, you weren't kidding about this place. Cold beer and great food," said David as the guys chowed down on some fall-off-the-bone barbequed ribs. The rest of the conversations throughout lunch were light and simple. Nothing personal was discussed. The band began playing soon after lunch was finished, which required a couple more rounds of beer. The band played a mix of country, bluegrass, and some eighties and nineties music which kept the guys quite entertained. After several hours, the men made their way back to the hotel all in one piece and sober.

"Hey, guys, thanks for a great lunch. I appreciate you spending your time with me and keeping me busy," said Tom.

"What else were we supposed to do all day?" laughed Jim.

"Yeah, our ladies are getting beautified," added Edward.

"You were the safe bet," joked David. The four men shook hands and each headed for their hotel rooms to take a nap.

Chapter 24

"Oh, my God! What an amazing day of pampering. One of us should get married at least once a month so we can enjoy this relaxing spa treatment," Luna said as she took another sip of Champagne.

"Oh, my goodness, yes!" replied Sara.

"It doesn't get any better than this!" Anne said as she closed her eyes and smiled.

"I could fall asleep right here. I'm so relaxed," added Diane.

"Um, I believe you were super relaxed and, may I add, totally glowing when we saw you this morning, missy!" laughed Luna as she opened one eye and pointed to Diane.

Diane just smiled and said, "I wonder how the guys are doing?"

"Nice way of changing the subject, Diane," joked Sara.

"Today is not about me or my love life. Today is all about celebrating our dear friend, Anne, as she begins a new chapter in her life," smiled Diane.

"You're definitely right, Diane. Let's all raise our glass to our beautiful Anne," added Sara.

"But we aren't finished with you," laughed Luna as she smiled at Diane.

After massages, mani-pedis, and a few glasses of Champagne, the girls were ready for hair and makeup. Each girl had their own makeup artist and hairdresser. The girls all agreed beforehand on how they would wear their hair, so there would be some uniformity in the way they looked. Anne, the bride, wore her hair in a loose hanging updo. Pieces of hair fell softly, framing her face. Luna, Sara, and Diane all wore their hair in loose curls. Their hair was up on the left side, held in place with a beautiful silver and crystal hair clip that was given to each of them by Anne as a gift for being in the wedding. Anne's wedding gown was an elegant off-the-shoulder, cream in color, body-fitting mermaid-style floor-length gown. It made a beautiful silhouette of her petite figure. The girls each wore a cocktail-length rose-colored dress which complimented their figures. Sara and Luna's dresses were halter-top style. Diane's dress was off the shoulder. Each girl looked stunning. After the girls were dressed, the photographer met them downstairs for a few photos in the outside gardens where the ceremony was to be held. After the pictures, Diane decided to check on David.

She called his cell phone which he promptly answered, "Hey, beautiful, long time no see or hear."

"I know," answered Diane. "So how was your lunch with the guys?"

"It was good. They're a great group of guys. So how was your spa day?"

"Oh, my goodness, it was fantastic! I really need to treat myself to that kind of day more often," laughed Diane.

"Well, sweetie, I can't wait to see you. I bet you look even more gorgeous than you did this morning when you left the room."

"Aw, I love you, David. So, are you dressed and ready to come down?"

"I just need to fix my tie and then I'll be down. Should I go to the lobby or make my way to the gardens to grab a seat?"

"Hmm, that's a good question. The ceremony starts in a half hour so I guess just make your way to the lobby and someone should gather all the guests and tell them to make their way outside. I'm sure you'll run into either Jim or Edward."

"Yeah, I'll do that. So, sweetie, are you going to tell me what you're wearing?"

"No," giggled Diane. "You'll see me at the ceremony like everyone else."

"Not even a hint? Man, Diane, you're strict!" laughed David.

"Yes, I am, but you still love me... right?" Laughed Diane.

"You know it, babe. Okay, let me go so I can tie this tie. See you in a few. Love you, Diane."

"Love you too, David."

David made his way to the lobby wearing a black fitted suit, crisp white dress shirt and a silk gold, silver and black paisley tie. He looked like he had just walked off the pages of GQ.

"Well, look at you, man. You sure clean up well," Edward said when he saw David.

David reached out his hand to greet Edward saying, "You don't do too badly yourself. Any sign of Jim?" asked David.

"Yeah, he went to call his mother to check on the boys. He'll be back anytime now."

Not a minute went by, when Jim jokingly said, "Look at you pretty boys standing around looking like you belong on the runway."

The guys all laughed. "So, how's it on the home front? The boys good?" asked Edward.

"Yeah, yeah. They're doing great. They haven't worn my mom out yet. I think she'll still be speaking to us when we get back," Jim said as he laughed and the guys made their way outside to be seated.

Soft music from the violinist was being played in the background of the beautifully decorated outside gardens. The wedding arbor that stood plain last night was decorated in beautiful burgundy, soft pink, and white roses along with pink and white peonies nestled in greenery and punctuated with baby's breath. A white cloth was draped over the arbor and fell loosely at the sides.

Tom and his brother, Michael, made their way next to the arbor, along with Marcus, his good friend who was performing the ceremony. Tom wore a light gray tux, white shirt, and a rose-colored bowtie. His brother wore the same colored tux but Michael wore a traditional rose-colored necktie. Both men wore a light pink rose boutonniere surrounded with a hint of greenery and baby's breath on their lapels. Tom looked around at the small gathering of close friends and family and smiled. He looked genuinely calm and ready to begin his new life chapter with Anne.

The violinist's music became louder as the ceremony was about to begin. The girls grabbed their bouquets of pink, white and burgundy roses and got in line to begin their procession down the aisle. The first bridesmaid to walk down the flower-lined aisle was Luna. Luna's smile beamed brightly as she walked slowly towards the arbor. As she walked past Jim, she gave him a wink and he gave her a thumbs up. Sara was waiting patiently for Luna to make it to the end of the aisle before she began her walk. As Sara began her walk, she quickly had a flashback of walking down the aisle as a bride. She quickly shrugged the emotion off and began to smile warmly at the people who were watching her every move. She spotted Edward and as she passed him, he put his hand on his heart and gave it a double tap as he watched her walk by. Before it was her turn to walk down the aisle, Diane hugged Anne and said, "I know I've said this at least ten times but you look absolutely beautiful. You deserve this beautiful day. Enjoy this moment and don't forget to walk slowly."

Anne laughed and said, "I'm ready. I can do this." Diane started her walk towards the end of the aisle, taking in the beauty of the gardens. Her eyes were wide and they appeared to be smiling as sweetly as the smile on her face.

David was in awe of the way Diane looked. As she walked past him he thought to himself, "My God, she is breathtakingly beautiful." Diane was in front of the arbor and looked out to see David. When their eyes met, David mouthed the words, "You look gorgeous. I love you." Diane gave David a sweet sheepish look. The music changed. People stood up and Anne slowly walked down the aisle towards Tom. Tom's eyes were transfixed on his bride and he wore a smile from ear to ear. Anne only looked in the direction of Tom and the saying, they only have eyes for each other, was an understatement. As Anne approached the wedding arbor, Diane stepped forward to hold her bouquet. Anne's bouquet was made of classic pink and white peonies surrounded with palm and palmetto leaves. As the sun set in the background, Anne and Tom recited their vows to one another and became husband and wife.

After the ceremony and after photos were taken, the small gathering of family and friends made their way into the reception hall. The wedding party and their significant others were all assigned to the same table but were casually talking amongst each other before sitting down.

"When are they going to start passing around hors d'oeuvres? I'm starving," said Jim.

"Who said there was going to be hors d'oeuvres?" remarked Luna.

"Say what? Seriously no little weenies wrapped in bacon or stuffed mushrooms?" Everyone laughed at Jim as the first tray of ham and cheese pinwheels and mini pizza rolls were being passed around by the waiters.

"Aw, yes, food," said David as he loaded up his small plate.

"Anyone want a drink? I'm heading to the bar?" said Edward.

"Yes, please," said Sara and Luna in unison.

"I'll take a beer," said David.

"And I'll have a white wine spritzer," added Diane.

"I'll go with you," said Jim as he put his last pizza roll in his mouth.

Luna laughed as she shook her head and said, "Aww, yes, he's all mine." Everyone laughed. David and Diane made their way to their table so they could sit down and eat their hors d'oeuvres.

"Wow, wasn't that a beautiful ceremony?"

"It sure was but there was one person who stole the show," said David as he softly touched Diane's face. "Babe, you looked and still look unbelievably gorgeous. You took my breath away when you were walking down the aisle."

"Oh, David, you're such a sweetheart. You always say the right things." Diane smiled as she kissed David's lips.

After dinner was served, the DJ started playing party music for the guests to begin dancing. Luna and Jim danced wildly as Anne and Tom swayed to the music holding each other. Edward and Sara seemed to be the only ones who knew the latest dance moves while David and Diane sat at their table watching. David patiently waited for the DJ to play a slow song so he could ask Diane to dance. After about twenty minutes, he got his wish.

"For all you love birds out there, this one's for you," announced the DJ. "The Way You Look Tonight," by Frank Sinatra began playing. The song couldn't have been more significant to the way David was feeling.

"I think they're playing our song," he said to Diane as he held out his hand and stood up. He nodded to the dance floor and said, "Shall we?"

"We shall," said Diane as she took David's hand and walked to the dance floor. David held Diane close to his chest. He placed his right hand just below Diane's waist and his left hand softly holding Diane's right hand. Diane's left hand was gently resting on David's right shoulder. As they danced, they felt every word and moved as one. Diane moved her left hand towards David's face and then to the back of his neck. When the song was over, they stood in the middle of the dance floor and were caught stealing a kiss.

"Hey, now, none of that nonsense," yelled Jim as everyone laughed. David and Diane laughed and walked off the dance floor. The night was filled with laughter, good company, and an overall good time. Everyone danced, ate and drank too much but, more than anything, made lasting memories. As the night began to wind down, everyone realized that there was no time tomorrow to meet up before leaving. Everyone had a different time to fly home. Hugs, kisses, plenty of handshakes, and a few tears filled the room.

"I can't believe the weekend is over," Sara said as she hugged Anne tightly.

"I know, what a great time," added Luna as she added herself to the hug.

"Such a beautiful wedding and so many good times," Diane said as she too added herself to the group hug.

"I want to thank you guys so much for making this all happen. You truly are the best group of friends any girl could have. I love you guys so much," Anne said as she began to cry happy tears.

"Okay, now, ladies, this is a happy day. Let's not get too sappy," Tom said as he walked over to his bride.

"Come on, Luna, my love. We have an early flight in the morning," said Jim as he tapped Luna on the shoulder.

"I know, I know but it's so hard leaving these girls," she said. Diane broke from the group hug and walked over to David and held his hand. Edward stood next to Sara with his arm around her waist.

Anne broke the ice by saying, "Well, okay, I guess this is goodbye. I love you all so much and thank you again for making our day so wonderful. You all send a text when you get home safely. Tom and I will be heading out for LA tomorrow evening and then flying to Hawaii Monday morning." The words "I love you" and "safe flight home" filled the room as everyone exited the reception hall.

The next morning, David and Diane were up early. They had a quick breakfast before making their way to the airport. Diane sighed and said, "Back to reality in a few hours, my love."

David paused for a moment as he thought about his Wednesday meeting with Lieutenant Colonel Jefferson before saying, "Yeah, I wonder what this week is going to throw at us." David leaned over to Diane, smiled, kissed her cheek and took her hand into his and held it the entire way to the airport. Not much was said during their twenty-minute drive. Diane thought it was unusual not to have a conversation and for David to be so quiet, but figured it was early in the morning and due to way too many beers last night. After checking in their luggage and going through the TSA check-point they finally grabbed a seat at their gate.

"We have an hour to kill before boarding. Would you like a cup of coffee or something?"

"No, babe, I'm good but I sure would love to know if there's anything wrong. David, what's up? You're really never this quiet."

David thought for a second and said, "Well, sweetie, there is something I need to talk to you about."

"David, you know you can tell me anything. What's wrong?"

"Well, Saturday morning after you left for your spa day with the girls, I received a call from Lieutenant Colonel Jefferson. He's the one I report to. He told me that we need to meet to discuss matters concerning the unit's deployment to the Middle East."

"What? Are you kidding me? David, No!"

David reached for both of Diane's hands. He held them tightly as he looked into her eyes and said, "It's just a meeting for now. We're going to go over details on Wednesday morning."

"Wednesday morning? As in this Wednesday? Like, three days from now Wednesday?"

"Yes, sweetie, but please don't start worrying just yet. It's just a meeting." David kept saying, "It's just a meeting" but was he trying to convince himself or was he trying to convince Diane? David was trying to downplay the meeting for Diane's sake but, deep down inside, he knew he was going to be leaving on a serious and dangerous deployment.

Chapter 25

It was a quiet flight home as well as the ride to Diane's house. Diane didn't know what to say and she knew David was not in the mood to talk about the meeting. Diane tried to make small talk and David talked a lot about the weekend. The mood was very tense.

As they approached Diane's street, Diane asked, "So, would you like to come in for a little bit? I could make you a sandwich? Are you hungry?"

"Thanks, babe, I really appreciate it but I'm going to head over to the bar and check on things there, but I'll call you later and, if you want, we can grab a bite to eat later."

"That sounds great. That will give me enough time to unpack and get things ready for work tomorrow." David walked Diane to her front door and placed her luggage in the kitchen. Diane put her sunglasses and purse on the kitchen table. She smiled at David and slowly walked over to him.

David hugged her tightly and said, "I love you and I'll see you later."

"I love you too, David. Thanks for a wonderful weekend. It really was great."

David kissed Diane on the forehead as he put both hands on her checks and said, "Get some rest, babe, and I'll call you in a bit." David turned and walked out the door. As she closed the door, Diane made a fist and hit the door. "Why? I just can't believe this is happening." Diane slid down to the floor where she sat and cried.

David sat in his truck for at least five minutes sitting silently while staring blankly out the window. He then started the truck and headed for the bar. Meanwhile, Diane had picked herself up off the floor and began to unpack. She decided to let the girls know through text message that she arrived home safely. Luna responded that she was home and Anne acknowledged she and Tom were getting ready to head for the airport. Sara and Edward were still in flight and wouldn't be home until a little later that evening due to a flight delay. Diane decided to message Sara separately from the other girls. She wrote, When you get home and settled, please give me a call. I really need to talk to you.

Diane wanted to know if Sara had heard any more news on US troops being deployed to the Middle East.

It was late in the afternoon and Diane hadn't heard from David or Sara. She needed to talk to someone and decided to call Jenny.

"Hello," answered a deep husky voice.

"Hey, Vic, it's Diane. How are you? Is Jenny home?"

"Hey, Diane. I'm good. No, Jenny is over at her sister's house. She'll be back in a couple of hours. You want me to have her call you when she gets back?"

"Yeah, that'll be great. Thanks, Vic. 'Bye."

"My goodness, I can't seem to get in touch with anyone today," thought Diane as she lay on her couch and closed her eyes.

When Diane woke up it was dark outside. She looked around in disbelief and then immediately checked her phone. Two missed calls and two messages. "Oh, my goodness, I can't believe I slept through the phone ringing!" Diane checked the first message which was from David. "Hey, babe. Where are you? Leaving the bar in about twenty then heading home to shower. Let me know if you still want me to pick something up for dinner and bring it over. Love you!"

"Are you kidding me? What time did he call? Crap, that was an hour ago." Diane immediately hit the call back button.

"Hey, you," began David, "Where have you been?"

"You aren't going to believe this but I fell asleep."

"Seriously, babe? I called twice and was getting a little worried. Well, do you still want me to come by with dinner? I just got home and was ready to jump in the shower. I can be there within the hour."

"I'd like that. I really want to see you," said Diane.

"Then I'm coming over but, to be honest with you, I was coming over either way," David said as he laughed then added, "So, what do you want me to pick up for dinner? You in the mood for anything special?"

"Well, I'm always in the mood for you," replied Diane as she smiled from the other side of the phone. "Well, I was asking about the main course. Dessert is a given," said David with a chuckle.

"You know, I'm in the mood for pork fried rice and an egg roll."

"Then, Chinese it is," said David. "I'll be over in about an hour."

"Okay, sweetie. See you then." Diane got up off the couch. She looked around the dimly lit room. The house was in order, clothes were unpacked, and she was ready for school in the morning. The only thing left was to shower and get ready for David and Chinese food.

About an hour later, as promised and on time, David knocked at the door. "I come with food!" David said as he walked inside raising the containers over his head and laughing. David put the food on the counter and took Diane into his arms. He gave her a big hug and even bigger kiss.

"Time for that later, big boy, I'm starving," Diane laughed as she wiggled away from David to the box of food on the counter.

"Oh, I see, you're only interested in the food and not me."

"Well, babe, for right now… yeah!" David and Diane both laughed and each grabbed a container and made their way to the couch. "Oh, this is good. This is really good!" Diane said with her eyes closed and a smile on her face. "So, how was the bar? Did it survive without you for the weekend?"

"It did. I'm lucky to have Joe as not only my business partner but also my best friend. I can count on him for anything and I'm sure he'll have no problem handling things while I'm gone."

"Speaking of that, David… "

"No, no, we're not going to speak of me leaving tonight. We're not going to speak about it until after I meet with Jefferson on Wednesday," interrupted David.

"I know, babe, but… "

"No buts," David said to Diane as he took away the container of fried rice she was holding and placed it on the nearby coffee table. The only thing I want to talk about is… "

"Well, who said we have to talk?" Diane whispered as she gently placed her index finger on David's lips. David smiled as he sat up straight and then leaned forward onto Diane. Diane eased down slowly on the soft pillows that were properly placed on her couch.

"Now, this is what I was thinking about!" David remarked as he and Diane enjoyed some couple time.

The living room was completely dark except for a hint of light that was coming from the stove light in the kitchen. David got up from the narrow couch and said, "This couch is comfortable to sit on but, damn, it definitely wasn't made for love-making."

Diane chuckled and added, "Well, was your butt between two cushions? I think not."

"Well, babe," David said as he got up and stretched "Lesson learned. This couch is for sitting and watching TV but definitely not for love-making." David grabbed his jeans and t-shirt and got dressed. Diane grabbed her shirt which was long enough to cover herself.

"Hey, you want to take some of this food with you for your lunch tomorrow?"

"Nah, thanks anyway, sweetie. Tomorrow is going to be crazy. I probably won't even have time for lunch. Remember, I have to go to the bar after work so I won't be able to see you tomorrow night."

"Sadly, I remember but you will be at school Tuesday, right?"

"Yes, ma 'am. That's the plan." David and Diane walked to the front door.

David kissed Diane goodnight and said, "I love you." "I love you too, David. Sweet dreams. Good night."

Chapter 26

Diane rolled out of bed bright and early for work and thought to herself, "Oh, lord, I wonder what I'm going to be walking into when I get into that classroom of mine?" Diane took a quick wake-up shower. She got dressed. She brushed her teeth and brushed her hair into a cute messy bun. She put on some mascara and a little blush. Diane grabbed a cup of coffee before grabbing some leftover Chinese food for lunch. She looked around the house, turned out the kitchen light, picked up her purse and made her way out the door. It was pretty early and she knew she'd have at least an hour to spare but knew from previous times walking into a classroom after being out can be a disaster. She made it to work in ten minutes and, of course, was the first one in the parking lot except for Mr. Green, the custodian. She sat in her parked car for a few minutes and decided to send a text to David, Good morning, my love. Hope you slept well. Have a great day. Call me when you can XOXO. David text immediately back, I love you, sweetie. I'll try calling during your break. Don't let those rugrats make you crazy XOXO! Diane laughed and made her way into the school.

Diane entered the office, signed in and gathered her things from her mailbox. She walked down the quiet hallway leading to her classroom.

"Hey, Miss Walker, good morning. How was your weekend?" yelled a friendly voice.

"Hey, Mr. Green. Good morning. Should I be afraid to enter my room?" laughed Diane as she answered.

Mr. Green laughed as he said, "You know, the room looked pretty good. They didn't tear it up too bad!"

"Fingers crossed," said Diane as she walked to her room. Diane unlocked her classroom door and slowly walked in and turned on the lights. "Well, well," said Diane with a smile on her face as she looked around. Diane walked over to her desk. The desk was neat and orderly. All the papers that Diane left for her students were paper clipped and graded. Diane looked around to make sure she was in the right room. She picked up the note written by the substitute.

"Dear Ms. Walker, thank you for leaving such well-written plans and directions. The children were a little rambunctious in the beginning but, once they knew who the boss was, they straightened up. It was a pleasure substituting for you. Mrs. Andrews."

"I did walk into the right classroom, right?" questioned Diane to herself. "Wow, I'm shocked! Hmm, this day is starting off great already." Diane walked over to the board, changed the date, and wrote her lessons for the school day. She sat down at her desk, read the note once again from the substitute and smiled to herself. Diane checked her phone out of habit and then realized she never checked her second message. It was from Sara. "Hey, girl, call me when you can. I need to talk to you ASAP!" And, just like that, Diane's day went from great to worrisome. "Damn! Why didn't I listen to her message?" said Diane as she closed her eyes, clenched her teeth and squeezed her hands tightly. Diane immediately tried calling Sara. Her call went right to voicemail. Diane hung up and sent a text to Sara's phone, OMG, I just heard your message. I'm so sorry I didn't get back to you. Call me when you can.

Diane sat back in her chair with her eyes closed and a gut-wrenching feeling in her stomach.

Diane's students came into class soon after, which was a welcome distraction.

"Miss Walker is back!"

"Yay!" yelled a couple of her students.

"I'm so glad you're back," said James, one of her more challenging students.

"Oh, James, that's so nice. Thank you."

"He's only glad you're back because that lady who was here was so mean," laughed Cal.

"Yeah, Miss Walker, she wouldn't let us breathe loud," sighed Mia.

"Oh, so you all were good only because Mrs. Andrews was strict with you not because it was the right thing to do. And, to think, she left a beautiful note about your behavior and I was going to reward you with extra recess time. Now I'm really going to have to think about it," laughed Diane.

"Aww, come on, Miss Walker," moaned the class.

Diane laughed and said, "It's all good. I'm still very happy that I came back to a clean classroom and a good report. Don't worry, we'll still have extra recess time."

As the class got settled into their seats, Jenny peeked her head into Diane's classroom and said, "Glad you're back. See you at lunch." Diane smiled, nodded and gave Jenny a thumbs-up.

"Girl, I smell Chinese food," Jenny said as she laughed then made a face.

"It's me. I'm guilty. David and I had Chinese last night. I had leftovers. Sorry to stink up your library," joked Diane as she sat across from Jenny.

"So, how was the wedding and the first weekend away with the cute boyfriend?"

"Oh, Jenny, the wedding was great. Anne made a beautiful bride. David really liked the girls and he really got along well with the guys. And can that man clean up well!" smiled Diane.

"Vic didn't tell me you called until like nine last night and I figured it was too late to call at that time."

"Oh, no problem, Jenny. That's okay; David was probably leaving around that time and, soon after he left, I went to bed."

"Is everything okay?"

"No, Jenny, it's not. David has a meeting on Wednesday morning and I know it's to discuss his leaving for the Middle East. Even though he says it's just a meeting, I know in my gut it's more. He's going over there to do something very dangerous, Jenny. I just know it!" Diane put her head down and began to cry.

"Oh, sweetie, it's going to be all right," Jenny said as she got up to sit next to Diane and put her arms around her. "Just wait until after the meeting. It could be just that, a meeting. Maybe they want his input. You know he's an important guy."

"Yeah, I know but we just started getting serious. I love him and he loves me and I want that to continue more than anything."

Lunch was almost over. Diane fixed her makeup in the bathroom, gathered her lunch which she hardly touched and thanked Jenny for listening, as she left to pick up her class from the cafeteria. The rest of the day was uneventful except for Diane's students, who received an extra fifteen minutes of recess time as a reward for behaving for the substitute.

Diane drove home knowing that she would not see David tonight. She knew he had a busy day at work and it wasn't over until he left the bar later tonight. She decided to stop at her favorite Greek restaurant for takeout for tonight's dinner. As she waited for her order, a Greek salad, her phone buzzed. It was a text message from David. Diane's face lit up as she read her message,

Hey, sweetie. Just checking on you and to let you know I've been thinking about you all day. I'm still running deliveries. I'll call when I'm on my way to the bar. Love you xoxo

Diane placed the phone to her chest, closed her eyes and smiled. "That must have been some message, Miss Diane, to get that reaction," smiled Alfred, the owner of the restaurant.

Diane gave Alfred a small chuckle as she took her salad and said smiling, "Oh, you could tell, could you?"

"Any look like that is true love. I can tell in the eyes," added Alfred as he smiled and winked at Diane as she left. "Hmmm, true love? Time will only tell," thought Diane as she got in her car and headed home.

Diane entered her house, dropped her keys and purse on the kitchen counter and placed her salad in the refrigerator for later. She kicked off her shoes near the door, picked up the remote and turned on the local news. She walked upstairs, changed into her infamous loungewear (sweatpants and t-shirt) and let down her hair from her messy bun. She galloped down the stairs, put on her flip-flops and went outside to check the mail. She opened the mailbox, "No mail, and no bills. I like it," said Diane out loud and smiling. She went inside and poured herself a glass of iced tea before plopping on the couch in front of the television. The local news reported on burglaries, assaults, traffic accidents, and embezzlement. "My God, seriously? Is there any good news to report?" Diane thought to herself. Just as she was getting ready to change the channel, the news anchor mentioned the Middle East. Diane froze in place, turned up the volume and began to listen intensely.

"Two U.S. service members were killed and two others injured Saturday when their vehicle was hit by a roadside bomb in southern Afghanistan, the Pentagon reported in a statement. The Taliban has taken responsibility for Saturday's attack. More than two thousand four hundred U.S. service troops have been killed in Afghanistan."

"Oh, no! I need to talk to Sara." Diane immediately picked up her phone and made the call.

The phone rang three times before Sara picked up and said, "Diane, I was going to call you. What's wrong? Everything okay?"

"Sara, I just saw the news about two more service members that were killed. What's going on? When is this going to end? Do you know anything? David has a meeting Wednesday morning with a Lieutenant Colonel Jefferson and I'm sure it's about him leaving on a dangerous mission."

"Okay, calm down, Diane. Has David told you anything about the meeting?"

"No, he doesn't want to discuss anything until after he meets with him. I can't get anything out of him and I'm so worried that he has to go over there and be put in harm's way."

"Diane, I honestly don't know what to say. Maybe they just want to meet with him because of his expertise. Just promise me, Diane, that you'll keep it together not only for yourself, but for David. Do you really think he wants to go? Do you think he wants to leave everything he has, especially leave you?"

"No, I know you're right, Sara, and I'm sorry to have lost it. I'm just so afraid."

"Look, sweetie, I know you're scared. I'll do everything I can to find out what's going on but, basically, what you hear on the news is what I know. I pinky-swear promise that if I find out anything, I'll let you know. Call me after David's meeting on Wednesday so I'm up to speed. Are you seeing David tonight?"

"No, he has to work at the bar tonight but he'll be calling later to say goodnight."

"Don't mention anything about the news. Just keep the conversation light."

"I will. I promise," Diane solemnly said.

"Diane," paused Sara, "You know how much I care about you. I'm here for you and if I find out anything, I'll let you know. Now, you turn off that damn news and watch a funny movie until your handsome boyfriend calls."

Diane laughed and said, "That sounds like a plan. Love you, Sara."

"Love you too, my friend. Good night."

Diane sat on the couch with her Greek salad and third glass of iced tea watching "Friends" reruns. When her phone rang, she paused the television. She was laughing while answering the phone and didn't even notice it was David calling.

"Hello," laughed Diane.

"Well, my goodness. Are you at a party?" questioned David.

"Oh, hi, honey. No, I'm just sitting here eating a Greek salad and watching "Friends" reruns."

"Well, it's good to hear you laugh. So, besides that, anything new?"

"Nah, I did speak to Sara a little earlier."

"Oh, yeah, how are things with her? What did she have to say?" David asked in a worried tone.

"Nothing really, we just did a little catching up." Diane didn't want David to know the real reason she called Sara.

"Well, okay then, sweetie, it's been crazy busy here, which is a good thing, but Joe and I haven't had a minute to ourselves. I just wanted to give you a quick call to let you know that I was thinking about you and that I love you."

"Aww, David, I love you too. I'll see you tomorrow at school, right?"

"You sure will," David said and added, "Well, babe, I really need to go. Sleep well. Love you. Good night!"

"Good night, David," said Diane as she blew a kiss goodnight into the phone.

Diane woke up bright and early. She had a good night's sleep and didn't let herself worry about David and his meeting. All she could concentrate on was what to wear to school and seeing David.

Chapter 27

As Diane walked into school her phone went off. It was a text message from David, Good morning, gorgeous. Hope you slept well. Making deliveries by myself today. Would you like a lunch date?

Diane smiled and immediately wrote back, Hi, honey. I would love a lunch date. We can split my salad.

David quickly responded back, No, that's fine, I was going to pick up burgers. Is that good?

Oh, David, that's perfect! Remember my lunch is at eleven-thirty-five a.m.

I know, babe, I'll be there. See you later.

Diane beamed as she walked past Mr. Green.

"Such a beautiful smile so early in the morning. What's going on, Miss Walker? You have something up your sleeve?"

Diane laughed and said, "No, it's just a good morning and I have a funny feeling it's going to be an even better afternoon."

"Glad to see you're in a good mood. I'm going to check back with you in the afternoon to see if you're still smiling," Mr. Green laughed as he walked away.

The morning was going smoothly. The children were all on task and Diane kept looking at the clock waiting for lunch-time. David never had lunch with her and she worried about what the other teachers would say. The only person at school who knew about Diane and David dating was Jenny and Jenny never told a soul. It was a beautiful fall day in Miami and would be a perfect day to eat outside and have a picnic, but Diane decided to have David come to her classroom to ensure tongues would not wag, but knew, as soon as one person saw him enter her classroom, the gossip and questions would start. Diane decided she could care less what people thought. She was in a committed relationship for some time now with David and, honestly, was ready for the world to know about it.

Diane lined her class up for lunch and walked them slowly to the cafeteria. She didn't see the truck and thought to herself that he was going to be late and they wouldn't have time together. She dropped the class off and went to the office to check her mailbox. She was stunned to see David standing there talking to Mr. Green while he was signing in as a guest.

"Well, hello, sunshine," David said as he smiled and winked at Diane.

"Hey, you," Diane said in a sheepish stunned voice.

"So, missy, this is why you were smiling ear to ear this morning," laughed Mr. Green. Diane smiled. Her eyes got wide and laughed as she quickly glanced at her empty mailbox.

"Okay, I'm good," Diane said to David. "We can go now." Diane grabbed David's arm. She blushed and smiled as she looked at Emma, the school secretary, as they left the office.

"I had no idea you were going to be so official and sign in as a guest. I thought you set up your deliveries to coincide with my lunch-time."

"No, babe, I'm on official-lunch-date with my girlfriend time," David said as he laughed and pulled Diane close. As they both walked down the hall to Diane's classroom, a few teachers stopped to glance at the happy couple walking together.

"Oh, geez, I can only imagine what's going through their minds and I just know I'll be the topic of conversation in the teacher's lounge," sighed Diane.

"Oh, babe, who cares. Want to give them something to talk about?" David said as he pulled Diane closer.

Diane giggled, "David, not here. The kids are watching."

With only twenty-five minutes left for lunch, Diane and David entered Diane's room. "What a nice classroom," said David.

"You've seen it before."

"Correction, my love. I've been in it before but the only thing I saw was you. I didn't look around. I was too fixated on kissing you to look around."

"Oh, yes," laughed Diane. "How can I forget our first kiss?"

"You better not," said David as he grabbed Diane to kiss her. Time was of the essence. They ate their burgers and drank their sodas way too fast but managed to get some talk in about David's meeting tomorrow.

"So, this meeting tomorrow, is it official? Do you have to dress in a uniform?" asked Diane.

"Yeah. I'll be dressed in my fatigues."

"Oh, okay, I bet you look mighty handsome in your fatigues, soldier," Diane said as she got up from her chair, kissed David on the cheek and gathered the burger wrappers off her reading table.

"Is that my cue that lunch is over?" asked David.

Diane laughed, "Well, I have five minutes left. Lunchtime flies and I still have to go to the restroom. Walk with me to the library so you can say hi to Jenny while I'm in the restroom."

"Sounds good but, before we leave, can I get a kiss and I don't mean a kiss on the cheek?" said David as he gently moved closer to Diane. Diane smiled and leaned in close to David for a short but sensual kiss. They walked into the library where Jenny was just finishing up with a class. Diane walked straight to the restroom and David took a seat next to Jenny's desk. Mrs. Donner was standing by the computers and smiled while fixing her skirt when she saw David. She was staring at him as if in a trance.

Jenny called her three times before walking over to her and said, "Mrs. Donner, your class is ready to go."

"Oh, my, I'm sorry. Yes, okay. Let's go, class," she said as she was quite visibly embarrassed.

"Geez, David, do you go anywhere without attracting women?" Jenny asked him as she gave him a gentle smack on his shoulder. "So, you had lunch with Diane."

"I did have lunch with Diane and I honestly don't know how you teachers do it all in thirty-five minutes. You take the kids to lunch. You go to the office to check your mailbox, you eat, you prepare for the afternoon and you make time to pee. You guys are my heroes. I couldn't do it!" Jenny laughed right as Diane was coming out of the restroom.

"What's so funny?"

"Your boyfriend here doesn't know how teachers can fit so much into a thirty-five-minute lunchbreak."

"If he only knew that teaching kids is a superpower!" laughed Diane as she quickly looked around, saw no one in the library and bent down to give David a kiss goodbye. "I have to go, my dear. Sorry, we didn't have much time. I'll talk to you later." Diane then softly said, "I love you."

"What was that? What did you say to me?" joked David. "Did you say you loved me?"

"David, you're crazy and, yes, I love you. There, I said it loud enough for everyone to hear," giggled Diane.

David smiled and said, "You better get going. I don't want you to be late on my account. I'll call you later from the bar." Diane walked to the door and, as she opened the door to leave, David yelled in a silly voice, "I love you too, sweetness!" Diane laughed, rolled her eyes, shook her head and walked out the door. David stayed a few minutes longer to visit with Jenny. "She's one special lady, Jenny, and I don't want to lose her."

"Well, then, don't fuck it up. Diane is a great girl. She's been through a lot. I can tell she really cares about you, David."

"And I really care about her."

Chapter 28

The dreaded Wednesday morning meeting was on Diane's mind as soon as she woke up. She hadn't slept well, even though she told David last night that she wouldn't think about the meeting until after hearing from him. Diane jumped in the shower, got dressed, and made a quick bowl of cereal and cup of coffee. She sat at her kitchen table staring into space, slowly eating her soggy cereal. Diane suddenly jumped when her phone began to ring. She quickly picked it up. It was David.

"Good morning, babe," answered Diane.

"Hey, beautiful. I thought I'd give you a call now because I have no idea when I'll be able to talk to you today. It's not too early, is it?"

"No, not at all. I'm actually sitting down eating a bowl of cereal and having a cup of coffee before I leave for work," Diane said as she picked up a spoonful of soggy cereal before pushing it away.

"Well, I just called to say have a great day at school. I'll call after the meeting but the most important reason for calling is to tell you I love you and not to worry about today."

Diane sat up smiled and said, "Aww, David, I love you but the worrying part is going to be a little bit more difficult but I'll try."

"Everything is going to be okay," said David in a reassuring voice.

Diane played with her cereal and then said, "I'm sure it is."

"'Bye, sweetie."

"'Bye, David."

The day dragged on for what seemed like an eternity. Diane watched the clock all day. There had been no word from David since his phone call that morning. Jenny was downtown for a meeting so she had no one to talk things over with. When school was over, Diane got her board ready for the next day and worked on her lesson plans for the following week. Winter break was in two weeks so planning was relatively easy. She didn't stay any longer than she had to. Usually, Diane was the first teacher to arrive and usually one of the last teachers to leave, but not today. Today, she could hardly concentrate and wanted nothing more than to leave, go home and wait to hear from David.

When she rounded the corner to her street, she noticed David's truck in her driveway. Diane perked up and then almost immediately a strange feeling came over her.

"Oh, my God, it must be bad," she thought to herself. "Why else would he be here waiting for me?" Diane slowly pulled into her driveway next to David's truck. She got out of her car. David got out of his truck.

"Wow, this is a surprise. I never thought I'd see you waiting for me. How did the meeting go?" Diane asked in a nervous voice.

David walked over to Diane, kissed her cheek and said, "I've been thinking about you all day and couldn't wait to see you so I thought I'd surprise you."

"Have you been waiting long?" asked Diane then continued by saying, "You should've called me to let me know."

"Then it wouldn't have been a surprise," laughed David.

"Yeah, I guess that's true," smiled Diane. "Come on, let's get inside," Diane said as she motioned to David with a nod of her head. David followed Diane to her front door. Diane slowly unlocked the door and both walked inside. Diane placed her purse on her counter and David leaned up against the counter. "So, how did it go?" Diane asked as she opened the refrigerator and took out a jug of iced tea. "Want a glass?"

"No, thanks, babe, but, Diane, we need to sit down and talk."

Diane poured herself a glass and, before putting the jug back into the refrigerator, she said, "Are you sure you don't want any?"

"Yes, I'm sure," said David as he walked over to Diane and took the glass from her hand and placed it on the counter.

He hugged her tightly and sadly said, "I'm definitely leaving in two weeks." Diane buried her head in David's chest and began to cry. After a few minutes, David gently lifted Diane's head off his chest and the two of them walked to her couch where they sat down. Diane sat facing David with her legs crisscrossed in front of her and her hands clenched together in her lap. David sat facing Diane but with only one leg slightly bent on the couch.

"So, tell me everything. Tell me, if you can, everything you're going to be doing over there," Diane said to David as she softly wept. David reached for Diane's hands and held them as he began giving her as much detail as he could.

"Well," he hesitated, "As I said earlier, I leave in two weeks. December 14th to be exact."

"Oh, my goodness," Diane sadly said, "You won't be here for Christmas or New Year's and that's exactly when my winter break from school begins." David hugged her as she began to cry again. "Oh, David, I just can't believe this."

"Well, the good thing is, if there is a good thing, I won't be seeing any type of battle. I'm there solely for my expertise to plan details and raids."

Diane looked up and said, "But I know that can be just as dangerous. You may not be actually fighting but I know since you're Special Forces you'll be planning and participating in those raids. I'm right, aren't I?"

"Well, yeah, you're right," David said as he pressed his lips together. "Don't try to candy coat this for me, David. I know what goes on over there. I watch the news and I know there're lots and lots of secret missions the

177

American people will never know about. It is dangerous. It is scary and I'm not going to be able to handle knowing that you're over there planning and taking part and being part of dangerous missions."

"Diane. Sweetie, I know it's a lot for you to take in right now but it's going to be all right. I promise to be careful. I promise to come back to you and, if there's any consolation, after this tour, I'm done. I'm retiring from the Guard. My obligation will be over. Just this last time. You have my word."

"How long will you be over there? Have they told you?"

David paused before answering, "It will probably be at least six months."

"Six months! Oh, my God, David! Are you kidding me?"

"No, sweetie, I'm not," David said somberly. Diane sat silently with her eyes closed, softly shaking her head from side to side with her hands placed in a praying position touching her forehead. David moved closer to her and put his arms around her as she sat with her head nestled just under David's neck. They sat quietly for a half hour. It was getting dusk outside as the sun began to set and the inside of Diane's house grew dark.

"Hey, beautiful," David began, "It's getting late. You've got to be getting hungry. Do you want to go out and grab a bite to eat or I can order something to be delivered if you'd like."

"I'm not hungry, David, but, please, if you want to order something, go ahead. Honestly, I really think I just want to go to bed. It's been a lot to take in. If you don't mind, I think I really just want to take a shower and be by myself."

"No, sweetie, I know. It's a lot to take in. I'll go. You get some rest and we'll talk tomorrow. I'll be at the bar tomorrow night but Joe's going to handle the weekend. We can plan something special, if you'd like?"

Diane smiled and said, "I'd like that a lot." Both Diane and David got up from the couch. Diane walked David to the front door. David place both hands gently on Diane's face and kissed her passionately.

"I love you, Diane Walker, with all my heart."

"And I love you, David Anderson." David walked to his car and, as he drove off, Diane slowly closed the door and began to cry uncontrollably.

Chapter 29

Diane's Thursday schedule at school this week was a breeze and exactly what she needed. She got to school at her usual time bright and early. She made sure that she wore makeup to cover her puffy eyes. She wasn't in the mood for talking to anyone except Jenny and Jenny didn't get to school until another thirty minutes. She waved and smiled to Mr. Green as if nothing in the world was wrong. She also exchanged good mornings with a couple of teachers who happened to be in the cafeteria as she walked by. She entered her room and, as the light came in from outside, she realized she didn't close the classroom windows before she left school yesterday. She shrugged her shoulders as if to say, who cares! She started walking slowly to her desk but stopped as she stared at the front board. She stared directly at the date which she also didn't change before she left yesterday. She dropped her purse on her desk and walked trance-like over to the board. She grabbed the dry eraser and quickly wiped the date away. "Ugh, I don't want to be reminded of that day!" Diane said to herself as she quickly but very neatly wrote the correct date. Diane took a deep breath as if to say, I got this, and walked over to turn the class computers on for her students.

About thirty minutes later, there was a knock on her door and then Jenny entered saying, "Hey, girl, good morning."

"Is it really?" answered Diane.

"Oh no," said Jenny as she sat down in a student's chair by the reading corner.

"He definitely leaves in two weeks," Diane sadly told Jenny and added, "What am I going to do?" With only ten minutes before her students were to arrive, Diane couldn't get into details.

"Oh, crap, Diane, I'm so sorry I didn't come to work earlier. We'll talk at lunch and don't you have an hour's break for music today?"

"Yeah, I do," replied Diane.

"Then we'll talk at lunch and, if we're not finished, we'll talk more during your break and, if we need more time. we'll talk after school." Jenny got up and gave Diane a much-needed hug and, before leaving, said, "You hang in there, sweetie. It's all going to be all right." Diane softly smiled, closed her eyes and nodded her head yes.

Diane went about her day as cheerfully as possible for her students. She had a wonderful rapport with them and like most young children knew when something wasn't quite right, so she had to hold it together. She knew keeping busy was the best thing to do and working was the best distraction. The morning seemed to fly by and lunch seemed to come quicker today than most days. She lined her class up, walked them to the cafeteria and went to the office to check her mailbox, before meeting Jenny in the library. When she entered the office, a bouquet of sunflowers and daisies was lying on the front desk. Diane admired them as she passed the desk to her mailbox. She took out an educational magazine and walked past the office volunteer and said hello.

As Diane began walking out of the office, she heard, "Excuse me, Ms. Walker." Diane turned around. "Those flowers came for you just a few minutes before you came in. They're really beautiful."

"Oh my goodness, really?" said Diane in a surprised tone. Diane smiled as she picked up the bouquet. She reached for the card and opened the tiny envelope.

It read, You are the light in my heart. You brighten my day and life. I love you, David.

Diane smiled as she held the card close to her heart. "Someone thinks the world of you. You're a lucky lady."

"Thank you," replied Diane. "I better go quickly and put them in water. I also have a phone call to make." Diane beamed as she quickly walked to her room, clenching her flowers. She grabbed a vase from under her classroom sink, filled it with water and placed the bouquet inside. She stepped back for a moment to admire the bouquet's beauty. She then immediately picked up her phone to call David. The call went right to voicemail. She left the following message,

David, what a wonderful surprise. I love my flowers. Thank you, babe. Text or call me when you get a chance. I love you.

Diane now only had fifteen minutes left of her lunchtime. She quickly went to the library where Jenny was waiting. "I thought you got lost or you changed your mind about talking," said Jenny as soon as Diane entered the library.

"No, not at all. I went to the office to check my mailbox and waiting on the front desk was this beautiful bouquet of sunflowers and daisies. They were for me from David," Diane told Jenny as she smiled then continued, "I took them to the classroom and put them in water and tried to call David but it went right to his voicemail. I'm sure he's super busy since he wasn't at work yesterday."

"Aww, he's such a sweetie and such a hard worker."

Diane nodded at Jenny and said, "I know, I only have a few minutes left but, Jenny, I honestly don't know what I'm going to do without him here with me. I'm so scared that something is going to happen to him over there. I'm upset that I won't be able to talk to him whenever I want to. Hell, I might not be able to talk to him for days at a time. Oh, Jenny, what am I going to do?"

Jenny went around her desk to give Diane another much-needed hug and said, "You are going to get through this. Diane, you're stronger than you think you are and David must be going crazy knowing that you're going to be here without him. You know that you can always count on me and Vic if you need anything. I know I keep saying this but you're going to get through this. I promise."

Diane stepped back from Jenny's embrace and said, "I know I will and I definitely know that I'm not the only girlfriend that has to let her boyfriend go over there, but it just hurts so much."

The rest of the day was pretty easy for Diane. She actually started her lesson planning for the beginning of the New Year. She figured that she wasn't going to do much over Winter break and probably wouldn't be in the mood to work so she wanted to get it out of the way. While doing her lesson plans, she kept looking at her phone to see if she missed a call or text from David, but there still was not a word or a reply from earlier.

The school day was over and Diane was getting things packed up and ready to leave, when her classroom door opened. Her heart skipped a beat hoping it would be David but it was Jenny.

"Hey, girl, you doing all right? Do you need me to stay, because you know I will?"

"Jenny, you scared the crap out of me. I thought you might be David coming to surprise me," Diane said with a chuckle in her voice.

"Did you hear back from him?"

"No, not yet. I guess he really is busy but he's never taken this long to call or answer a text message. I'm getting worried."

"Don't worry! He's fine. He's probably really busy like you said and he's probably getting things lined up for when he leaves."

"Yeah, you're right, Jenny, but see how I'm worried because I haven't heard back from him in a couple of hours; how am I ever going to get through not hearing from him for days?" Not a word was spoken for a couple of minutes. Jenny had no words. Diane walked over to the sink where her beautiful bouquet was resting in a vase. She picked up the flowers and said, "These are going to look fabulous in my living room." She smiled at Jenny and walked over to her desk. She took her book bag out of her desk drawer, grabbed her keys from inside the pocket and silently walked with Jenny down the hall to the office to sign out. Jenny knew it best to wait to see if Diane wanted to talk. Jenny and Diane said their good nights to the office staff who were still working and slowly walked to the parking lot. Finally, Diane spoke and said, "Jenny, thank you. You really are a great friend and thank you for putting up with me and all my crap. I know I'm a mess and I'm sure I'll be messier."

"Messier?" laughed Jenny. "I never heard of anyone referring to themselves as messier."

Diane laughed then smiled at Jenny and said, "You know what I mean."

"I do and you're lucky that I like messy. Have you seen what I'm married to?" Both Jenny and Diane laughed as they got into their cars.

Diane started her car and quickly pulled out her phone to call David again. "Pick up, pick up," Diane said out loud as the phone began to ring.

"Babe," answered David. "I swear I was just going to call you. I've been slammed all day and when I got a few minutes to call, I knew you were teaching so I waited because I knew it wasn't a good idea to call during one of your lessons. I know I should've sent a text and I'm sorry I didn't."

"No, babe, that's okay. Don't worry. I figured you were busy," Diane said as she made a face, rolled her eyes and giggled to herself.

"So, you got the flowers."

"I did and I absolutely love them. When did you order them?"

"Aww, sweetie, did they brighten your day? I know you were feeling pretty down last night. I know they're your favorite and I just wanted to put a smile on your face so I ordered them as soon as the florist opened up this morning."

"The flowers are beautiful but the card, oh, David, the card melted my heart."

"Well, I meant every single word," said David.

"I know you did," Diane softly whispered. After a short pause, Diane asked, "So, are you still going to the bar tonight?"

"I am but I have a little surprise for you."

"A surprise for me? Well, do tell," Diane said as she laughed.

"Well, began David, "Do you have any plans for the weekend?"

"Only if they involve you," answered Diane.

"Good, because I made reservations in Sanibel for Friday and Saturday night."

"Oh, my goodness, David, really? That's fantastic!"

"I wanted us to have some quality time together before I leave and I mean no television, no radio, no phones, nothing, just the two of us enjoying each other on the beach."

"Oh, that sounds great! Can we leave right now?" Both David and Diane laughed.

"Babe, I can't wait to be with you but, right now, I need to finish up my last delivery and then head to the bar. I need to go over a number of things with Joe before I leave but I'll call before you go to bed."

"I totally understand, David. I'll talk to you later. Thank you again for the beautiful flowers. I love you."

"I love you too, Diane. I'll talk to you later." Diane hung up and didn't even realize she had driven home during their conversation. She had a smile on her face and was feeling much better. She was very excited about the weekend and had to tell Jenny and then call the girls to catch them up on what was happening.

Chapter 30

The bright yellow colors of the sunflowers and daisies lit up and added a pop of color to Diane's living room. She stood back and admired the flowers one last time before heading to her bedroom to change into her comfy after-school sweats. Diane plopped on her couch and was very tempted to put on the early news but decided against it and turned on an old recording of The Late Show. She began to call Jenny but then decided to text her instead. "I've put poor Jenny through too much today," she said to herself as she began texting,

I heard from David. He was super busy all day just like we thought. He's going to the bar tonight but… we're going to Sanibel for the weekend!!!! Soooo excited!!! Talk to you tomorrow.

Jenny responded almost immediately,

OMG!!!!! So exciting. I'm so happy!!!!!

Diane smiled and then decided to group text the girls,

Are you all up to FaceTiming tonight? I have a lot to tell you! Does seven work for you all?

Within five minutes, Diane heard back from all three girls and they all responded with a thumbs up. Sara texted Diane separately,

Does this have anything to do with David? Is he heading overseas?

Yes and yes, responded Diane then added, I want to make sure I tell everyone together.

Sara quickly wrote back, I totally understand. Just want to be prepared. Talk to you in a bit.

Diane made a salad and poured herself a glass of wine. She sat down and gathered her thoughts. She wrote down talking points to have on hand when she talked to the girls. She didn't want to leave any of the details or information out. She knew they would have tons of questions and would demand answers.

Diane looked at the clock. She had five minutes before making the call so she decided to pour herself another glass of wine and got comfortable on her couch. Diane sighed, grabbed her phone and started the group video chat. The first to answer was Sara.

"Hey, there, I'm here and ready to talk," Sara said eagerly.

Next to answer was Anne, "Hey, guys," she said in a cheerful tone.

And, last, of course, was Luna who joined the group yelling, "Boys, don't you disturb me. I'm on the phone with my girls. If you're bleeding, grab a Band-Aid and tell your daddy!" The girls all laughed.

Diane started by saying, "Hey, all. I'm so glad you were able to talk this evening. I really need my girls right now and this was the best way to get every one's input."

189

"Oh, my goodness, Diane, of course, we were going to make time for you," said Sara.

"Honey, you know we're all here for you," Anne sweetly responded.

"We're here to listen and you know we're here to give our two cents," added Luna.

"I know, I know, but it's after work for all of you and I know you're tired, so please know I appreciate this so much," said Diane.

"Okay, spill. What's going on? Start from the beginning," Luna eagerly interrupted.

"Okay, well, you all know that David has been given orders to go back to Afghanistan. He leaves early next Saturday morning. This is our last weekend together for a long time. He surprised me and told me today that he made reservations for the weekend in Sanibel. He wants a total disconnect weekend. No phones, no television, no radio, no nothing!"

"Damn girl, be ready for some amazing sex," laughed Luna.

"Oh, yeah, he's got love on his mind!" added Sara. Anne just laughed and agreed.

"Oh, my goodness, guys, get your mind out of the gutter!" chuckled Diane then added, "Of course, that's what's on his mind and mine too!" All the girls laughed out loud. "But, seriously," Diane quickly began, "I'm scared. I'm really scared. I'm scared he won't come back. What if something happens to him? I won't be able to talk to him when I want. I may not talk to him for days, maybe weeks. I just don't know what I'm going to do without him," Diane said as she began to cry.

"Why couldn't we have this conversation in person?" said Anne sadly.

"Sweetie," began Luna, "I'm so sorry and in a very rare moment, I don't know what to say except I'm so sorry and I feel awful for you both."

Sara jumped in and said, "I'm sure David feels horrible too. I'm sure he's just as worried and scared. It's a small consolation but you always have us and you know you can always come up to New York and stay with me for a while."

"I know I have you guys. You're my rock," answered Diane sadly.

"Listen, how about you try and I know it's going to be hard to do, but try not to think about him being away for now. Just enjoy the weekend that you two are going to share together," Anne softly said.

"And don't forget the amazing sex!"

"Damn, Luna," laughed Sara. "Do you think of nothing else?"

"Is there anything else?" laughed Luna.

The girls spent the rest of an hour trying to take Diane's mind off of David's leaving and as soon as Luna's twin boys started running in and arguing, that was their cue to wind things down.

"Thank you, guys, so much for taking time this evening and talking to me. This meant the world to me."

"Are you kidding?" snapped Anne, "That's what friends are for."

"Damn right. Remember when one of us is hurting, we're all hurting," added Luna.

"We love you, Diane, we're here for you and, remember, my spare room is all yours when you're ready to visit," Sara reminded Diane.

"You're the best, best friends anyone could ever ask for. I love you all so much. Thank you, guys, again and I'll keep you all posted."

"You can keep the details of your, what we know is going to be, triple-X-rated weekend to yourself," laughed Luna. All the girls laughed as each one said goodbye and hung up.

Diane took one last sip of wine from her glass before putting the glass in the sink and walking up the stairs to her bedroom. As she undressed to take a shower, her thoughts went right to David and she began to cry. She walked into the shower and let the warm water run softly over her body. As she was getting out of the shower and heard her phone ring, still wet and dripping water, she ran into her room to answer the phone. It was David.

"Hey, you," she answered, "I was just thinking about you."

"Oh, really, well, you sound out of breath. What have you been doing without me?"

"David Anderson, you devil you! I had to run to my bedroom from the shower to get my phone. I literally just got out of the shower when I heard my phone ring. So, I'm a little out of breath."

"So, you're standing there dripping wet and naked while you're talking to me?"

"I sure am," Diane said in a sultry voice.

"Baby, why are you doing this to me? You're such a tease," David said as he sighed.

"I'm not teasing. I'm telling you the truth," Diane said with a smile on her face.

"Okay, since I can't be there and enjoy the view, I'm changing the subject." Both Diane and David laughed. "So, babe, what did you do tonight? Are you excited about the weekend? You really don't need to pack too much. It is a clothing-optional kind of weekend."

Diane snickered and said, "Well, I talked to all the girls earlier. We video-chatted to catch up."

"Aw, that's nice. How are the girls doing?"

"They're all doing well and give you their love."

"As much as I hate leaving in a week, I'm glad you have your friends that you can lean on and keep you company."

"Yeah, I don't know what I'd do without them. They are my rock."

After a slight pause, David said, "Well, sweetie, my break time is over. I wanted to make sure I called you before you went to bed to say goodnight. I never thought I'd get an added bonus of having the image of you dripping wet and naked while talking to me."

Diane laughed as she said, "See, I'm full of surprises. I love you, David, and I can't wait to see you tomorrow and spend the entire weekend with you."

"I love you too, sweetie. I'll call you before I pick you up. Do you think you'll be able to leave on time?"

"I'll be out of school tomorrow by three-thirty."

"Great, I should be at your house by four to four-fifteen."

"I'll be ready!" said Diane cheerfully.

"I love you, Diane."

"I love you too, David. Good night."

Before Diane went to bed, she took out her overnight bag and began to pack. As she was packing, she thought out loud to herself, "Hmm, a couple of swimsuits, a couple of sundresses, a shawl, a hat, sunglasses, a cover-up, and a couple of shorts and t-shirts. Oh, and a couple pairs of sandals. That was fast and easy!" she laughed to herself, jumped into bed and went to sleep.

Chapter 31

The school day couldn't come to a close quickly enough. As Diane left, she popped into the library to say a quick goodbye to Jenny. "Girl, I'm so sorry I didn't get a chance to see or talk to you today. Old battle axe had me doing purchase orders for the spring book fair all day."

"Oh, Jenny, no problem. I totally understand. I just wanted to stop by to say, have a good weekend."

"Well," said Jenny laughing. "We both know you'll be having an excellent weekend with that good-looking, hunk of a boyfriend."

Diane giggled, smiled and, in a girlish way, shrugged her shoulders and said, "I will definitely try!"

Both Jenny and Diane laughed. "Okay, you, get out of here and go start that fantastic weekend."

"See you Monday, Jenn, and thank you," said Diane as she left the library and quickly walked out of the school building for home.

Before starting her car, Diane looked at herself in the rearview mirror. She had a smile on her face from ear to ear. She thought about the romantic weekend she and David would have. She got an excited chill through her body that felt almost electric. "All righty then," she said

195

out loud to herself. "Let me get the heck home and get this love fest started." Diane giggled, started her car and quickly pulled out of the parking lot, as she began happily singing along with the songs on the radio.

As Diane approached her driveway, her phone rang. It was David. "Hey, handsome. I've been thinking of you all day."

"Well, hello, beautiful. Are you ready to get this weekend started?"

"Oh, I sure am. I'm actually pulling into my driveway right now."

"That sounds great sweetie. I should be over in about a half hour. Do you still need to pack? Because, if you do, remember don't pack much. It is a clothing-optional weekend!"

Diane giggled as she quickly answered, "Oh, yes, I'm packed. I did that last night and, yes, I remembered about the clothing requirements or lack of."

David responded, "Glad you remembered because if there's more than one overnight bag, I'm going to conveniently forget to put it into my truck." Both David and Diane laughed.

"No problem," said Diane as she smiled to herself then added, "All I need to do is take a quick shower and get into some comfortable traveling clothes."

"I sure wish I was going to be in that shower with you," David said in a sexy tone.

Diane shivered and responded, "Well, I guarantee there will be more than one shower time over the weekend."

"Oh, you can bet on that!" David said then added, "I'm hanging up now so I can get my rear over there. I can't wait to be with you, Diane. I'm already getting hard just thinking about you."

"Well, then, hurry up and get over here," demanded Diane.

"Okay, sweetie. Love you and I'll see you very soon."

"Love you too, David." Diane got out of her car and ran to her front door. She did a little dance as she went inside. She dropped her purse, kicked off her shoes and ran upstairs to shower. All the while giggling to herself. Diane stepped out of the shower and dried off. She applied baby oil all over her body. She brushed her hair into a loose ponytail and applied very little makeup to her radiant skin. She went to get dressed then stopped and thought to herself, "Hmm, clothing optional weekend. Well, then, that means no bra and definitely no undies. I think I'll just slip this sundress on and that's it!" Diane smiled in a sexy evil way to herself and thought of some wickedly fun things to do to David during the drive.

David arrived at Diane's house wearing a pair of shorts, flip-flops and a tight-fitting t-shirt. He was definitely dressed for a casual weekend. Diane greeted him at the door with a huge hug and kiss. David picked Diane up and spun her around. Diane smiled as she dropped her neck back, exposing it to David. David began kissing

Diane's neck which made her weak in the knees and sent chills through her body, making her nipples hard.

"Oh, David," Diane softly said, "If you continue to do that we're never going to make it out of here."

"How about we start our weekend early and I take you upstairs?" David said as he continued kissing Diane's neck.

"Oh, David, there's nothing more I would want but I really want to get to Sanibel before sunset so we can sit on the beach and watch it together."

"Well, when you make a suggestion like that, how can I say no, that sounds like a wonderful idea but taking you upstairs and making love to you is still my first choice."

Diane chuckled as she kissed David on his nose and said, "Don't you worry, I have plans for you, mister." David smiled as he grabbed Diane's overnight bag and started for the front door. Diane grabbed her purse and followed David outside. She locked her door, set her alarm and walked to David's truck. Like the gentleman he was, David opened the truck door and helped her inside.

David had an easy-listening radio station on but it was for background noise mostly. Both David and Diane decided they were going to keep the weekend topics to simple, everyday stuff. There would be nothing discussed about David's deployment. This was a weekend for the two of them to connect on a level that would sustain both of them for months.

Chapter 32

They had been driving for about an hour and were on Interstate 75 when Diane looked in the passenger's side mirror.

"Hmm, not too many people on the road today. There isn't a car behind us," Diane said in a sneaky voice as she cuddled up to David.

"Yeah, I noticed the same thing. We must have left at the right time," said David as he smiled at Diane. Diane got a bit closer and put her warm, moist mouth on David's earlobe and began to suck on it ever so gently. "Oh, wow, Diane! What are you doing?"

"What's the matter, sweetie, don't you like it?"

"Oh, my God, I love it but you're making me hard."

"Well, let me check for myself," chuckled Diane as she slowly moved her hand to David's thigh and then to his rock-hard bulge in his shorts. "Yup, mission complete," laughed Diane as she slowly began to stroke his rock-hard penis.

"Diane, if you keep doing that I'm not sure we're going to make it to Sanibel in one piece or we might have to pull over to finish what you started. You're driving me crazy, woman!" David said as he took a deep breath and slightly moaned. Diane, not taking her eyes off of him, slowly unzipped his shorts to expose David's hot, pulsating, very large dick. She moved her hand slowly up and down his shaft and gently squeezed his full, clean-shaven balls.

"Diane, I swear I'm going to burst all over the front seat. I don't believe I'm saying this but you have to stop."

Diane stopped and seductively said, "Well, I just wanted to get you in the mood and give you a little sample of what's to come."

"No, no, don't get me wrong," David quickly responded. "I love, loved every minute but if you were to continue, either I'd crash the truck or I'd need to pull over and take you right on the side of the road."

Diane laughed. "Okay, okay. I understand. I'll try to behave myself for the remaining car ride."

"Well, we're almost there. And then you won't have to behave yourself for the entire weekend," said David who was still broken out in a slight sweat as he grabbed Diane and stole a kiss.

Twenty minutes later, David pulled up to a small cottage on the beach. "We're here, sweetie."

"Oh, my goodness, it looks great! And it's right on the beach. Oh, David, I love it already!"

"Well, so far, it's everything the website said it would be. Let's go inside and check out our weekend love nest!" Both David and Diane entered the cottage. They looked around and smiled at each other. It was everything they needed. The cottage living room was decorated in whites, creams and soft blues, and pale yellows for pops of color. The bedroom had a king-size canopy bed. The room was decorated in soft gray and light peach décor. The windows were draped with soft sheers, letting just enough sunlight to shine inside. It had a very romantic feel. David and Diane smiled at each other as they walked outside to the back porch.

"Oh, my stars, look at this view. David, however did you find this gem? This is absolutely beautiful." David went over to Diane and scooped her up and spun her around.

"Are you happy, sweetie?"

"Oh, my God, yes. David this is fantastic and the sunset is going to be epic."

"Well, that's what I'm counting on. Let me get the bags from the truck so we can get this weekend started. From the looks of it, we have about another hour and a half before sunset. I want to make sure everything is ready."

"Everything ready?" questioned Diane.

"Yes, ma'am. I have dinner being delivered in about a half hour and I'm trying to time the sunset to our dessert. This weekend is all about us. I'm going to show you just how much I love you, Diane Walker."

"Oh, David, I love you so much and thank you."

"Thank you for what? I haven't done anything yet."

"Oh, yes, you have and even before our weekend begins, I want to thank you for a lovely time."

Twenty minutes later, there was a knock on the door. David rushed to answer the door. A young man and young woman, dressed in black slacks and white button-down shirts wearing smiles on their faces, introduced themselves.

"Hi, good evening. Mr. Anderson?" asked the young man.

"Hi, yes, I'm Mr. Anderson but please call me David."

"We're Wes and Belle from Evening Delights and if you're ready, we'd like to set up your picnic dinner," said Belle in a sweet voice.

"Oh, yes, please come in." Diane had just come out from the bedroom where she was putting away her things.

"Oh, my, what's this?" asked Diane in a very surprised tone.

"Well, my dear, this is Wes and Belle and they're here to set up our picnic dinner." Diane smiled as she walked closer to David and gave him a hug.

"Is there anything you need from the kitchen?" Diane politely asked of the two.

"No, we have everything. We just need to know where you'd like us to set up," responded Wes.

"And the sooner we know, the sooner we can set everything up and let you guys get started enjoying your romantic dinner," added Belle with a wink.

"Well, in that case," smiled David. "You guys can get started right now setting up out back, near the water."

"Perfect. We should be done in about fifteen minutes. We'll knock to let you know when dinner has been set up."

"Thanks so much, guys. We really appreciate it." David walked out the door with Wes and Belle to discuss last-minute details. Diane sat on the couch biting her bottom lip as a huge smile lit up her face. David walked back in and slowly walked towards Diane. Diane jumped up off the couch and wrapped her arms around David's neck and gave him a long deep kiss.

"This is more than I ever expected and we haven't even begun the weekend," Diane excitedly whispered into David's ear.

"Oh, babe, this is just the beginning. I told you I wanted this to be a memorable weekend."

"Well, it already is," Diane said as she closed her eyes and smiled.

A few minutes later, there was a knock on the door. Both David and Diane answered the door. It was Wes and Belle. "You're all set up," smiled Belle.

"If there's anything else you need or if you have any questions, please don't hesitate to call us," Wes said as he handed David his card.

"I'm sure it's going to be exceptional. Thanks, guys. We really appreciate it," David said to Wes as he extended his hand to him and, then to Belle, giving each a very large tip.

Before heading out to the beach, Diane quickly ran to the bedroom to grab a shawl that she placed over her shoulders. David and Diane slowly walked hand in hand to the back of the cottage.

"Oh my goodness!" gasped Diane. "This is the most romantic setting I've ever seen! David, this is absolutely gorgeous! It's like it's right out of a movie!" David put his arm around Diane's waist as she leaned her head on his strong shoulder.

A large blanket was spread on the sand. Hurricane lanterns illuminated the soft pillows that surrounded the blanket. A wicker tray and basket sat in the middle with a vase of white roses, two wine glasses and a bottle of wine just waiting to be opened. A charcuterie board filled with fresh jams and jellies, crackers, fine cheeses and different meats awaited the loving couple. David took Diane's hand and walked her over to the awaiting blanket. He helped her sit down and soon sat by her side.

Diane sat staring out at the beautiful waves crashing nearby and said, "This is so surreal. I honestly feel I'm dreaming." David smiled, opened the bottle of wine and poured them each a glass.

As he handed Diane her glass he asked, "Are you happy, baby?"

Diane took the glass from David and responded. "Happy? That's putting it lightly. David, I don't think I've ever been happier." David softly brushed the hair from Diane's face and kissed her lips gently.

"I love you, Diane."

"I love you too, David."

David and Diane enjoyed the cheeses, meats and other tasty treats from the charcuterie board. "Are you done with the first course?"

"First course? Oh, my goodness, David, that could have been dinner," laughed Diane.

"Oh, no, babe, that was just the appetizer. We have the main course and dessert still to come."

Diane giggled then said, "Okay, bring it on but I'm so full!" David reached into the wicker basket and took out two covered dishes, each containing roast chicken, grilled asparagus and wild rice.

"Oh, David, that looks delicious but I'm never going to be able to eat all that."

"You know, you're right. How about we seal these dishes back up and have this meal tomorrow night?"

"Or, we can eat it after we build up an appetite later tonight," Diane said as she snuggled into David's chest.

"I love the way you think," paused David. "But, can we at least have these for dessert?" David smiled as he pulled chocolate-covered strawberries from the basket. "It's perfect timing," he began. "The sun is setting. The waves are softly crashing. We have wine in our glasses and I'm with the most beautiful woman in the world, that I madly and deeply love by my side."

"How can I say no to that? David, I'm not often lost for words but, right now, I'm speechless. I could not have asked for a more romantic night." Diane kissed David and David gently placed a strawberry close to her lips. Diane smiled and slowly opened her mouth to take a bite. The strawberry oozed juice down the side of her chin. David quickly and softly licked the juice from her chin with his wet, warm tongue and then entered her warm awaiting mouth. Diane let out a soft moan as she and David embraced.

"I think it's time to take this party inside," said David as he drew Diane in closer for another kiss. Diane smiled with her eyes closed and nodded her head in agreement. David and Diane quickly picked up their picnic basket and grabbed the bottle of wine. "Leave the other stuff. We can get it in the morning," said David as he took Diane's hand, then the two of them walked back to the cottage.

Chapter 33

As they both reached the entrance of the cottage, David stopped and quietly asked, "Diane, sweetie, can you wait right here for a moment?"

Diane, with a smile on her face and a gleam in her eye, softly answered, "Of course but what do you have planned now?" David laughed mischievously and took the basket and wine to the kitchen counter. He opened the basket and searched until he found the fun bedroom foods that he ordered. Hidden in a box at the bottom he found caramel sauce and lollipops. "What's taking you so long?" a very anxious Diane asked.

David smiled and replied, "Don't you worry, my love, I'll be there in a minute. I'm just checking on a few things that I'm sure you're going to love." David put the caramel sauce and lollipops on the counter, then took out a bag of grapes that he quickly put in the freezer, and a can of whipped cream and cherries that he placed in the back of the refrigerator along with tonight's leftovers.

"Oh, yes, for tomorrow night!" he sneakily said to himself.

David grabbed the goodies. As he walked over to Diane, he had a very sexy yet scheming look on his face.

"Oh, boy, I see trouble written all over this handsome face of yours," Diane said as she grabbed his face and kissed him.

"Me? Scheming? Why, Miss Walker, what do you mean?" David laughed as he held up a bottle of caramel sauce and a small bag of lollipops.

"David, you devil you!" David took Diane's hand as they walked to the bedroom.

David and Diane entered the bedroom, where a beautiful king-size bed was eagerly waiting for them. The sun had set but there was a hint of moonlight coming in from the window. David walked over to the back of the room where he placed his goodies on the nightstand. He then walked back to Diane who was waiting patiently with a warm smile on her face. David stared straight into Diane's inviting eyes. He kissed her cheek then the tip of her nose. Diane quietly giggled like a schoolgirl. It was a nervous giggle. She innocently bit her bottom lip as she sat down on the edge of the bed. David joined her. David slowly placed his right hand on the back of Diane's neck and drew her in softly to his awaiting warm, wet mouth. Her body melted in his arms as she released a slight moan. David began removing her sundress which was the only thing covering her awaiting perky bosom and clean-shaven lady parts. Diane reached for David's t-shirt which she lifted over his head. As she looked deep into his eyes, she took control for a short time as she gently grabbed and massaged David's crotch. She felt the firmness of his aroused cock. As she unzipped his shorts, she could feel the throbbing of his penis just waiting to pop out like an overwound Jack-in-the-Box. Both completely naked, David took Diane's hand and led her to the bathroom. "Why are we in the bathroom, David?" Diane asked inquisitively.

"Just wait right here. You'll see and I promise, once we get started, you'll understand why."

David led Diane into the shower stall. He gently pinned her against the wall. Diane gasped as her warm body touched the cool ceramic tile. David held Diane's arms over her head with his left hand.

"Close your eyes for me and tell me what you feel." Diane did as she was asked. As soon as David dripped the caramel sauce on her breasts, Diane's nipples became hard and erect. "Oh, my goodness, David."

"Keep those eyes closed. I'm not done." David then drizzled more sauce on her firm abdomen which began running down to her already moist pussy. David added more sauce to her inner thighs as he told Diane in a sexy voice.

"Ok, now open your eyes." Diane smiled as she slowly opened them one by one. "Now, spread the sauce all over your body." Diane looked directly at David. She softly squinted her eyes, gently bit her bottom lip and then moved her tongue over her lips, as she used both hands to spread the sticky caramel sauce over her body. David grasped his already hard cock in enjoyment.

"Now it's your turn, Mr. Anderson." David stood ready and willing to get his turn. Diane started at David's neck. The drizzled sauce began making its way to his abundant pecks. Diane squirted more sauce from the bottle which made its way to his rock-hard abs. and began dripping on his stiff staff. Diane poured the remaining sauce into her hands as she made her way to the inside of his thighs and to his clean-shaven balls.

"Okay, now spread the sauce all over YOUR body."

"I have a better idea," said David as he took Diane into his body. "Why don't we let our bodies massage it in, then we can lick it off slowly from each other's body?"

"I love how your mind works, David."

David began with deep kissing. His wet warm tongue ran over Diane's gums, around her tongue then across her lips. Diane returned the favor, by first caressing his face, kissing his neck then tugging and nibbling at his earlobes ever so gently. Both made moans that excited the other and they both wanted to please each other only more. David slowly began taking in Diane's firm full breasts one at a time, while each time lightly sucking and licking off the caramel sauce. Diane arched her back and moaned louder as David made his way to her taut abdomen and then inner thighs. Diane placed her hands on top of David's head as he began to orally please her with his warm tongue. Diane's body convulsed and she let out a scream as she reached her peak of orgasm.

"Oh, my goodness, David," Diane sighed. "That was unbelievable!" she said as she caught her breath.

"You liked that, didn't you?" David said in a devious tone.

"Well, yes, I did and now I'm going to show you just how much I enjoyed it on you."

David smiled and eagerly said, "I'm ready!"

With a not-so-innocent smile on her face and a slightly raised eyebrow, Diane pushed David up against the cool tile.

"Hey, now," David said chuckling. "You're not playing."

"No, I'm not," said Diane as she began licking and gently sucking on David's neck. David closed his eyes, smiled and began enjoying the ride. Diane pushed her still erect nipples into David's chest and, with both of her hands, grabbed around his back to bring her closer into his body. She ran her warm tongue over his hard nipples and teased as she flicked her tongue and tenderly bit at them. She slowly moved her tongue to his well-flexed abs and, with her right hand, began to stroke his erect organ. After taking a good amount of time with his special member, she leisurely made her way to his sticky sack which she softly caressed. Diane knelt down on her knees to take his sweet, sticky shaft into her moist mouth. David moaned in complete euphoria which made Diane want to please her man even more. Diane stood up, grabbed David's hand and placed it between her sticky inner thighs. David's fingers explored her insides, making Diane squirm with joy and then tasted each finger one by one.

"I think it's time to take this party to the bedroom," David said ready to explode.

"I totally agree, David, but I think a quick warm shower is definitely in order before getting into those sheets."

"Babe, I don't think I can wait that long. I'm ready to burst right now!"

"Well, we can't let that happen now, can we?" began Diane as she thought for a second and said, "You're a strong man. You can hold me." Diane started the shower. The water quickly warmed and trickled out like light rain. David moved closer to Diane. He picked her up as she straddled him under the rainfall shower head. Diane dropped her head back as she slightly arched her upper body to take all of him inside. David moved his hips in a pumping motion and brought her in close, as he held her bottom at the same time, making both partners satisfied. David didn't last long as he could no longer hold in his excitement. David let out a primal yell as his warm juices flowed into Diane. As sensitive as his cock was, he didn't stop until Diane was completely finished, releasing her sweet cum.

David and Diane slowly showered each other then grabbed the plush, warm towels to wrap and dry themselves. They made it to the bed, where their weak, very satisfied, numb bodies both fell quickly to sleep.

Chapter 34

The morning light softly shone through the linen curtains and the sound of the calm ocean water from the incoming tide gently rushed back and forth made for a beautiful way to start the day. David was the first to rise. He gently placed a kiss on Diane's cheek. Diane opened her eyes with a soft smile. "Good morning, sunshine," said David as he slowly brushed the hair from Diane's forehead.

Diane made a soft moan, smiled, and yawned as she stretched out her arms and said, "Good morning to you handsome. Did you sleep well?"

"Like a baby," said David smiling and looking down at Diane. "So, babe, when you're ready I have fresh coffee, fresh muffins and fruit in the kitchen for breakfast."

"David. What? How did you manage to do that?" Diane said as she got up from bed and put on her robe.

"Well, I didn't," laughed David. "It is all part of the weekend food package I ordered. Wes and Belle were back early this morning to get the things from last night and they also delivered the breakfast. Oh, and since we didn't eat the dinner from last night, I cancelled the pasta I ordered for tonight."

"Good call. We have more than enough food," added Diane as she sat down to pour herself a cup of coffee and dig into the muffins and fresh fruit.

David joined her and said. "I was thinking about spending the day on the beach. And, if you're up to it, renting a couple of wave runners for fun. Hey, when you live in Florida during the winter and it's a beautiful eighty degrees, you have to enjoy it."

"That sounds amazing. I'm glad I packed my bathing suit."

"And if you didn't bring one, well, that would be okay too!" Both David and Diane sweetly smiled at each other as they finished breakfast.

Dressed for the beach, David and Diane jumped into David's truck and headed out to find a place to rent a couple of wave runners for the day. Not too far from their beach cottage, David pulled up to a small marina. The sign posted at the entrance read: wave runners and boat rentals, parasailing and the best pelican watching and sunsets on the gulf coast.

"How about this place?" David said as he pulled off the main road and onto a gravel road.

"Looks like they have a lot to offer. Sure, David, let's check it out." David followed the palm tree-lined road until it stopped. David parked the truck. There were a few other cars in the lot. David and Diane got out of the truck and followed the music through the trees, which opened up to the most gorgeous view of the gulf. "Oh, my goodness, are you kidding me right now? This place is amazing!" Diane said as she reached to take her sunglasses down from her face.

"Welcome," a young man said as he walked over to David and Diane. "What can I help you with today?"

"We'd like to rent a couple of your wave runners and maybe even be interested in parasailing."

"Oh, excuse me," interrupted Diane. "I don't know about that. I'm not quite set on the parasailing just yet!" The men both laughed.

"Well, folks, I'm Jerry and wave runners I can definitely get for you and maybe, after you think about it, I can help you set up for a parasailing adventure. Follow me."

Diane softly punched David's shoulder, bit her bottom lip, smiled, shook her head and whispered, "You're crazy. No way am I doing that."

David smiled as he put his arm around her waist and said, "You're too cute, babe."

After signing the necessary insurance forms and a quick lesson on how to operate the machines, David and Diane were ready to start enjoying a day on the gulf coast. Diane was all giggles as she straddled the machine.

"This is so cool. I can't wait!"

David raised both arms in the air and let out a powerful yell with a mischievous smile on his face and then pointed to Diane and said, "You're going down, Walker!" Diane laughed as she followed David's lead out into the open waters.

David and Diane spent a couple of hours on the water, having fun racing each other and doing circles around each other. They also explored the mangroves and the large riding area around the coast. They were also lucky enough to see bottlenose dolphin and a family of manatees. Diane enjoyed the spray of the salty water on her face and David felt an exhilaration of freedom as he crashed through the waves.

As they drove the wave runners back to their starting point and got off the machines, they both looked like little kids. You could see on both their faces that they had an amazing time.

"So, how was it?" asked Jerry.

"Oh, my goodness, Jerry, so much fun!"smiled Diane as she unclipped her life jacket.

"It was great, man. We had a fantastic time," added David.

"So, how about that parasailing? You interested?" David looked at Diane and smiled.

"Well, babe, what do you think?" Diane crunched up her nose and shook her head no. "Not today, Jerry. We'll leave it for another day."

"No problem, folks. You guys have a great rest of your day and if you're looking for a place to grab a drink and some lunch, there's a pretty cool place just down the road on the left." David and Diane smiled and waved as they walked towards the truck. David grabbed a couple of towels from the back cab. Diane toweled off and ran her fingers through her wet hair.

"That was so much fun," said Diane as she zipped up her shorts.

"That really was. I haven't done that in years," added David as he pulled a t-shirt over his head and hard-rock abs. "You hungry, sweetie? Let's check out the place that Jerry recommended."

"Sounds good to me!"

David and Diane drove for a couple of miles until they came upon this tiki bar-looking restaurant. They pulled into the parking lot, where they could hear a calypso band playing in the background. David and Diane smiled at each other, held hands and walked up to the bar and grill which was located right on the water. Pelicans sat on the dock waiting for the right moment to dive for fish. They were seated close to the water but close enough to hear the soft Caribbean music.

"David, this is fantastic! What a cool place!" said Diane as she looked around and swayed to the music.

"The best places are the hidden gems. This is definitely a find."

A young waitress came up to their table with two menus and a smile. "Good afternoon, folks. I'm Sadie and I'll be your server today. Can I get you started with some drinks?"

"Hi, Sadie. Yes, drinks would be great. I'll have a Coors Lite and, Diane, what are you drinking?"

"Hmm, let's see. I think I'll have a margarita."

"Will that be frozen or on the rocks?"

"Frozen"

"Fantastic and, sir, it's two for one right now. Would you like both beers now or do you want to wait for the second one?"

"I'll wait. Thank you."

"Excellent! Can I get you an appetizer to start? The conch fritters and hush puppies are wonderful."

"How's the fried calamari?" asked David.

"Everything is great here!" Sadie said with excitement.

"Well, Sadie, you sold us. We'll have the calamari," said David.

"Oh, and the conch fritters and hush puppies too," added Diane.

"I'll go get your drinks and put your food order in."

"Thanks, Sadie," said Diane as she handed her the menus.

David reached for Diane's hand. They intertwined their fingers and smiled deeply into each other's eyes. David took a deep breath and said, "I'm so glad we did this. I'm so glad we went away."

"I must say, David, you really have outdone yourself this weekend. From the surprise dinner on the beach last night and the wave runners today, I'm having the time of my life. Thank you for this." David sat up in this chair and leaned into Diane to give her a kiss just as Sadie arrived with the drinks.

"Aww, you guys are so cute!" said Sadie as she placed the drinks on the table. "Food will be out shortly."

David took a long gulp of his beer. "Oh, yes, that's actually what I needed."

Diane took a sip of her drink, smacked her lips and said, "That's a really good margarita!" They both looked out at the water and smiled. Seagulls were flying overhead and pelicans sat on the wood rails of the dock. "David, this is so nice. So relaxing. I'll remember this day for a very long time."

"I wanted to give you a weekend to think about while I'm gone. One that would put a smile on your face when you're hopefully missing and thinking about me," David sheepishly said as he blew Diane a kiss.

"Well, that definitely won't be a problem," Diane said as she returned the air kiss.

"Okay, folks, food's here," Sadie said as she placed the calamari, conch fritters and hush puppies on the table.

"Wow, this looks and smells amazing!" said Diane as she moved her drink out of the way and reached for the plates that were off to the side.

"Dig in and, if there's anything else you need, you let me know. Hey, are you ready for your second beer?" Sadie asked David.

"Yeah, that sounds good," David replied as he finished the last sip in his glass. Sadie took the glass and then politely asked Diane if she was good with her drink.

"I'm good. Thanks. Oh, man, David, this smells fantastic!" Diane said as she put a little bit of each on her plate.

David dug in as he looked up to the sky and said, "Those seagulls better not even think about swooping down to try some." David and Diane laughed as they enjoyed their lunch.

After lunch, David and Diane walked around the outside of the restaurant which was tucked away from the busy road to take in the scenery. It was late afternoon when they returned to their weekend cottage on the water.

As David pulled into the driveway, he looked out towards the water and said, "Looks like we're going to be able to witness another beautiful sunset in a little bit. Do you want to go inside to grab a blanket and the wine and wine glasses?"

"Yes, most definitely. That sounds great! I'll grab the blanket and you get the wine and the glasses," directed Diane.

Diane spread the blanket out onto the sand and as close as possible to the water without getting splashed by the waves. David handed Diane a wine glass and poured each of them a glass of wine. The two snuggled close in silence. Diane rested her head on David's shoulder and David had his arm wrapped around Diane as they both gazed out into the calming waters.

Diane broke the silence by softly saying, "This is so relaxing. I could sit here with you forever. This is probably one of the best days I've had in a very long time." David softly brushed Diane's hair out of her face with his hand. Diane sat up and tenderly placed both of her hands on David's face and sweetly said, "No matter what, Mr. David

Anderson, I will always love you and I'll be patiently waiting for you with open arms when you come home."

"I love you so much, baby," said David as he passionately started kissing Diane on top of the now sand-covered blanket.

"Let's take this inside before we get sand in places that sand shouldn't be," recommended Diane as they both laughed, picked up the blanket and walked back to the cottage.

Diane dropped the sandy blanket outside by the front door before she and David entered the cottage. David rushed to put the wine glasses and wine bottle in the sink then quickly went back to Diane, grabbed her hand and walked her to the bedroom. Diane and David were still wearing the same clothes from their amazing day which they wiggled out of before quickly entering the shower. Diane giggled and David smiled as they let the warm water run over their bodies. David pressed his hard body against Diane and immediately started exploring her mouth with his wet warm tongue. David slowly moved down to her neck and, with the water cascading down upon Diane's body, her already hard nipples were more erect. Diane jumped up and straddled David.

She whipped her wet hair and in a soft moan said, "Take me to the bed."

David responded, "With pleasure, my love. With pleasure!"

Their slippery wet bodies made moving across one another easy. It was as if they were gliding on each other.

David stopped caressing Diane for just a moment and, looking down upon her radiant, glowing face said, "I'm going to miss making love to you and holding your beautiful body in my arms."

Diane smiled as she looked up at David and gently whispered, "I'm so lucky to have you in my life. I've waited so long to feel this way. Thank you for walking into my life." And, with that last spoken word, David and Diane spent the rest of the night making love and holding each other until they fell asleep.

Chapter 35

As the morning sun peaked through the sheer curtains hanging from the bedroom window, David was already dressed and lying in bed watching Diane sleep. Sensing David's presence, Diane, with her eyes still closed and a smile on her face, reached for David. She slowly opened her eyes and, with a quizzical look and in a quizzical tone, she asked as she sat up, "Why are you dressed? What's wrong? Is everything all right?"

"Well," began David, "As luck would have it, I need to get back in town sooner than later. Apparently, Joe called late last night and left a message that a pipe broke in the kitchen and the bar is flooded."

"Oh, no, David. That's awful."

"Yeah, I don't even want to think of the mess and, of course, the timing couldn't be worse. I'm so sorry that we need to cut our day/weekend short."

"David, I've had the time of my life this past weekend. Taking care of the bar is more important right now. I just need to jump in the shower. I can be ready within a half hour."

"Baby, you're the best. Take your time. I'll straighten up a bit and put everything back in its place according to the directions the owner left, and we can grab a quick coffee and breakfast on the road." As David cleaned out the refrigerator and freezer, he noticed his frozen grapes and jokingly said to himself, "Damn, we didn't get to use these!"

The conversation going back was fun and upbeat, even though David had no idea what he was going to walk into when he got to the bar.

As David pulled into Diane's driveway, she said, "Now, you're sure you don't want me to go with you and help out?"

"I'm very sure. I have no idea how long I'm going to be there and the extent of the damage. Joe already called a plumber but it's Sunday, so who knows when someone will get there and, besides, you have work tomorrow. I could be there all night. I'll call you later and, Diane, thank you for being so understanding. I love you."

"I love you too, David, and again thank you so much for this weekend. It was fantastic!" David kissed Diane at her front door and left.

The day became night and still no word from David. Diane kept herself busy by doing laundry and making a quick stop at the grocery store. She kept checking her phone for a text or a call from David. She wondered if this was just a precursor to her future while David was away in the Middle East.

Around nine at night, David finally called. Diane anxiously answered the phone. "Hey, sweetie. How is everything?"

David responded, "Oh, babe, what a day!"

"Oh no!" began Diane, "So, I guess the damage was pretty bad?"

"Yeah, but we're going to be okay. The pipe is fixed. Thank God! That took forever. We had to call two separate plumbers and then they had to work together which was real fun but, in the end, it worked out. There really wasn't too much water damage. The chairs and tables will be just fine and, more importantly, so will the kitchen. We decided to stay closed tonight so everything can dry out properly. Everything should be fine for tomorrow."

"Oh, wow, David, I'm so happy!"

"Yeah, me too. That's one less thing I will need to worry about when I leave." There was deafening silence for about thirty seconds. Neither David nor Diane knew what to say after that. "So," David said as he tried to start up a new topic of conversation. "Are you ready for school tomorrow?"

"Well, if I'm not, I better be," laughed Diane. "The week before Winter break is brutal on us teachers."

"Oh, I can only imagine," David sympathetically said. "But, Diane, honestly, who is more ready for the two weeks off? Teachers or students?" David and Diane laughed. After talking and reminiscing about their fun and romantic weekend, which was hard to imagine took place less than twenty-four hours ago, it was time to say goodnight. Both David and Diane had to get up early the next morning for work.

"So, sweetie, any chance of seeing you at school tomorrow?"

"You know, babe, I really don't know. I have a lot of loose ends to tie up before Tuesday. Basically, tomorrow is my last day with the delivery business because, on Tuesday, I need to meet with Jefferson to get all my necessary paperwork in order. But, you'll definitely see me tomorrow night."

"Well, that's good. At least I have something to look forward to, especially if those little rug rats drive me crazy!"

"Don't let them make you crazy, babe."

"Easier said than done!"

David laughed then said, "I love you, Diane, and thank you again for being so understanding about today. I really was hoping to spend the whole day with you."

"I know, honey, me too but things happen. I'm just really glad that if it had to happen, that it happened today and not Friday night."

"Oh, you know it, because my poor boy Joe would've had to deal with it all by himself!" laughed David. Diane laughed along with David as they said their goodnights and hung up the phone.

"Hey, girl!" yelled Jenny as she saw Diane walking in the hallway. "So, did you have an amazing weekend?"

"Oh, Jenny, it was fantastic!"

"Well, I will definitely be heading over to hear all about it during lunch!" Jenny winked at Diane as she made her way to the library. Diane got in her classroom and was so thankful that she was all set-up for the day. As she was putting her backpack in her desk drawer, she heard her phone ding. It was a text message from David, Good morning, sunshine. Have a great day. Love you. Diane smiled and quickly wrote back, I love you too xoxoxo

Diane and Jenny spent their entire lunch talking about David and Diane's fabulous weekend.

"You and Vic have to go there," Diane insisted. "It was just wonderful. The cottage was so quaint and it was right on the beach. Talk about romantic ambience."

"Well, you have definitely convinced me, girlfriend. Who couldn't use a little spark in their relationship?" Diane and Jenny laughed as they looked up at the clock and realized their lunch break was just about over. "Ugh, time goes by so fast," moaned Jenny.

"It sure does and I still have to use the bathroom," laughed Diane.

The rest of the school day was uneventful. Diane checked her phone over the course of the day but there was no word from David. She knew he was going to be busy but thought he would at least have time to send her a text message. At the end of the day, Diane tidied up her room and was excited she finished her lesson plans for after Winter break. She walked out of her classroom and walked to the office to sign out. She made idle chit-chat with a couple of teachers and office staff before heading to her car. Before she started her car, she checked her phone one more time. "Damnit, David. Call me. Please don't bail on me tonight," Diane said as her heart sank.

As Diane pulled into her driveway, David's truck followed. Diane saw his truck in her rearview mirror. A huge smile from ear to ear appeared on her face. She jumped out of her car and ran over to him as he was getting out of his truck.

"Oh, wow, David, that was perfect timing!" Diane said as she threw her arms around David's neck.

"I was hoping to beat you home. I wanted to set all this up for you." Diane looked in the truck and saw flowers, two bags of take out and a bottle of wine.

"Oh, sweetie, you're the best."

"Well, I figured if we stayed in we'd have more time together."

"Like I've always said, I like the way you think, Mr. Anderson." Diane helped David bring in the bags. Diane reached into the pantry for a vase for her beautiful bouquet of daisies and sunflowers. David unpacked the bags containing their dinner and began to open the bottle of wine. "Are you ready to eat now?" asked Diane. "It's a little early, isn't it?"

"Well, it is a bit early. You're right but I was hoping we'd get a little love-making in after dinner."

"Well, well, well, that sounds like a plan to me but, seriously, David, you never do a "little" love-making!" David smiled and picked Diane up and spun her around.

"You know what? How about we change the plan? How does making love first, then dinner sound?"

"Again, David, I like how you think," giggled Diane as she took off running up the stairs and David quickly followed.

"Hey, where are you going?" David said to Diane as he gently pulled her close to his chest.

"I thought I'd jump in the shower and get the school funk off of me."

"No, I want you just the way you are right now. School funk and all!"

"Ew, David, seriously?"

"Yes!" David said as he brought Diane close and began undressing her. First, her blouse and, then, her bra. Diane wiggled out of her slacks and eventually stepped out of them, leaving just her laced thong to be removed. Diane then returned the favor by unzipping David's pants. His bulging member was trying to escape his underwear and tight jeans, which put a wicked little smile on Diane's face as she grabbed his manhood and winked at him. David quickly removed his shirt and both he and Diane were left looking at each other like two hungry boxers in the ring, waiting for the other to make the first move.

"Let me take a moment and just look at you and enjoy your beauty. Damn, Diane, you're so gorgeous. How am I ever going to stand being apart from you?"

Diane smiled sweetly and said, "I'm not going to think about being away from you tonight. I just want to enjoy making love to the man I love."

David reached over and held Diane close and whispered in her ear, "Do you know how much you mean to me? I can't imagine life without you. My God, Diane, I love you so much!"

Diane responded by saying, "David, no matter where you are, you will always be in my heart. I can't imagine life without you either. I love you, David." And with those words of endearment, David and Diane made love tenderly and affectionately to one another.

By the time they got out of bed and showered, two hours had gone by. It seemed like an entire night had passed but it was now a normal dinner time. Diane put on her robe and David slid on a pair of shorts he had at Diane's house. He poured the wine as Diane heated up their dinner. They sat mostly quiet, staring at each other and falling in love with each other all over again.

On his way home, David couldn't help but think about the words that he and Diane said to each other.

"We both said that we couldn't imagine life without each other! What if something happens to me? Damnit, I love her but why did I continue falling in love with her? Is it right to have her put her life on hold until I get back? Who the hell knows when or if I will be back? It's too late, David. You totally fucked this up!"

David met with Lieutenant Colonel Jefferson first thing Tuesday morning to discuss his orders, and to fill out and make sure all of David's paperwork was properly in order and submitted. David was told to report to the Homestead Air Force Base at fifteen hundred hours (three a.m.) tomorrow. David drove home, all the while knowing that today may be the last day he ever sees Diane. "I need to make this day count, but she's working and I need to get my gear ready and get a good night's sleep," David said to himself as he grew more and more frustrated.

It was Diane's lunch break so she took a chance on calling David. David quickly answered the phone when he saw Diane's number appear.

"Hey, babe, I'm so glad you called. I've been thinking about you all day!"

"Well, I've been thinking about you too. How did it go with Jefferson? Did you find out all the necessary information for tomorrow?"

"Yeah, I did and I'm pretty pissed at the fact that we only have a few more hours left together and you're working and I'm here getting all my crap together and, to boot, I need to be at the base by three a.m."

"Three a.m.? Oh, my God, David!"

"Yeah, that means a very early night for me. When I spoke to Jefferson last week, he told me it would be a late-night flight not early morning. Hell, I might as well stay up all night and sleep on the plane."

"Now, David, that sounds like a plan."

"Well, babe, I was kidding. Tomorrow is considered a work day. The Army doesn't care how early it is. If I'm scheduled to report at three a.m., then I better be prepared to be ready to work!" After a short pause, David asked, "So what time do you think you can be home?"

"There's a short faculty meeting right after school. I'll leave right after that so, hopefully, I'll be home by four."

"Babe," David began, "We're going to make this work. We will spend a quality last night together."

"As long as I get to hold you and kiss you and tell you how much I love you before you leave, then I'm good."

"Well, I'm hoping you'll actually show me how much you love me too!"

"Aw, David, you know that's a given. So, I'll see you at my house after four."

"Okay, sweetie, see you then."

Chapter 36

"If MaryAnn asks one more question, I'm going to kill her," whispered Diane to Jenny, "I can't believe today is the day Ms. Marshall decides to have a faculty meeting to explain Curriculum Night, which isn't until way after we come back from Winter break. I'm getting ready to grab my bag and walk out."

"Don't you worry, my friend, because I'll be walking out right behind you!" said Jenny then added, "I'm giving it five more minutes and then I'm out of here!"

Ms. Marshall looked out at the teachers and asked, "Are there any more questions?"

The teachers all looked at MaryAnn and said, "No!"

"Okay, then, teachers, see you all tomorrow. Have a good night." Diane and Jenny both looked at each other and hightailed it out of the meeting. They walked quickly to the parking lot so as to not get caught up in any lingering conversations.

"Now, look, Diane, if you need to talk after David leaves, especially tomorrow, you know I'm here for you and you know I'm a great listener."

"You are not only a great listener, Jenny, you're a great friend. I think I'm probably going to be taking you up on the talking and listening offer. It's going to be so lonely without him."

Jenny hugged Diane and said, "It's all going to be all right."

Diane hugged Jenny back tightly and said, "I sure hope and pray it is." Diane looked at her watch and frantically said, "I've got to go!" Diane jumped into her car, waved to Jenny and headed home to see David.

When Diane pulled into her driveway, David's truck was already there and, since he had a key to Diane's place, he was inside waiting.

"Oh, babe, I'm so sorry for being late, the damn meeting ran over," said Diane as she entered her house. David put one hand up as if to tell her he was on the phone. Diane put her hand over her mouth and then whispered the words, "I'm sorry." David had a serious look on his face. He kept nodding in agreement and kept repeating, "Yes sir." As the conversation was winding down David's last words were, "I understand, sir. I will, sir. Goodnight." David placed his phone down, walked over to Diane and gave her a big hug that lifted her off the floor. He then put both his hands on her cheeks and kissed her lips.

"Well, hello, big boy," Diane said as she continued, "That sounded a little intense. Is everything all right? Who were you on the phone with? Jefferson?"

"Yeah, well, there's been a slight change in plans. Seems like Jefferson had it right the first time. We are flying out at night, unfortunately, it's tonight at eleven-thirty. Babe, I have to now be at the base by ten!" Diane just stared at David in disbelief, saying not a word. "Diane, I'm so sorry," David said as he hugged Diane. "I never thought our last night together would end up so rushed."

"David, first of all, it's not our last night together. We're going to have many years together after you get back. This is just a little set-back. We had a great weekend and fabulous time last night. We still have a couple of hours."

"But I didn't want to rush this evening. I wanted it to be special. I didn't want to keep looking at the clock. I'm going to need to grab a couple of hours of sleep before I leave because I know it's going to be a very long night and very long day tomorrow."

Diane thought for a moment and said, "I can't believe I'm being so calm about this, but, David, let's go grab a couple of burgers, bring them back here and then spend some quality time with each other before you need to go home. The only thing that has changed is the time. We're still here together so let's make every minute count."

"And this is why I love you so much. Diane Walker. You, sweetie, are incredible."

David and Diane quickly got into David's truck and drove to the closest hamburger joint with a drive-through. On the way home, Diane sat as close as she could to David in his truck and began rubbing his inner thigh.

"You know you're making me crazy, right?"

Diane laughed. "Why, Mr. Anderson, whatever do you mean?"

"Oh, you'll know exactly what I mean, when I get you home!"

Diane smiled and said, "Well, let's get this truck moving!"

When they reached Diane's front entrance, David said, "You know these burgers are going to have to wait right?"

"That's what we have microwaves for," laughed Diane as she and David threw the bags of burgers and fries on the counter and headed up to Diane's room.

As David and Diane entered the bedroom, Diane turned to David and said, "David, tonight I want to make love like last night. I want it to be slow and sensual. I want it to last. I want it to be the thing I remember as I'm sitting with my eyes closed thinking of you on those nights without you." David placed his index finger over her lips then he placed his hand at the back of her neck and drew Diane close. He began passionately kissing Diane. Her eyes closed and her body went limp. David scooped her up and placed her on the bed. Realizing they were both fully clothed, each broke from the moment and undressed, but doing so while staring into each other's eyes, making the act more erotic and sexy. David, not known for speaking during love-making, had much to say tonight. In between kissing Diane's warm wet mouth, David softly whispered, "I love you, Diane." Diane smiled. He continued, "I love your eyes." He kissed her eyes. "I love your nose." He kissed her nose. "I love the corners of your mouth." He kissed the corners of her mouth. "I love your neck." He kissed and licked her neck which made her body tingle. "I love your breasts." He kissed and gently suckled her breasts. Diane grew more and more moist. David slowly traced an invisible line with his warm tongue from her breasts to Diane's now extremely wet vagina.

Diane stopped him and said, "I want you. I want to feel all of you inside of me." David smiled and obeyed her command. He gently mounted Diane and inserted his manhood with ease. Diane and David's bodies moved in perfect harmony as each of them moaned in satisfaction. David and Diane did not want this time together to end but nature took its course, as they both climaxed and yelled out in unison.

David held Diane closely without either saying a word. Diane had a tear fall down the side of her face as she lay in bed already missing David. She pulled herself together, sat up and gazed at the clock.

"David, it's five-past-seven. What time do you need to start getting ready to go home to get your things?"

"At least by eight." David said in a solemn voice. Diane lay back down and rested her head on David's chest. He stroked her hair, not to calm Diane, but to calm his own nerves. After several minutes, David said, "How about those burgers and fries?"

Diane laughed and said, "Sounds good right about now. I think we worked up an appetite." Diane grabbed an oversized t-shirt and put it on.

"Do you mind if I shower here before I go? It will give us a few extra minutes and one less thing I'll need to do when I get home."

"No, not at all. Do you want any company?"

"Babe, usually I would jump at that offer but if I have you in that shower, you know we're not getting out anytime soon."

Diane smiled and agreed. "I'll just go downstairs and heat up the food."

"Sounds good. I won't be long." David stood under the warm cascading water having so many emotions running through his mind about Diane and leaving her, without knowing when and if he'd return. With his eyes closed, he kept shaking his head from side to side as if to say no.

David and Diane ate their burgers without much conversation. It was just about eight o'clock when David stood up and took Diane into his arms. "I guess it's time for me to go." Diane stood there and nodded her head. "Diane, my love, I will write and call as often as I can. There will be times when I won't be able to get a letter out. You have to promise me that if you don't hear from me for a week or two, you won't freak out, worry, and think the worse."

"I promise, David, but I'm going to be honest with you. I know it's not going to be easy for either one of us and I will try very hard to stay positive. The day you came into my life, I knew you were special and, as we grew closer, I knew you were the one that I would love for the

238

rest of my life! I can't imagine my life without you. David, I love you so much!"

David and Diane embraced for the last time before David left and, as he left, he softly said, "Just remember, Diane, no matter where I go and no matter how far away I am from you, I will always find my way back to you. I love you, baby!" As David walked towards his truck and left her home, Diane's eyes filled with tears and she began to cry.

Chapter 37

After David left, Diane had a very hard time being by herself. Diane grew more and more nervous with each passing day that went by without hearing from David, but things were about to change. David had been gone for five days and, for five days, Diane went without hearing from him and, when she did hear from him, the call ended abruptly. She had no idea how she was going to manage being away from David for so long. The phone call was also the beginning of David knowing that he couldn't let Diane put her life on hold for him.

The Phone Call

Diane's phone rang. An unknown number appeared. Diane's heart seemed to stop as she picked up the phone and frantically asked, "David? David, is that you?"

"Hello? Diane? It's me, David. Can you hear me?"

"Yes, David, I can hear you. Oh, my God! I'm so happy to hear from you! I've been so worried. Are you okay?"

"Yes, sweetie, I'm fine. I'm just very tired. I haven't slept in three days."

"Oh, my goodness, David, I'm so sorry! These past five days seem like five years. I miss you so much."

David dropped his head and closed his eyes as he said, "I miss you too, Diane." There was silence on both ends. David sadly said, "Look, sweetie, I just have time for a quick call. I just wanted you to know I arrived safely. I'm so glad I got to hear your voice."

"Oh, me too, David. I just don't know how I'm going to get through this."

David shook his head and then said, "I love you, Diane. I love you so much. I'll write as soon as I can."

"Promise?" Diane quietly asked.

"I promise," said David as a loud crackling noise began to interrupt their conversation.

"David? David, can you hear me? What's that noise? David, I love you!"

"Diane? Diane!" The phone went dead.

After the abruptly ended phone call, David just knew deep down inside that he couldn't let Diane live in fear of not knowing. After thinking long and hard, he decided to write several upbeat love letters to Diane and would mail one letter every other week, then he decided he would selfishly stop all communication with her. He knew it was wrong. He knew it would destroy her. He knew he was taking the cowardly way out. He knew he was being a prick but, deep down inside, he thought he was doing the right thing. He loved Diane so much that he thought letting her go was the best thing for her. Boy, was he wrong!

Chapter 38

Months after David left, Diane sat lonely, depressed and extremely sad on her living room couch. The letters had stopped, as did the occasional surprise phone calls. Her life was put on hold and became very dark, until she received a call and a harsh voicemail from Sara.

"Hey, girl, it's me, Sara. You remember me, right? You're not picking up the damn phone when I call. I'm not sure if you're listening to your messages. I'm not sure if you're ignoring me and the other girls. Hell, we don't even know if you're dead or alive. We're worried about you, Diane, and because we're worried, the girls and I have decided that if you don't pick up the freaking phone and call me back in five minutes after getting this call, I'm going to call the police and have them go by your house to check on you. So, tick tock, tick tock!"

"Holy shit! Really?" said Diane as she sat up on the couch after hearing the message. Diane took a deep breath and, with much hesitation, called Sara back. "Well, well, well, it's about fucking time, Diane!" Sara sarcastically said as she answered the phone. "What the hell is going on with you? Have you seriously just given up? What happened to calling me or the girls when you need us?"

Diane interrupted Sara and said, "Okay, okay, I didn't call you back to get a lecture. I'm sorry. I'm just… " Diane paused.

"Just what, Diane? You're what?"

"I'm sad. I'm miserable. I'm depressed. I miss him so much! There're days I cry so hard that I can't breathe!"

Sara stopped Diane from saying anymore and sternly said, "All right, that's it. I'm booking you on the next flight to New York. You're spending time with me!"

"No, no, no, Sara, I can't."

"Really, Diane, you can't? Tell me exactly why not. Why can't you come? You have plans? You have the entire fucking summer off," snapped Sara. Not a word was spoken on either end until Sara said, "Diane, I'm sorry for yelling at you. I know I don't know what you're going through. Neither of us girls do, but I do know that the girls and I love you very much and we're very worried about you. Luna is a basket case and Anne calls me in tears when they can't reach you. Please come to New York. I have some vacation time saved up. It'll be fun and we'll do stuff to get your mind off things. C'mon, Diane. What do you say?"

There was silence on the phone but, after a couple of minutes, Diane finally said in a pathetic, fragile voice, "Okay, I'll come."

"Oh, my God, really? That's great! I'll call the airlines and book your flight for tomorrow."

"No, Sara, that's all right. I can get my own ticket."

"No, ma'am Miss Walker. It's my treat. Look at it as an early birthday present and this way, if I book it, I know you'll definitely get on the flight! So, let me get off the phone so I can do this thing! I'll send you all the information."

"Sara," Diane said softly. "Thank you."

"No, Diane. Thank you for agreeing to come. I love you or, should I say, we love you. Luna and Anne are going to be very happy too! Oh, and by the way, pack for at least seven days."

Diane closed her eyes, smiled and said, "You're a great friend. I love you!"

"Yeah, yeah, yeah, that's me!" chuckled Sara as she hung up. Diane sat on the couch clutching the phone to her heart as she stared into space, then whispered to herself, "Time to get off your ass, get into the shower, wash your hair, pack and rejoin the living!"

New York

After an uneventful flight, Diane landed in the Big Apple. She made her way through the crowded airport to the baggage claim area. As she stood waiting for the carousel to start up, she heard loud cries of joy. She turned around to see what was going on, only to find a solider in uniform being reunited with his family. Diane quickly turned back around, as her heart sunk deep into her chest. She closed her eyes, bit her lip so she wouldn't cry and shook her head as if to shake the sight from her mind.

Diane was startled by the start of the baggage carousel and Sara's familiar voice,. "Diane, hey, girl!" shouted Sara as she rushed up to Diane.

"Hey, Sara," Diane said as she broke down in Sara's embrace.

"Oh, boy, it's worse than I thought," Sara whispered to herself as she wiped tears from Diane's face. "Let's get your luggage and get you to the apartment."

The drive to Sara's apartment wasn't long at all but the lack of conversation made it seem like an eternity. Diane broke the silence by solemnly asking, "Did you see the soldier? Did you see his happy family? It just broke my heart when I saw that all unfold. I wanted that so badly to be me. I'm sorry, Sara. Maybe it was a bad idea for me to come."

"What the hell are you talking about? You just got here! You haven't even made it to my apartment. So, you had a little setback. There's nothing wrong with that. I'm sure I would've done the same thing. It's normal and very understandable. Now, just shake it off and try to think of the amazing time we're going to have," said Sara as she held Diane's hand and reassured her that everything was going to be all right.

Diane got settled in Sara's upstairs guestroom. She took a quick shower and unpacked her suitcase. Sara came up to the room and said, "I thought we would eat in tonight and call the girls. I'm sure they would love to hear your voice."

"I'd love to talk to them but can we do it tomorrow night? Tonight I'd just like to relax with a good dinner and a glass or two of wine."

"You know, Diane, I think we can make that happen," laughed Sara as she continued, "So, what do you want for dinner? I have Italian, Chinese, Mexican, and Indian takeout menus."

After finishing a delicious, huge dinner of baked ziti, salad, garlic knots, and a nice bottle of Merlot, Diane asked Sara how her relationship with Edward was going. Sara was a little hesitant to answer, because she and Edward were doing really well and even talking about a future together.

She didn't want Diane to think she was rubbing salt into her wounds, but Diane softly said, "It's okay, Sara. If you're happy, I want to hear all about it. Don't be afraid to tell me. I'm not going to go off the deep end. I want you to be happy. You deserve it, especially after what you've been through with that nasty divorce."

Sara smiled, then paused and sheepishly said, "Well, it's going very well. I honestly now believe I can be happy again with Edward. I was so afraid to put myself out there and get serious with someone, but he makes it so easy and if I can put myself out there, you can too, Diane."

"It's way too soon, Sara. I'm still so much in love with David. There's been no closure, so it just makes it that much harder for me to let go. Anyway, enough of that, I want to hear more loving stuff about you." The girls laughed and opened another bottle of merlot. "So, Sara, where's Edward? Will I see him anytime this week?"

"He's actually back in Nashville setting up a security detail for, hmm, I forgot who!" Sara said giggling then added, "It must be the wine."

"Well, I'm all about forgetting right now, so pour me another," Diane said as she held out her empty glass.

Two and a half bottles of merlot later, the girls were giggling and laughing at just about anything the other said. "Sara," Diane began in a mellow tone. "Thank you for this. I know it's only day one but I really, really needed this. I needed you and I need the girls. I'm so sorry that I avoided you and ignored all your phone calls. I just thought that I needed to be by myself, not realizing that was probably the worst thing I could've ever done."

"Well, that's all in the past now. You're on the right road to healing. See what a good bottle of wine and a good friend can do for you?" Diane smiled and gave Sara a big hug then both girls made their way to the kitchen to put their dishes and their wine glasses in the sink.

"We'll get these in the morning," Sara said as Diane nodded and made her way to her room. Sara stayed in the living room to call Edward.

Chapter 39

Back home in Miami

"What the freaking hell?" Jenny said as she looked at her cell phone as it rang.

"What's wrong?" Vic asked.

"I think David is calling me!"

"Anderson?"

"That's what the caller ID says."

"Well, then, answer it!"

"Hello?" Jenny said in a quizzical tone.

"Jenn, it's me, David."

"Oh, my God! David! What the hell? Where are you? What's going on?" Jenny stared at Vic with a stunned look.

"I know, Jenny. It's been a long time."

"Yeah, like six or seven months," Jenny interrupted. "How are you and Vic? You guys doing all right?"

"We're doing just fine but I'm sure you didn't call for that. What's going on, David? And, if you don't mind and forgive me for sounding rude, but why are you calling? Are you somewhere in the Middle East?"

"No, Jenny, I'm home."

"You're home? Wow, that's great!"

"Yeah, well, honestly, I've been home for a couple of weeks."

"Oh, my goodness, Diane must be over the moon. I bet she is thrilled and beyond excited."

"Well, that's the thing. Diane doesn't know I'm back."

"What? David, come on, seriously? You've got to be kidding me. Why not?"

"Well, that's what I need to talk to you about. Is there any chance we can meet somewhere to talk?"

"Geez, David, you know that Diane and I are good friends. She would hate me or even stop talking to me if she knew that I knew you were home and didn't tell her."

"I'll explain everything, Jenny. I promise."

"Oh, man," Jenny said in a disturbed tone. Then, with hesitation, continued, "Okay, David. Why don't you come over for dinner tonight? We can all catch up as you spill your guts and, all I'm going to say is, there better be a good reason coming out of your mouth. Be here around six."

"Thanks, Jenny, I really appreciate it. I'll see you guys later."

"Aw, man," Jenny said after she hung up the phone then turned to Vic and said, "This shit better be good or I'm going to smack the crap right out of him!"

David arrived at Jenny's around five-forty-five with a six-pack of beer and a bottle of wine under his arm. Vic met him at the door and, grabbed for the six-pack, before reaching out to shake David's hand.

"How the hell have you been, buddy? Come on in." Jenny came out of the kitchen and met David with a smack on his arm and then with a big hug.

"David Anderson, you have a lot of explaining to do."

"Damn, Jenn, let the man at least sit down and have a beer before you start on him!"

"No, man, it's okay. I probably deserve it but I will have one of those beers first." Vic, Jenny and David walked to the living room and sat down.

"Okay, you have your beer and you're sitting down, now start talking," Jenny demanded. Vic shook his head and chuckled. David took a large swig from his beer bottle and a deep breath.

"All right, I'll start from when we got back from our weekend in Sanibel. As you know, because I know Diane told you all or most of what happened that weekend, that it was great but, when we got back, I started doing a lot of soul searching. I've never loved any woman as much as I love Diane. We got back early Sunday and I only had until late Tuesday night before I took off. I didn't know how long I was going to be gone and, basically, I didn't even know if I was coming back. To see the look on her face that Tuesday night before I left was more heartbreaking for me than I thought it would be. I didn't want to leave her. We both broke down. Diane was inconsolable. She was sobbing so hard that she was having a difficult time catching her breath. When I finally left, I told her how much I loved her. I told her I would write as often as I could and try to call when it was safe and when it was possible. I didn't want to leave her but I knew I had an obligation to my country and I could not fail. I sat in my truck and, I'm not ashamed to say, I cried and I may have hit the stirring wheel a few times pretty hard out of anger." At this point, Jenny was in tears and Vic was holding her tight. David continued explaining, "Before I boarded the plane the next morning, I called Diane to tell her again that I loved her very much but she never answered her phone. I figured she was in the shower getting ready for school. I did leave a message and I hung up."

"But I know you guys have talked and written letters since then," Jenny said wiping her tears away with her apron.

"Oh, yeah. We spoke often but things changed the night I left her house. When I was on that flight to Afghanistan, I knew I couldn't put her through the not knowing if I was okay every time she watched the news and heard of troops being injured or killed, so I slowly started phasing myself out of her life."

"You did what? Why would you make that decision without talking to her first? David, Diane has been a basket case for the last six months. With all due respect, you had no right to phase yourself out of her life. Diane has been deeply depressed. She has stopped going out. She has stopped talking to friends. All she did was throw herself into schoolwork. And now that it's summer break, who knows what she's going to do? This once vibrant young woman is in such a very dark place. Her friends, Luna, Anne, and Sara, have a hard time getting in touch with her.

I do know that Sara, who has called me a few times, worries about her and wants Diane to go to New York to spend time with her. Maybe she'll go and, hopefully, it will do some good." David sat quietly with his head down.

He drank the last of the beer in the bottle, stood up and said, "I've got to go."

"What do you mean you've got to go? You haven't had dinner," snapped Jenny.

"I know and I'm sorry but I think it's time to call the girls. I don't know which one to call first but I know it doesn't matter who I speak to; I'm definitely going to get a well-deserved ear full." David stood up along with Vic and Jenny. He shook Vic's hand and gave Jenny a kiss on the cheek and a hug, before saying, "Thank you. Thank you both for allowing me to come over and pour my heart out. I have a lot to think about and I need to make a few phone calls. Wish me luck because I'm sure as hell going to need it."

"But, David, what does this mean? What are you going to do?" asked Jenny.

"Jenny, my dear, I'm going to try to win back my girl. I'm going to beg for forgiveness but I know I first have to go through the girls. Wish me luck."

"Let us know how it goes."

"I sure will," said David as he left Vic and Jenny's home.

"Babe," Vic began, "Do you think he has a shot?"

"Honey, I have no clue but I sure wish him luck because, after the girls find out he's been home for the past couple of weeks and hasn't gotten in touch with Diane, I'm afraid they're going to rip him a new one! And it's going to be well-deserved"

On his way home, David started to have second thoughts about contacting Diane and the girls. He began talking to himself out loud, "What if Diane has moved on? What if she wants nothing to do with me? What if she can't forgive me? Aww, shit, I fucked it up royally. I was only thinking of myself. I got scared. I was so freaking selfish. What I put Diane through is inexcusable and I honestly can't blame her if she tells me to go to hell!"

David got home, cracked open another beer and paced back and forth deciding what to do. After several minutes, he finally decided to call Luna. He figured she was the one that would give him the most shit and also the one who would be the most honest, and that's exactly what he needed. He needed someone to give him an honest opinion of what to do or not do.

Chapter 40

"David Anderson, if this is you, you better be calling to tell me that you've been in a coma for the past few months and I'm the only person and number you remembered!"

David stayed silent and instantly regretted calling Luna, but he took a deep breath and said, "Hey, Luna."

Luna quickly interrupted, "What the hell are you calling me for, David? I should hang up the damn phone. I really don't want to talk to you and I really don't care about what you have to say."

"Please, Luna, please don't hang up. I really need to talk to you. It's important."

"Fine, David, talk but this better be good!"

David began by saying, "First of all, I'm so sorry. I'm really sorry for… "

Luna again angrily interrupted and yelled, "David, just stop there. Just let me get this off my chest. You take Diane on this super romantic weekend before you leave. You wrote to her weekly and called her when you could and Diane, although sad, was handling you being gone pretty well. She totally understood the secrecy of your mission but then, after a couple of months, everything stopped cold without explanation. That, sir, is just wrong!

You've made no contact with her for months. She didn't know if you were dead or alive. Sara had to call in a couple of huge favors to find out about your status. Then to find out that you were indeed alive and well AND that, even though your mission was secret, it didn't require you to stop all contact with your loved ones. So, tell me, David, what the fuck happened? Why, David? Why did you stop all contact with Diane?"

"Because I love her."

"Oh, horse shit, David. Don't give me that line of crap! If you loved her you wouldn't have stopped all contact with her and made her think you were dead or MIA! So, buddy, you better rethink that "I love her" statement!"

"I know, Luna, it doesn't make sense but you've got to believe me. I had no idea when I was coming home. I had no idea where I was going to be sent. I had no idea if I would even come home in one piece or come home the same man she fell in love with. So, yeah, I took the easy way out or, at least, that is what you and everyone else thinks, but you've got to understand that this was the hardest decision I ever made. I knew it would be hard on her, extremely hard, but I also knew she had amazing friends to help her get through it."

"Well, let me inform you, Mr. Anderson, she didn't let us help her. She wouldn't take our calls. She wouldn't answer our texts. She threw herself into work. She has no life. She's depressed, sad and in a very dark place. You talk about being scared of coming back not the man you were when you left, well, guess what? She's not the woman she was when YOU left! Thank God that Sara finally got her to go to New York for a visit and, hopefully, this visit will help her get her mind off of you and begin to heal her broken heart."

"But that's not what I want. I want her back and I'll do everything I can to make her realize how very sorry I am for what I did."

"Look, David, I really don't know if that's a good idea. You crushed her heart. I mean, don't get me wrong, I can hear it in your voice that you seem genuinely sorry for the way you handled this but you did some horrible damage to her heart, soul and mind. Let me ask you, how long have you been back from Afghanistan and are you completely out of the Army where you never have to go back into combat?"

"Yeah, I'm totally done. My obligation was officially over two weeks ago."

"Wait, what? Are you telling me that you've been home for two weeks?"

"Yes, Luna, I've been home for two weeks."

"And, David, have you tried to reach out to Diane?"

"Yes and no, Luna."

"Oh, man, what the hell is that supposed to mean?"

"Well, every time I pick up the phone or drive by her house, I just tell myself NO but I can't do this anymore. I can't be without her. Please, Luna, please tell me what I need to do to make things right again."

"Listen, David," began Luna, "I'm going to be very honest with you. I can't tell you how to make things right with Diane. That's between you and her and I'll stand by her no matter what. I do know that she loves you and hasn't stopped, but I also know that she's heartbroken that you cut everything off without even a word and I really don't know how she's going to react to the news that you've been home for two weeks and haven't contacted her. Look, let me think about this and let me run this by the girls to get their input. I can't promise you anything but I'll get back to you and let you know what we think and how you should move forward. But do know that you fucked it up royally."

"Yeah, I know I did, Luna. I do appreciate anything you and the girls can do. I do love her, Luna, and if I have to spend the rest of my life proving it and making up for what I did, I will."

Luna hung up the phone and sat in disbelief for a few minutes while trying to dissect their conversation.

"Aw, screw it," she said, then picked her phone back up and began her group text with Anne and Sara, You're not going to believe who just called me begging for forgiveness and professing his love for Diane! He spilled his guts to me! It's way too long and intense to discuss over texting. We three need to talk. He wants our input on how to get her back!!!!!

Anne: WTF??????? Is he crazy???????

Sara: Are you kidding me???? Can't talk right now. Give me a few minutes to make sure Diane is asleep.

Luna: Sara, call me when you can. Anne, I'll patch you in so we all can talk.

Sara: Sounds good.

Anne sent a thumbs-up emoji.

About an hour later, when Sara knew Diane was fast asleep, she sent Luna a text message. The girls talked and discussed what David told Luna and, at times, it got pretty heated but, after about an hour ,they came to the conclusion that it wasn't up to them to decide what was right for Diane.

According to Luna, "She's a grown-ass adult." The girls figured that David does need to explain his actions to Diane and only she can decide what's right for her life.

"We'll stand by her no matter what she decides," Anne said many times. "Diane would absolutely kill us if we decided for her what to do about David. He fucked up and fucked up big, but I do understand where he was coming from but he went about it totally the wrong way,"

Sara said, "Fucking men! They always think they know what's right and think they should make the decisions in the relationship. I sure do hope, only if she forgives him, that she grows some balls and becomes more accretive," said Luna before adding, "I'll call David tomorrow but I should first toy with him for a bit and make him squirm."

"Luna, I'm sure you will," laughed Anne.

"Hey, let us know how it goes with him and, by the way, Diane and I will FaceTime with you guys tomorrow night. Love you all. Good night!" said Sara as she hung up.

Chapter 41

"Well, good morning, sunshine," Sara said to Diane as she staggered into the kitchen. Diane laughed as she used her long fingers as a comb to tame her hair.

"Sara, I love your bed. And your pillows, my goodness, they're so comfy. I slept like a baby."

"Well, thank you but do you think it had anything to do with the two bottles of wine we drank last night?"

"Hmm, good point!" laughed Diane.

Sara laughed too as she poured a cup of coffee for Diane. "So, my friend," began Sara, "What would you like to do today?" Even though Sara wanted to stay home and talk to Diane about David and ask her a million questions to feel her out to see if she even wanted him back in her life, she knew she couldn't but that was the reporter in her. She also knew that the subject of David was bound to come up tonight when all four girls got together over FaceTime.

"Well, Sara, I've been doing a lot of thinking and, well, don't laugh, but since I'm in the Big Apple, I'd really love to… "

"Dear God, please don't say it," interrupted Sara.

"I want to take a Big Red Bus tour," yelled Diane as she laughed at Sara.

Sara closed her eyes and shook her head. "Seriously, Diane?"

"Yes, I'm serious. I want to ride on top of a big, red double-decker bus and see the city."

"I better find my baseball cap and my darkest sunglasses. I wouldn't want any of my friends or colleagues to see me but, you know, I bet it will be fun. I've never seen the city like a tourist before."

"See that, we're definitely going to have fun! And isn't that the whole reason I'm here? I can't wait!" laughed Diane.

After a full day of doing "touristy" things, both Sara and Diane were beat. "I honestly never realized being a tourist could be so exhausting," began Sara as she took off her baseball cap and sunglasses and laid them on the kitchen counter, then asked, "How about something easy for dinner tonight? You feel like a pizza?"

"Sure," said Diane, "But only if I treat."

"Whatever," yelled Sara as she walked to the bathroom to take a shower. "Oh, wait! I guess you'll need the number for the pizza delivery. It's on the side of the refrigerator."

"Okay, thanks. Oh, Sara, by the way, does half pepperoni and sausage and half veggie with extra cheese still work for you?"

"It sure does."

The pizza arrived soon after both Sara and Diane were in their pajamas and beginning their second glass of wine. "Oh, my goodness, Sara, this pizza smells amazing."

"Nothing like a New York-style pizza. So, Diane, you ready to call the girls and face the music?"

"Geez, can I have a slice before we call and I'll probably need another glass of wine too!" laughed Diane as she reached into the box to grab a couple of slices.

"Hey, stranger," yelled Luna. "Girl, I missed you so much! You look great!"

"Aww, thank you, Luna. I've missed you too. Hey, Anne, good to see you, my friend."

"Hey, Diane, it's so good to see your beautiful face."

"And what am I? Chopped liver?" laughed Sara.

"Ladies, may I just start off by saying how truly sorry I am for alienating all of you, especially when I needed you the most and especially when you continued reaching out to me and I didn't respond. I look back now and I can't believe I did that to you all."

"Don't you worry about that anymore, Diane! We understand," Anne said softly.

"Honey, we were just so damn worried about you and all we wanted to do was wrap our arms around you and let you know everything was going to be okay," said Luna then continued to ask, "Do you want to talk about it or him now?"

"You know, Luna, I'm having such a wonderful time talking to you guys and seeing your happy faces. I don't want to ruin that by talking about something sad."

"I totally respect that but can I ask you just one little question and then I promise to not mention another word."

"Sure, Luna, what's the question?"

"Do you still love him?"

Without hesitation, Diane quickly answered, "Yes, yes, Luna, I do. I still love him."

There was a brief moment of silence until Sara jumped in and said, "Hey, I have a question."

"Really? You have a question? What?"

"I want to know if you're going to tell Luna and Anne what you made me do today in the city."

"Oh, boy, this sounds like it's going to be good," laughed Anne.

"Oh, wait, I better pour a glass of wine," yelled Luna.

"Hold on, let me get the bottle for us," chuckled Sara. All four girls laughed out loud while they shared stories and caught up on each other's lives. Diane held firm and didn't discuss David.

After about an hour and a half, Diane said, "My God, I really needed this tonight. You guys are the absolute best and I truly love each and every one of you so much, and I promise to never not let you know what's going on with me. If I feel bad, I'll call. If I need to vent, I'll call. If I need to yell and get things off my chest, I'll call and if I just need to laugh and hear your voices, I'll call. And I promise to pick up the phone when you call and answer a text. Not only do I promise, I pinky promise!" rambled Diane in a very tipsy voice.

"Here, here," began Luna, "Now, everyone, raise your glass." The girls all raised their glasses.

"To friendship," said Sara.

"To happiness," said Anne.

"To being there for each other," smiled Luna.

"To great times with great friends. I love you all," shouted Diane. The girls all took a sip then Diane added, "Talking to you all is all the therapy a girl needs. To the best girlfriends a girl could have. Thank you all for this and, now, I think it's time for me to say good night!"

The girls laughed and Luna said, "Sara, get that lightweight drinker to bed!" The girls all threw kisses, said good night and then hung up.

After making him wait a good twenty-four hours, Luna decided to call David with information about her call to the girls. "Hey, Luna, thanks for calling. So, did you speak with the girls? What did they say? Do you think I have any kind of chance to talk to and explain things to Diane?"

"Hold on there, cowboy. Take a breath. Relax! I did talk to the girls and all three of us, as you know, are not very happy with you and the way you treated our best friend, but we do know that Diane still loves you and we feel she deserves to make up her own mind if she ever wants to see or speak to you. We do feel that you should contact her and see what happens from there."

"Oh, my God, that's great! Do you know when she'll be back from New York?" David excitedly yelled.

"Well, as a matter of fact, I do, but why, David? What do you have planned? Do not, for God's sake, make a scene anywhere! Contact her only after she's been home and settled for a few days."

"I know, I just want to start thinking of when and what to say to her."

"Well, you better start off with the truth. That's what you say to her and the truth is something you don't prepare for, you just say it!"

"No, of course. I'll definitely be speaking from my heart. So, Luna, when is she coming home?"

"She flies back home this coming Tuesday. David, I swear, you probably only have one chance to explain yourself, so don't fuck it up. We've also said that whatever Diane decides, we will stand with her and back her one hundred percent. Do not ask any of us to do anything on your behalf like talking you up because we won't do it. You got yourself into this and only you can make it right!"

"I know, Luna. You and the girls are right. It's up to me to make this right. Look, I really appreciate you and the girls talking this over and getting back to me. No matter what happens, Diane is one lucky woman to have such great caring friends."

"Well, thank you, David. The four of us have a special bond and we'll do anything we can to help each other out. Good luck, David, and good night." Luna hung up the phone, rolled her eyes, shook her head and said, "Poor bastard."

David was over the moon when he got off the phone with Luna. "She still loves me!" he yelled as he quickly went online to check all flights coming in from New York next Tuesday.

Luna quickly texted Anne and Sara, I spoke to David. He was thrilled but he also promised me that he wouldn't pressure Diane or do anything over the top. He said everything is up to her.

Anne: He has a very long road ahead of him. He's got to do a lot of rebuilding.

Sara: I'm still feeling out Diane's thoughts about him. She's come a long way in just a few days and I sure as hell don't want her to go back in the wrong direction. He really did a number on her heart!

Luna: She's got a good head on her shoulders. Only she knows and can decide what's right for herself. We just need to be there for her either way. Like I said, it's her decision but it's our job to back her!!

The week in New York seemed to fly by. Sara and Diane had the time of their lives shopping, eating out, visiting museums and enjoying all the tourist spots. They also just hung out in Sara's apartment relaxing and talking about the future, which was good for them both.

"So, are you really thinking about going back to school?"

"Yeah, I am. I think it'll be good for me. It will take my mind off of things and keep me busy. It's a long two months off of work by myself and I definitely need to do something. I don't know, maybe I'll take a class at the community center for now, then weigh my options in the fall."

"Well, Diane, my friend, I think it's a great idea to keep busy. You know the saying about idle minds!"

"Yes, I sure do, Sara."

After a brief pause, Sara asked, "So, Diane, any more thoughts on David?"

"Honestly, Sara, you have kept me so busy this past week, I haven't had the time to think about him. At night, you've kept my wine glass full so, when it's time for bed, all I had to do was close my eyes. No time for David thoughts."

Both Sara and Diane laughed then Sara jokingly said, "Hmm, I don't remember you ever saying no to any of the wine I poured into your glass."

"You're so very right. I've never complained about too much wine!" Again, there was a brief pause then Diane turned to Sara and softly said, "But, seriously, Sara, I really need to thank you for this week. It's like you threw me a life preserver. You truly saved my life. I was going down a dark path and to think it was all because of a guy."

Sara got a little nervous hearing Diane's last statement and asked, "But you still love David, right?"

"I do but I've been working on trying to forget about him because, obviously, he's forgotten about me!" Sara wanted to quickly change the subject because she didn't want to blurt out that David is back home and wants her back in his life but then she thought to herself, "If she wants him out of her life, that is completely up to her and David will be shit out of luck!"

"Well, Diane, let's not talk about him on our last night together."

"Yes, Sara, I totally agree. How about I go pack my bags, shower then we can heat up the left-over Chinese food?"

"Now, that sounds good to me and don't you worry, I'll have the wine glasses ready!"

"That's my girl!" said Diane as she left the room.

"Aw crap!" Sara began as she murmured to herself, "She's trying to forget about David! You know, that's his problem. I'm not getting involved unless it's to support her. Keep it together and remember you and the girls are to support any decision Diane makes!"

Chapter 42

"All right, we're here. Are you sure you don't want me to come in with you? I don't mind staying with you before you check-in. We can have some coffee."

"Sara, I'm sure and, besides, I checked in online this morning and have TSA pre-clearance. I'm good. Stop worrying. I'll be fine." Sara pulled her car over to the curb and both Diane and Sara got out. Diane opened the back door to get her bags. Sara and Diane smiled at each other and then squeezed each other tightly.

"You're the best friend any girl could ever have. I love you, Sara."

"And I love you, Diane. Make sure you call me when you get home and settled. Oh, and pinky promise me right now that you will call me or one of the girls any day and any time you need to talk."

"I pinky swear promise," said Diane as she and Sara stuck out their pinkies and sealed the promise. Both friends smiled at each other and Diane slowly walked into the airport.

Diane's flight was surprisingly on time and she could only hope for it to be uneventful. As soon as she sat down, she buckled her seatbelt, closed her eyes and was ready for takeoff. There were millions of things running through her mind, and the many upcoming decisions she had to make made the three-hour flight home go by quickly. The flight landed and the passengers were given the location for baggage claim. Diane made her way through the busy airport. She stood patiently waiting for the conveyor belt to start so she could retrieve her bags and call for an Uber to go home. Her mind quickly went back to last week, which seemed like an eternity ago, when she witnessed the reunion of a soldier and his family. As the conveyor belt started up and the luggage began to come out, Diane felt a familiar presence around her. She looked left and then right. She didn't notice anything or anyone familiar so she shrugged off the feeling. Diane spotted her bags but, before she could move forward, she felt a tap on her shoulder.

"Excuse me, ma'am, would you like some help getting your bags?" Diane's eyes got wide. Her mouth dropped open and she stared straight in front of her almost frozen in shock. She knew that familiar voice. Diane turned slowly around with her eyes closed as if she was making a wish. She opened her eyes. She gasped.

She placed her hand over her mouth and, with a slight smile, whispered, "David."

"David?" Diane said shocked and surprised, then added, "What are you doing here?" Diane paused then sharply said, "Why are you here?"

"Diane, sweetie," David said nervously and began, "I'm here to pick you up!"

Diane anxiously looked around and then, in a very harsh tone, said, "To pick me up? Oh, no, David, that's not going to happen." Diane waved her hand in the air to punctuate her statement. "I can't do this, David. I can't do this here and, as a matter of fact, I don't think I can do this again with you." Diane stepped aside, shook her head and walked over to where she saw her luggage coming out on the conveyor belt.

"Diane!" David called as he followed behind her. "Can we please talk? If not now, maybe after you get home and settled?"

Diane grabbed her luggage. She looked at David and sternly said, "David, right now I want you to leave me alone. I don't know how you knew I'd be here but I think I have a pretty good idea who told you. Look, you hurt me. You hurt me badly and it's taken every inch of my being to sort things out. I've come a very long way in the last couple of months and I have no intentions of going backwards. So, if you don't mind, step aside and let me leave!"

"But, Diane," David said as he sadly watched Diane walk away.

Diane's heart was beating uncontrollably. She broke out in a slight sweat as she quickly saw and walked over towards the UBER driver's car that matched the description on her phone.

"Frank?" Diane questioned as she walked up to the open car window.

"Yes, ma'am. Are you Diane?"

270

"I sure am."

"Fantastic, let me get out and get your bags," Frank said as he leaped out of his car.

Diane was safely in the backseat and decided to quickly look around outside the car window to see if David was anywhere near. Once the airport was out of sight, Diane took a deep breath and sent Sara a text message,

Arrived safely! Had quite the shock and surprise waiting for me at baggage claim… David!!!!!

After a few seconds, Sara texted back, WHAT?? Are you fucking kidding me?? Are you with him now???

Too much to text, Diane's text began, I'll call you later. Probably a group call. I need a few answers and HELL NO!!! He's not with me!!!

Diane stared straight out the car window unable to comprehend what had just happened and growing more angry trying to figure out who amongst her friends told David where she was and when she'd be home.

The UBER ride home was quiet and uneventful. Frank, Diane's driver, sensed a conversation with her was out of the question. He didn't even engage in small talk and Diane definitely appreciated it.

Diane got home, locked the door behind her, then placed her keys and her purse on the kitchen counter and carried her suitcase almost zombie-like up the stairs to her bedroom. She fell face down on the bed and started to cry. "Why? Why now, David? Why in the hell would you do this to me? Why?" Diane clenched the pillow with both hands and screamed angrily into it, saying, "And which one of my friends would betray me and tell him where I was? Damnit, who would do that to me?" Diane cried herself to sleep as she sobbed uncontrollably.

Chapter 43

The next morning, Diane rolled over and startled herself as she realized she had fallen asleep with her clothes and shoes still on. Diane jumped out of bed, walked into the bathroom, looked into the mirror and said, "Oh, dear God!" Diane's eyes were swollen and her mascara was smudged around her eyes, making her look like a raccoon. Her face was streaked with tear lines from the makeup left on her face after crying herself to sleep. Her hair looked like tangled spaghetti as she tried to tame it with a comb away from her face. Diane closed her eyes in disgust and walked over to the shower where she immediately undressed and started the warm water.

With a towel wrapped around her hair and dressed in her robe, Diane felt like a brand new person. She made her way down to the kitchen to make a pot of coffee and grab a breakfast bar. "What is that sound?" Diane asked herself as she quickly turned to the beeping sound coming from her purse. "Oh, shit! Really?" Diane said as she picked up her phone from her purse's side pocket. "Eight text messages and two voicemails from Sara. Oh, man, she is going to kill me!" Diane poured herself a cup of coffee and stood at her kitchen counter, began to read her text messages and listen to her voicemails from Sara.

On the other side of town, David was waking up sore and with a major hangover headache. David had drowned his sorrows and frustrations at the bar. He was in no shape to drive home, so Joe insisted he stay the night in the back room on the cot to sleep it off. He didn't get the chance to tell Joe what he did at the airport and, maybe that was a good thing, because he knew Joe would've laid into him. He also knew he had picked up the phone several times to call Diane but actually decided against having the calls go through, which was another good thing but his best decision last night was not calling Luna. Even though he knew he needed to tell her that he did everything she told him not to do, he just wasn't ready to hear her scream. He decided to call her after a warm shower and hot cup of coffee.

"Dear God, David! So soon? What now?" answered Luna.

David wanted so badly to hang up the phone but sheepishly replied, "Hey, Luna."

"Don't hey Luna me, David. Just get to it. What did you do? What happened?"

"Before you yell at me, please just hear me out," David seemed to beg as he continued, "I went to the airport to pick up Diane."

"You fucking did what? Damnit, David! Didn't I tell you to give her time after getting home? Didn't I tell you to take it slow? What the hell is wrong with you?" Luna was fuming.

"I know, I know, I messed up, Luna, but I wanted to see her so badly and explain myself and my actions to her, but she wanted nothing to do with me and told me to leave her alone."

Luna interrupted, "What did you expect her to do, greet you with open arms? Fuck, David, you broke the girl's heart. She had every right to tell you to leave her alone."

"Yeah, I know, but I had to give it a try and I know now I went about it totally the wrong way."

"Well, if you would've listened to me and the girls and waited for her to settle in after a few days, things may have been different."

"Well," David began, "She wanted to know who told me where she'd be. I didn't say a word but one of the last things she told me was she had a good idea who it was."

"Oh, that's fucking great, David. Just great!" Luna said sarcastically.

"Now Sara, Anne and I need to do damage control. If you would've just listened and waited. Damnit, David! I can't believe this shit! I need to get off the phone and make a call to the girls."

"Luna, I swear I'm so sorry. I didn't want any of this to happen. I just wanted to make things right with Diane. I wanted to hold her in my arms again. I wanted to tell her how very sorry I am and how much I love her. I never meant to put you and the girls in the middle. I know you said that it was up to Diane and that you and the girls were staying out of it and that you would support her in any decision she made. I screwed up and now I think I've not only messed things up for me, but caused a huge problem between you, the girls and Diane. I'm so sorry. I guess I'm just a real fuck-up. Maybe it would've been best for everyone if I just listened to my heart in the first place and let her go to find someone better suited for her."

Luna, in a very unforgiving tone, said, "Oh, please, David. Give me a fucking break." She abruptly hung up the phone.

Chapter 44

Diane had finished her coffee and finished reading Sara's very concerned text messages and listened to her voicemails. She knew it was time to make the group call to tell them what happened at the airport and to find out who told David where she'd be and why they did it.

Luna had just hung up with David and was still fuming when she saw the incoming group call. Her heart was beating as she answered the phone with a somber, "Hey, girl."

Soon after, both Sara and Anne joined in. "Hey, guys, I hope it's not too early and I hope you all have a few minutes to talk." All three ladies agreed they had time to talk.

Anne, who knew nothing of what happened at the airport with David, was the first to speak, "So, how was the flight home? And what's on the agenda for this week?"

"Well," started Diane. "I guess it wasn't you, Anne."

"Wasn't me, what?" asked Anne in a concerned tone.

"Well, one of my three best friends apparently had a conversation with David and told him that I'd be at the airport yesterday. So, he decided it would be a good idea to surprise me after all these months. He wanted to pick up where things left off like nothing ever happened, but I shut him and his idea down pretty darn quickly. So, come on, which one of you was it? Now I know Anne didn't do it and Sara seemed very shocked when I texted her from my UBER so that leads to Luna. So, Luna, was it you?"

Luna quickly gathered her thoughts. "Now, Diane, don't you jump to any conclusions until you know the entire story and the facts, and I mean all of the facts! You know, as a matter of fact, I want to be able to see your face and look you in the eyes when I'm telling you what happened. So, can we all FaceTime?"

Everyone was now on FaceTime. Luna took the initiative and began, "Okay, where do I begin? Let's see. While you were in New York, David called me. I was shocked and had a few choice words for him from the get-go. He explained to me why he did what he did and how much he regretted doing it and wanted to explain it all to you in the hopes of getting you to understand and to forgive him."

Diane interrupted and asked, "What did he say? Why did he put me through months of not knowing? Why didn't he call me? Why didn't he contact me? No offense, Luna, but why you? Why did he call you?"

"All very good questions but not for me to answer," said Luna in a very solemn tone. "He called mainly to find out what we (us girls) thought of him contacting you. Look, Diane, I made it very clear to David that it wasn't our call. That if he did make contact with you then it

278

should be after you got back home and settled from New York."

"So, you told him I was in New York?"

"I believe I said that I was glad that you finally joined the living and took Sara up on her invitation to go to New York for a visit but I didn't come right out and tell him. I did, however, tell him that we would stand by you in any decision you made, but, I swear, I told him that he needed to do a lot of explaining to you and not to think that we would help in any way."

"So," Anne began, "Are you telling us that he met you at the airport?"

"Yes, he sure did," said Diane.

"Wow, that boy knows he really messed up. Well, what actually happened?" Diane retold the story of what happened at the airport to the girls.

Afterwards, Luna added a few things, when she said, "David called me this morning explaining what he did and how he didn't listen to a word I told him. He apologized to me but I was so damn mad at him that I basically hung up on him, but I do know he's hurting and I'm not taking his side. The bastard just doesn't know how to go about talking to you, Diane. I know he feels extremely guilty."

"Which he should," interrupted Sara.

"But," began Luna, "Maybe I shouldn't say anything but, when I asked him why he did what he did, he said because he loved you."

"Because he loved me?"

"I know I shouldn't have said anything but, yes, that's what he said. This is why you two are eventually going to need to talk, especially you, Diane, if you're going to get closure."

Diane shook her head and closed her eyes and said, "I know, but not right now. Maybe after a few weeks but, right now, it's just really too raw."

Chapter 45

The next day, Jenny decided to call Diane to tell her some school news and to come clean about David. She wanted to make sure that Diane knew David was home and what was discussed when he went over to her house.

"Hey, girl, good morning," Diane answered the phone in a cheerful tone. "You must have been reading my mind. I was going to give you a call. How's your summer going?"

"Oh, Diane, it's so good to hear your voice. It's been going pretty good. You know me, I've cleaned every closet, rearranged all the drawers and washed all the windows, and that was just in the first week." Diane and Jenny laughed. "Well," began Jenny, "I called for a few reasons. The first one was to see if you're free for lunch. There are a few things I need to talk to you about."

"Hmm, is one of them David Anderson?" Diane asked in a curious way.

"Yeah, that's definitely one thing but not the only thing. I need to talk to you about our fabulous principal, Ms. Marshall, and what she has planned for us this coming school year but, mainly, I need to talk to you about David."

"I figured as much. I need to catch you up on things unless he's already done so."

"Let's just say, we need to have a nice long talk over lunch."

"Well, Jenny, I'm good today, if you are?"

"Today definitely works for me. Around twelve-thirty at the deli on 144th?"

"Perfect," said Diane, "I'll see you then."

Diane arrived first and got a table in the back. She figured there was going to be some intense talk and wanted some privacy.

As Jenny walked in the door, Diane stood up, waved her hand and yelled, "Jenny, over here." Jenny was all smiles as she and Diane embraced. "You look amazing," Diane said to Jenny.

"You don't look too bad yourself," Jenny said and added, "See what a few weeks without kids will do." Both ladies laughed and sat down. "Before we get talking about work and David, tell me all about New York."

"Oh, honestly, it was a blast. I made Sara do all the touristy things like go to museums, shopping, eating at all the cool little restaurants but, the best part, was having her take a city tour on the Big Red Bus."

Jenny laughed and said, "I'm so glad you went. It sounds like you had lots of fun. Okay, what do you want to hear first? Work stuff or David stuff?"

Diane thought for a second then said, "Let's order something to eat and then get work stuff out of the way because something tells me we're going to need a lot of time to discuss Mr. Anderson."

"Okay, Jenny, what's up with Ms. Marshall? Has she come up with a school-wide theme?"

"As a matter of fact, she has. She is set on the Busy Bee theme and she's recruited me to help. She also asked if you're up to the task to help out and set up a committee. You know how much she loves to delegate."

Diane chuckled, shook her head, yes, and added, "She sure does but you got to love her. Tell her, I'm in!"

"Great, because I think she already knew you would!"

Both Diane and Jenny laughed then Diane said, "Okay, I guess it's time to get serious. Tell me about David and what he did."

"All right, here goes. While you were in New York, David called me. At first, I was like, oh my God, he's calling from Afghanistan but, no, he was calling me from here. I was totally shocked. I even remember telling him how over the moon and happy you must be to have him home, but when he told me that you didn't know, I became extremely angry. I reminded him how close we were and how horrible I felt knowing he was home when you didn't!"

Diane quickly stopped Jenny and said, "Don't feel bad. He also called Luna. Yeah, he called my friends and apparently poured his guts out to you and her but not to me!"

"I'm so sorry, Diane."

"No, no, it's not your fault. It's like he didn't trust me enough to contact me to discuss what was going on with him so, instead, he thought showing up to a crowded airport was the answer and that I would just drop everything and forget all the crap he put me through the last several months!"

"Yeah, Diane, he definitely went about it the wrong way. Vic and I had him over the house for dinner so he could explain what happened but he didn't even stay long enough to eat. He just sat in the living room explaining everything that happened and, after pouring his heart out, I can say, as he was leaving the house, he said he was going to try to win his girl back and wouldn't stop at anything until you forgave him. I did tell him how sad and depressed you had become and when I said that, he added that if he had to spend the rest of his life making up for what he did to you, he would!" Diane just sat there in silence biting her bottom lip. Her eyes were closed and her left hand seemed to be holding up her forehead. Jenny broke the awkward silence by saying, "Diane, I'm so sorry for bringing this up but I really thought you needed to know what happened and how he still feels."

"Seriously, Jenny, I'm good. I'm just thinking. What makes this whole mess so hard is the fact that I still love him but I'm just not sure if I love him enough."

"No one says you have to do anything right now. I know it's easier said than done, but just get on with your life and enjoy your summer before school starts and Ms. Marshall gets a hold of you!" Diane started to laugh. Then

284

Jenny added, "If David keeps popping into your thoughts then, maybe and only if you feel comfortable, the two of you can sit down and talk things out. Hey, if for nothing more than to bring closure to this mess. David has a lot to prove to you, Diane, and personally, I think you need to get a lot of questions answered."

"You're right, Jenny. I have a lot of thinking to do. Thank you so much for this. I truly appreciate your friendship."

Jenny held Diane's hands and looked her straight in the eyes and said, "All right, now let's get off this subject and decide on what piece of cake we're going to share for dessert."

Chapter 46

"You did what? Man, are you crazy?" Those were the first two questions that came out of Joe's mouth when David finally explained to him why he got drunk Tuesday night. "What did Diane do? What did she say?"

"She told me to leave her alone. Well, her exact words were that she couldn't do this here at the airport and then she told me she didn't think she could do "us" again. Damnit, Joe, I really fucked things up and I don't for the life of me know how to fix things."

"Look, man, I'm definitely not an expert on love or women but you really need to give her some space. This may not be what you want to hear but, David my man, you did fuck up royally when you let Diane think the worst. You stopped all correspondence with her. What was the poor girl to think? And then, without a word or a heads up, you just go to the airport thinking she's going to run into your arms like nothing happened. Look, man, like I said, give the lady some time and space. Let her think about things. Let her clear her head. Think about doing something romantic. Write her a letter. Yeah, write her a love letter telling her how much you miss her and love her.

And, send her a bouquet of her favorite flowers. Come on, man, what can it hurt?"

"At this point, Joe, nothing can hurt."

After working the night shift at the bar, David was exhausted and was not in the love letter-writing mood. He decided to sleep on the idea and tackle it in the morning. His thoughts were only on Diane as his mind began to drift as he lay in bed. He soon fell asleep and started dreaming of making love to Diane. In the dream, Diane was laying on her back. He was resting on one arm as he was leaning over her. He began to softly touch her cheek as he brushed her hair away from her beautiful face. He gently kissed her sparkling eyes and tenderly gave her nose a little peck. He made his way to her lips where he passionately explored her mouth. Her long soft neck was next on his radar. He delicately kissed her neck which sent tingles through her body and made her nipples hard and erect. He put his warm, wet mouth on her full breasts and tenderly tugged on each breast, which caused Diane to make soft erotic moans. Next, he traced her belly button with his wet warm tongue. He made his way to Diane's awaiting and inviting womanhood. He took his time to please her, then continued tracing her legs and finished by taking into his mouth and suckling each of her cute, stubby toes. He then mounted her as she wrapped her strong athletic legs around his muscular body, and they began to make passionate love to one another.

David woke up hot and sweaty, along with having a hard-on that could choke a horse. "Son of a bitch!" David said as he sat up in bed. "If that doesn't put me in the mood to get Diane back then I don't know what will!" David slipped out of bed and walked slowly to the shower, where he took things into his own hands.

Feeling refreshed and stress-free, David made his way to the kitchen to make himself a cup of strong coffee. He began thinking of what to write in Diane's love letter and, after several crumpled-up pieces of paper, he knew exactly what to do and what to say,

Dear Diane,

I know I messed up. I'm so very sorry. I miss you and I do still love you very much.

I miss and love the way your hair falls in your face and how I brush it softly back behind your ears.

I miss and love the sparkle in your eyes when you look at me.

I miss and love your full sweet lips when I kiss you.

I miss and love your soft long neck especially when I kiss it which causes you to tingle all over.

I miss and love your beautiful full breasts.

I miss and love your slightly "outie" belly button.

I miss and love your long athletic legs, especially when they're wrapped around me.

I miss and love your cute stubby toes and how you paint them with bright colored polish.

I miss our long talks and love how we would talk about our goals and future plans.

I miss and love how special you made me feel in a room full of strangers.

I miss and love how we expressed our love for one another, especially your soft moans of joy.

I miss and love everything you stand for.

I'm sorry for hurting you and if I have to spend the rest of my life making up for all the pain I caused you, then I most definitely will.

Please give me a chance to explain myself.

With all my love. Forever,

David.

David read the letter back silently and then again out loud to himself. He debated whether or not to share it with anyone. Should he let Joe read it? Should he call Luna and the girls? Or should he let Jenny read it? "No, this time I'm doing this on my own. My decision, my words," David said as he put the letter in an envelope and placed it on his kitchen counter, where it stayed for the next couple of weeks.

Chapter 47

Over the past few weeks since coming back from New York and having her altercation with David, Diane was trying to keep busy, but thoughts of David popped into her head several times during the day. "He sure did listen to me. I'm really surprised he hasn't tried to contact me, hmmm!" Diane thought to herself. Diane's thoughts quickly faded as her phone rang.

"Hello, Ms. Marshall. How are you doing?"

"Well, Miss Diane Walker, it's good to hear your voice. How's your summer been?"

"It's been pretty good. Catching up on cleaning and doing some reading and planning for the upcoming school year."

"Excellent! Well, that's why I'm calling. Are you doing anything this Thursday? I would love to have you and Jenny come by the school to help plan out our new school theme. Lunch is on me and I promise to give you comp time during the school year."

"Well, Thursday sounds good to me. I have no plans. What time do you want me there?"

"How about ten? Does that work for you?"

"Sure does. So, I'll see you Thursday, Ms. Marshall."

"Okay and I expect some great ideas from you girls!" Diane chuckled and said goodbye.

Thursday morning came way too fast. Diane got up and jumped into the shower. As the warm water fell on her soft body, her mind wandered as she drifted in thought about David. She closed her eyes and remembered David's touch as she soaped up her body. David was the only man who knew her body so well. Diane was caught off-guard as she could hear her phone ring from her bedroom. Diane quickly gathered her thoughts and turned off the water. She grabbed a towel and wrapped it around her wet body. She looked at herself in the mirror and asked her reflection, "What the hell was that all about? Get yourself together, Diane." Diane walked over to her nightstand where her phone was charging and saw that it was Jenny who called. She listened to her message, smiled and said, "Jenny always seems to know what's best for me!"

Diane pulled into the school parking lot. She scanned the lot looking for Jenny's car. When she saw Jenny's car, she gathered her purse and notebook and began to exit but not before getting a glance of herself in the rearview mirror.

After exchanging pleasantries with the office staff and custodians, Diane made her way to Ms. Marshall's office, where she cheerfully said hello and hugged both ladies.

"Well Diane, you look well rested and eager to start the new school year," said Ms. Marshall as she sat down and handed Diane a pageful of her thoughts for the new school year's theme. Diane glanced at Jenny and smiled.

The ladies were going back and forth with ideas, when a familiar male voice could be overheard coming from the main office. Diane stopped talking. Fear poured over her face. Her eyes got wide and she took a deep breath.

"Diane, are you all right?" asked Jenny.

"Yeah, I'm good but I think David is out there, whispered Diane.

"Who's David? Is he that gorgeous delivery man you were seeing?"

"Oh, my goodness, Ms. Marshall! How did you know that?"

"Darlin', not much gets past this ole broad!" All three ladies giggled. Ms. Marshall got up and walked to her office door. Diane mouthed the words "What is she doing?" to Jenny. Jenny just shrugged her shoulders and threw up her hands.

Ms. Marshall walked out and said, "Well, good afternoon, young man. I heard an unfamiliar male voice and was curious."

"Yes, ma'am. I'm David Anderson. I do most of the deliveries to your school from the county."

"Well, all right then, Mr. Anderson. We are no longer strangers. I'm glad I was able to put a face with the voice." Ms. Marshall smiled turned around and walked back into her office, where Diane and Jenny were both sitting with their hands over their mouths. Ms. Marshall went back into her office making sure, this time, her office door was closed.

She sat down at her desk and said, "That's one good-looking man, Ms. Walker, and he seems to be quite the gentleman too." After a slight pause and mischievous look, Ms. Marshall continued and said, "Well, enough of that, so what am I ordering us for lunch?"

After several hours at school, Diane and Jenny decided to call it quits. Before they left, Ms. Marshall gave them each a small project to complete in time for the beginning of school. Diane couldn't wait to talk to Jenny about the close call with David. Both ladies stood in the parking lot talking.

"You know you're going to run into him sometime during the school year. You can't hide from him, Diane. You have to decide what you're going to do."

"I know. I know I need to do something but I just don't know what. I've definitely cooled off from the airport fiasco and I guess I could talk to him to get closure, but I just don't know how to go about it. He's definitely listened to me about leaving me alone. Maybe he's moved on."

"Well, I don't think so but what the heck do I know? Time will tell. Well, girl, I better get going. Vic should be home soon from work and I have no clue what to make for dinner. Looks like Domino's is going to get a call." Diane laughed and waved goodbye. Diane got into her car and started for home.

As Diane turned into her driveway, the mail truck was right in front of her house. Diane quickly got out of her car to greet the mail carrier. "Hey, how's it going?" Diane said as she smiled.

"Hi there. Good afternoon. Here you go," The mail carrier said as he handed Diane a small stack of mail. Diane entered her house and dropped her purse and the stack of mail on her kitchen counter. Diane quickly walked upstairs to her room. She changed into her jogging clothes, put her long hair in a high ponytail and set out for a long run to clear her head. About an hour later, Diane came home. She went into the kitchen and poured herself a glass of water. She walked right past the mail lying on her counter and sat down to catch the local news. "Ugh, so depressing," she said as she turned off the television and decided to go upstairs to shower. About an hour later, Diane came down to make herself some dinner. She decided on a tuna sandwich and a salad. Before she sat down to eat, she gathered her mail so she could look through it as she ate. "Let's see what I have today. Junk, junk, bill, junk, letter from David? Oh, my God. A letter from David!" Diane threw it down then picked it up again. Her heart was beating. Diane looked at the clock. It was seven p.m. "The girls should all be home," Diane said to herself as she picked up her phone. Diane sent the following text message, Are you all available to video chat? Everyone except Luna texted back within a few minutes. She finally responded,. Give me about ten minutes. Getting the boys settled and ready for bed. Is this a wine or no wine call? Definitely a wine call! answered Diane.

Diane patiently waited as fifteen minutes slowly went by. She sat on her couch with a glass of merlot and David's unopened letter.

Luna made the call and everyone quickly joined in. "Hey, ladies, so how's it going?"

Diane quickly jumped in and held David's letter up to the phone and said, "I received this today!"

"Oh, my goodness, is that a letter from David?" asked Anne.

"Yes, it sure is," answered Diane as she closed her eyes and bit her bottom lip.

"What does it say?" Sara quickly asked.

"I have no idea. I haven't opened it yet."

"What in the holy hell are you waiting for?" demanded Luna.

"I wanted to read it with you all and I wanted to see your initial responses."

"Okay, well, we're all ears so read it already," snapped Sara.

"Let's hear what the poor bastard has to say," insisted Luna.

Diane began to read the letter aloud. There were slight murmurs of sweet ews and aws coming from the girls. Diane stopped a couple of times to catch her breath and, as she finished reading the letter, she held it to her chest as tears ran down her cheeks. No one spoke a word; not even Luna had a comment.

Sara was the first to speak, "Oh damn, I need a drink."

"Wow, Diane, that was really a heartwarming letter," Anne softly whispered.

"Yeah, I've got to give the guy props. He wrote from his heart," Luna said as she took a sip of wine.

"So, Diane, what are you going to do?"

"Oh, Sara, I just don't know. I was at school today meeting with Jenny and my principal about the upcoming school year and, while in the principal's office, David was in the main office delivering things. I froze. I didn't know what to do."

"Did he see you?"

"No, Anne, but Ms. Marshall went out there to see him because she saw the look on my face when I heard his voice. She played it cool. She introduced herself and, of course, when she came back into her office she said how handsome he was and that he was a complete gentleman."

The girls sat in silence until Sara asked, "So, Diane, what do you think you're going to do?"

Diane smiled then gently responded, "I think I'm going to sleep on it and, to be honest, I'll probably reread this letter a couple more times, but, and I repeat, but, I can't let him off the hook for what he did and for how he made me feel."

"I totally agree," said Anne.

Luna quickly jumped in and added, "May I give you my two cents?"

"Just two cents?" laughed Sara.

"Of course, Luna. What are your thoughts?" Diane said as she shook her head and smiled.

"Well, I really think, for what it's worth, you need to sit down with him and talk about what happened. I mean a down-and-dirty conversation. Listen to what he has to say and see if he really means it. Let him apologize for all the right reasons. You know I'm one hundred percent on your side and you know I'm not saying to forgive him just because he wrote a sappy love letter. Let him work for it! But at least hear him out. David knows he fucked up royally. Firstly, for how he handled the whole Afghanistan debacle and, then, for what he did at the airport. Diane, sweetie, you will never get closure if you don't hear him out. Honestly, what do you have to lose? He's the one who has to prove himself to you again. He did tell me (when he called) and he also wrote it in the letter that, if he has to spend the rest of his life making up for what he did to you, then he really must mean it. I say, when you're ready, call him and set up a time and place to talk things out."

"Diane, I'm going to have to agree with Luna," said Sara. Then she added, "You need closure. No one is saying that you're going to quickly forgive him and that you'll jump into his arms and everything will be like it was. Hell, you may find out that it's over, that you can't forgive him and you just don't feel the same as you did because the hurt is too much, but at least it will be on your terms after hearing him out. It will be your decision to make and yours alone!"

"You see, I've told you guys a thousand times. You're the best girlfriends a girl can have. Thank you so much.

I'm so glad I shared the letter with you. I'm going to digest all of this and I'll let you all know what I decide to do."

Anne reluctantly asked, "I hate to seem like I'm pressuring you, but can you tell us at least what you're leaning towards doing?"

Diane smiled then gave a small chuckle and said, "I'm going to call him but I don't know when. I do need to hear him out because the boy does have a lot of explaining to do!"

Chapter 48

Diane tossed and turned all night. She picked up David's letter several times during her sleepless night and reread the letter each time. She reread it again when she got up from her bed. She asked herself, "Do I call him or text him?"

Diane made her way downstairs to her kitchen. She poured herself a glass of orange juice and sat down on her couch. "Okay, it's Friday. If he has the same schedule he had before he left, then he's out all day today with deliveries and will be super busy at the bar tonight and tomorrow night. Oh, man, should I wait until Sunday night?" Diane was now pacing back and forth in her living room. Diane stopped pacing and thought, "I need to report back to school in only two weeks! Oh, God I know I'm going to eventually run into him at school just like Jenny said. UGH! I better try to make contact with him before then."

Diane called Jenny to share the news about David's letter. "Oh, my goodness, Diane! That's beautiful. Sounds like it came right from his heart. So, what are you going to do? Are you going to call him?"

"Yes, I'm going to call him but I know he's going to be extremely busy with deliveries today and the bar tonight and tomorrow night. I need to touch base with him before going back to school. I know we'll eventually run into each other and I really don't need an awkward scene in the hallway."

"Why don't you first reach out to him by text?" asked Jenny. "Let him know that you received his letter and that you'd like to talk. He can call you when the time is right."

"That's a great idea, Jenny. Now to decide when to do it!"

Later that evening, David showed up at the bar. "Hey David, how's it going?"

"Hey, Joe. Long day like most Fridays. Bar looks packed already."

"Yeah, we have a bachelorette party and a "Dirty Thirty" party! It's going to be a crazy night. I can feel it," laughed Joe.

"You know the letter I wrote to Diane? Well, I finally mailed it. She should've gotten it already."

"So, I'm figuring she hasn't let you know that she got it."

"She probably saw it was from me and threw it out!"

"Oh, come on, man, give her the benefit of the doubt. Maybe she hasn't read it. Maybe she's waiting for the right time to touch base."

"Or maybe she just wants nothing more to do with me!" David sadly said.

Joe closed his eyes, dropped his head into his chest, put his hands up in the air and said. "I'm sorry, man. Don't give up. Just give her some time." David made his way to the back of the bar to mix some drinks and to get ready for the night.

Diane was sitting on her bed. "Okay, it's now or never." She began writing her text to David. It was short and to the point,

I received your letter. I think we should talk.

David had his phone on silent but felt it vibrate in his pocket. He ignored the vibrations while he was mixing and pouring drinks. He was laughing it up with the customers and never gave his phone a second thought. He never would've guessed that Diane would be texting. Diane waited for over an hour after texting him. She had no right to jump to any other conclusion than he was busy at the bar. She figured he'd see her text in the morning. To help her sleep, Diane decided to take a sleep aid. She didn't want to toss and turn like she did last night. Diane was fast asleep within twenty minutes.

Two and a half hours had gone by since Diane sent her text. David finally got a break. He grabbed a barstool at the end of the bar, took his phone from his pocket and took a big gulp from his beer bottle.

"What the fuck, man? Are you kidding me?" David yelled as he looked at his phone. "No! I missed her text message! Shit!"

"Hey, man, watch the language. What's the problem?" asked Joe.

"Diane. She sent me a text and I missed it. She wants to talk."

"How long ago?"

"Oh, man, like two and a half hours ago!" David quickly looked at his watch and said, "It's way too late to call now. I sure hope she doesn't think I'm blowing her off."

"She isn't going to think that. You just sent her a love letter. She knows how busy the bar gets on Friday nights. Just send her a text now explaining what happened so she'll get it when she wakes up."

"That's a great idea, Joe! Thanks, man."

David went back to the office where he could gather his thoughts and, after several minutes, sent the following text,

Diane, I'm just seeing your text now. The bar was crazy busy. I'm sorry. I would really love the opportunity to talk with you.

David stayed at the bar for another hour and, even though he knew Diane would not respond, he kept checking his phone every few minutes.

Diane woke up after a full eight-hour sleep feeling rested and refreshed. She glanced down at her phone as she walked to the bathroom. "Oh my goodness! He did text back!" she said as she put her phone down, smiled to herself and confidently walked into the shower.

After her shower, Diane was still smiling. She quickly threw on a pair of jeans and a t-shirt. She piled her hair into a bun on top of her head and applied a small amount of mascara to her pretty brown eyes. She made her way downstairs, sat at her kitchen table and sent a group text to the girls,

I sent him a text last night. He responded after I went to sleep. Read it this a.m. I'll try again later.

All three ladies sent a thumbs-up emoji. Sara sent a private message telling Diane to keep her posted and how important it was to get all the facts before making her decision.

Diane knew she had the upper hand but was going to take her time calling David. She also knew how important it was to think about what needed to be said. Diane began to make talking points.

It was midafternoon by the time Diane felt she was ready to finally touch base with David. She had her list of things that she needed to get off her chest and things she needed answers for. Diane tried several times to call his number but could not go through with it. She was too nervous and her heart was beating too fast. She sat down after pacing back and forth in her living room and decided to give it another try. She picked up her phone, swallowed hard, closed her eyes and pressed the talk button. The phone was ringing. David's phone rang two times before he picked it up.

"Diane? Diane, is that you?"

Diane hesitated for a second then said, "Yes, David, it's me."

"Oh, my God! Thank you, Diane. Thank you for calling me. It's so good to hear your voice." Diane closed her eyes and everything that she had written down went out the window.

She was going to play it cool but a wave of hurt came over her and the only thing that could come out of her mouth was, "Why, David? Why did and why would you put me through such pain? How could you just stop all communication with me? I thought you loved me. What you did was mean and hurtful. I just don't understand. I honestly can't wrap my brain around what you did." Diane didn't want to cry but she began to sob and her voice became soft and low.

David, who was sitting on his couch at home, dropped his head into his chest and the only words that could come out of his mouth were, "I'm so sorry. I messed up."

"Messed up? That's an understatement," Diane said sarcastically. There was silence on both ends of the phone.

David broke the silence by saying, "Diane, you're right. As a matter of fact, you're one thousand percent right and I definitely owe you an explanation, but I really want to see you in person to give you a proper apology and tell you the reasons behind what I did, which I know now was so wrong."

"David, I'm not sure if I'm ready to see you."

"I totally understand, Diane, but please give me the chance to explain and, afterwards, if you never want to see me again then at least you'll know the reasons, but, Diane, please know that if you ever decide to give me another chance, then I will spend the rest of my life making up for my stupid mistakes. I love you, Diane. That has never changed and will never change."

Diane put her hand on her heart and closed her eyes as tears rolled down her face then whispered, "Tomorrow."

"What?" asked David.

"I'll see you tomorrow and we can talk," said Diane softly.

"You name the time and the place. I'll be there."

"How about the park near my house? There's that bench by the duck pond. We can meet around two. If that works for you?"

"I'll be there. Thank you so much, Diane."

"'Bye, David. I'll see you tomorrow."

Diane hung up her phone and took a deep breath. David jumped off his couch and fist-pumped into the air. Diane, not feeling like talking and going over the very emotional conversation, sent a group text to the girls saying,

Spoke to David. Meeting him at the park tomorrow to hear him out. I don't feel like talking but I'll let you know how it goes… Don't worry, I'm fine.

Diane copied her text and sent it to Jenny.

Diane tried hard to keep it together for the remaining part of the day. She went for a jog and then, later, went to her favorite Chinese restaurant for takeout. It was pretty much a quiet and uneventful day after her conversation with David.

David arrived at the bar late afternoon. As soon as he saw Joe, he said, "She called me."

"Who called you?"

"Diane called me and she agreed to see me so I can apologize and explain my actions to her properly. Joe, man, I can't fuck this up. I need her back."

"Well, then you better not fuck it up. Speak from the heart but, just remember, she's probably going to need time. I'm sure she's not going to just jump into your arms like nothing happened. She may need some time to think things through and, if she doesn't accept your apology right away, don't get upset. You need to understand what she went through. Just think if the shoe was on the other foot."

"No, man, you're right. I'll be as patient as she wants me to be if it means I get my girl back. Joe, I've never loved a woman more than I love Diane."

For the most part, David kept pretty busy throughout the night which kept his mind off of meeting with Diane. It was only on his drive home that David got nervous. He had thoughts of Diane telling him to drop dead and to go fuck himself. "Crap, what if she does that? What if she doesn't want to see me and tells me to go to hell? No, that's not going to happen. Diane will listen to everything I say. She'll think about it. Oh, man, she's got to think about what I say and give me a second chance!" David hit the steering wheel and yelled, "Damn it, David, why the hell did you fuck up a fantastic thing?"

Diane sat in her bed reading David's letter over and over. Before going to sleep, she said out loud to herself,

"Oh, David Anderson, this better be good. You better have a very good reason for doing what you did!"

Chapter 49

David arrived at the park twenty minutes early. He found the bench near the duck pond and was glad that no one else was nearby. Diane arrived a few minutes later. "Somethings never change. You're always early," Diane said as she walked towards David.

David smiled and said, "You look beautiful as ever, Diane."

"Thank you, David," said Diane as she sat down next to David on the bench. It took all of her self-control not to hug and kiss him and not let go. David could feel movement in his loins but suppressed his feelings to take Diane into his arms and make passionate love to her. You could cut the sexual tension between the two with a knife.

David slowly took a deep breath, closed his eyes and said, "Diane, I'm not going to make excuses for what I did. I'm not going to be long-winded. I'm going to speak from the heart." David paused and gathered his thoughts then continued, "I was scared. Diane, I've never been scared about losing anyone more than I was about losing you. Like I told Luna and Jenny and just about anyone who would listen, that I had no idea when I was coming home. I had no idea where I was going to be sent. I had no idea if

I would even come home in one piece or come home the same man you fell in love with. I know, Diane, that a lot of people say I took the easy way out but you've got to understand that it was the hardest decision I ever made."

Diane interrupted, "David, wait a minute. Hold on a second. I just still don't understand why. Why would you just stop all communication with me? I still can't believe, with everything we meant to each other, that you would do that to me, to us, without any explanation! You said you loved me."

"I still love you, Diane. I still love you!"

Diane stopped and just stared sadly at David then continued, "David, you know I loved you unconditionally with all my heart. I knew the casualities of war but what I can't wrap my head around is the fact that you didn't think I was strong enough to handle you being gone or if you came back different. That tells me that you doubted my love for you because, if you thought our love was strong, then we wouldn't be here doing this right now."

"Look, Diane, I know I messed up big time. I know I made a huge mistake. I know I was selfish but, after that first call I made to you, you seemed so sad, so worried and so scared. I know I made the decision to end all communication without even consulting you, but please understand how sorry I am, my reasons, however lame, were made because of how much I love you."

Diane rolled her eyes, shook her head and said, "David, I've never doubted your love for me but it's the trust that's been broken. You not only broke my heart but you broke the trust that I had with you and, once the trust is broken," Diane paused then continued, "It's very hard to get it back and I think for us to ever work again, it's going to take time. We're going to have to start from the very beginning. I mean, all over again, like meeting for the first time. I need to regain my trust in you."

David looked deeply into Diane's eyes and said, "I will prove myself to you. I promise to work hard to regain your trust and if you ever doubt my love for you, just reread my letter. I meant every word, Diane."

"I know you did, David." Diane gently held David's hand and smiled then said, "School starts back in a couple of weeks. Maybe I'll see you there but, David, I really need time to think about us and sort things out."

"Most definitely. Take as much time as you need," said David with a smile. "Diane, thank you for today. Thank you for letting me explain and apologize to you in person." Diane stood up from the bench, smiled at David, and stared directly into his blue eyes, nodded her head and, without saying a word, turned around and slowly walked away.

Chapter 50

It had been two weeks since the last time David and Diane had contact with one another. David was giving Diane the time and space she requested and Diane was concentrating on the upcoming school year but, at times, she was also thinking about and missing David.

Teachers were due back to school. Diane was back to work early and eager to get her classroom ready for the new school year. She dusted off bookshelves and rearranged tables and desks. She put up new bulletin boards that were bright and inviting for her students. She continued to think of David and what they discussed at the park. She knew she wanted to work things out with him but she also knew that building back trust was going to take time and they were going to have to begin slowly from the bottom up.

While making her way to her classroom from the main office and having no other thought on her mind except how to make this school year the best for herself and her students, Diane was soon to get a surprise. As she opened the doors leading to the outside walkway to her classroom, she saw David's truck. She immediately felt butterflies in her stomach and her heart began beating quickly. She thought to herself, "Oh, my God, I see the truck. He's here. Oh, how do I look? How's my breath? Am I having a good hair day?" It was déjà vu all over again.

David jumped out of his truck, tugged on his belt to readjust himself and slid his hands over his flat chiseled stomach to smooth out his tightly fitted t-shirt. Diane smiled and quickly reminisced when she met David for the first time.

David was in her direct path. Their eyes met. Diane was transfixed on David's smile. "Hi there. Good afternoon. I'm David," he said as he wiped his hand on his tightly fitted pant leg and then extended it to Diane as a greeting.

"Hi there. I'm Diane," she said as she met her hand with his. They looked at each other and held the stare into each other's eyes a little longer than a usual greeting. They smiled and then both let go of their hands.

"Well, then", said David. "I guess I better be going. I have to deliver these books to the library. It was nice to meet you, Diane."

"It was very nice to meet you too, David," Diane said with a huge smile on her face. She squinted her eyes, bit her bottom lip, took a deep breath, chuckled to herself, turned around and began walking away.

"Hey, Diane," yelled David making Diane turn back around. "Maybe next time, let's see if we can talk a bit longer and get to know each other a little better."

Diane smiled as she nodded and said, "You know, David, I think I'd like that very much. I would love to get to know you better!" David winked, smiled, then walked away with the biggest grin on his face.